Haunted by her mother's death, sixteen-yea
night. By day, she peddles bootleg vodka to ri
the wrong side of Brooklyn Bridge, a place
meltdown, strict curfew laws, and violent disarray.

Penny's chance meeting with Quinn, a rabble-rouser dabbling in
counterculture graffiti, sets in motion a deep love affair and the start of a
seemingly impossible revolution. Inspired by a childhood memory, the
two of them craft powerful messages hidden in the folds of hundreds of
paper airplanes. They plan to launch them from the rooftops of derelict
buildings even as the unforgiving militia hunts them from below.

Will hope take flight in a crumbling world, or will their efforts devastate
them all?

ORIGAMI WAR

Toni J. Spencer

A NineStar Press Publication

www.ninestarpress.com

Origami War

© 2022 Toni J. Spencer
Cover Art © 2022 Jaycee DeLorenzo
Edited by Elizabetta McKay

Printed in the USA

ISBN: 978-1-64890-510-0

First Edition, July, 2022

Also available in eBook, ISBN: 978-1-64890-509-4

CONTENT WARNING:
Depictions of mental Illness, substance abuse/dependence, alcoholism, graphic violence/mutilation, intimidation and physical violence against women, homophobic language and behavior, and no HEA.

In memory of Nik, who always loved my tales of misfits and madness.

Chapter One

THE STREETLIGHTS THAT ran the length of Brooklyn Bridge had long since been defunct, and the nights had become so black even the city in the distance gave nothing away. A scattering of blocks in shadow, like a once-prized Lego set, accumulating dust atop the bookshelf. Occasionally, a spotlight broke from a cloud and ran the gauntlet of alleys and nooks before disappearing from whence it came.

Penny perched precariously on the edge of the bridge gazing across the bay, waiting for her mind to sway back into the present and catch her up on the events of the night. An inhale of breath, her own, sharp and cold, jump-started her brain. The brick in her hand, nuggety and rough, was tied in the middle with twine. Cheap and thin. She fingered it with shivering hands and followed its coil as it snaked around her leg and ended in a bow at the ankle.

The sleepwalking had been escalating in distance and danger over the last few weeks. Where she had once woken in the lobby of her apartment building, sleepy-eyed and drowsy, she now found herself miles from home with knives in hand and blood on her knees. Her present predicament, though, was a new and dark incarnation of her nightmares. To find herself harnessed to a ledge, with wobbly knees and the plight of a harrowing demise, chilled her to the bone. A blush of heat warmed her forehead, trickled down her cheeks, and spread like a fire in her belly. A tear rolled off the end of her nose, and regret overwhelmed her entire being.

She crouched, dropping the brick beside her. The knots, having been tied in a daze, were easy to untangle, and the pain in her fingers, riddled with cuts, was easy to ignore, given the circumstances.

Her breath broke the silence of the night and ushered in an orchestra of sounds that moments ago she had been unaware of. The waves lapped far below. A military chopper thundered in the distance. A footstep slapped the sidewalk. She sprang to her feet and scanned the walkway. Brick in hand. Weapon if necessary.

She heard the voice before she saw the person. Another footfall, a rush of breath.

"Hey," said the shadow.

Penny jumped. Fear engaged.

The silhouette lifted its arms. "Don't shoot; I'm harmless."

Penny raised her brick as the shadow morphed into a human with a perfectly symmetrical face, framed by a mop of unruly hair. The girl was certainly not old enough to be a serial killer, possibly Penny's age, maybe a year older. Seventeen, eighteen? Her face was kind, and the girl smiled in the darkness. Well, what passed for a smile in these times. How long had this girl been watching her; how much had she seen? Penny lowered her brick before spotting the shopping bag. Did the pretty girl have a severed head in there? She lifted the brick back up.

"You know it's past curfew," said the stranger. "You shouldn't be out here alone."

"No kidding." Penny stepped backward, toward Manhattan. Toward home.

"So, what's with the brick?"

"Protection." Penny thrust it in her direction, satisfied only when the girl flinched. Not a serial killer after all. She dropped the brick, all the way down.

"Can I have it?"

"No," said Penny, stupidly possessive. "Get your own brick."

"I'm not going to kill you with it. I promise."

There was that smile again.

"What do you want it for?" asked Penny.

The girl lifted her bag and jiggled it. Metal on metal, the sound of a broken bell. "Got some evidence I need to dispose of."

Penny raised an eyebrow.

"Nothing sinister. Take a look." The girl tossed the bag at Penny who stepped out of the way so it crashed to the ground. "Nice catch."

"Wow. A comedian." Penny hoped the girl registered her sarcasm.

"See," the girl said, pointing to the spray paint cans that littered the bridge walk. "Not a threat."

Penny rolled a paint can beneath her shoe. Pink-colored paint. Nothing sinister. "So you're a vandal, then?"

"Of sorts, although I prefer the term campaigner of freedom."

"Ha, good luck with that." Penny handed over the brick despite her obvious disapproval.

The girl crouched at Penny's feet, shoving the cans back in the bag. She placed the brick on top, tied the package fast, and walked to the edge of the bridge. "So, you're one of those 'resistance is futile' types, then?" she asked.

"I sure am," Penny said, following her.

"Good luck with that." The girl grinned as she dropped the bag into the gloom below. Penny shivered as it fell, heard the impact, felt its pain, and when she lifted her eyes, her close physical proximity to the girl surprised her. She should be more careful.

"So you're just going to pollute the Hudson with empty paint cans?" said Penny.

"Not usually, but I went on quite the bender tonight. If I get busted with these things, it's lights out for me."

"That sounds a bit dramatic."

The girl laughed and offered Penny the palm of her hand. "I'm Quinn."

Penny hesitated. She was determined to impress upon this girl two things. One, that she had manners enough to not leave this stranger hanging, and two, despite those manners, she was a reluctant participant in this introduction and would protest by way of the limpest handshake known to mankind.

"I'm Penny," she said, finally accepting Quinn's handshake.

An unmistakable bolt of electricity shot through Penny's fingers, and the world spun, just for moment.

"Penny like the coin?" said Quinn.

"Sure. I guess."

Quinn shook Penny's hand, apparently unaffected by both the dead-fish salutation and the obvious warmth that emanated from their joined fingers. "Well, Penny like the coin, it's nice to meet you."

"I guess," Penny repeated. "Considering you're not a serial killer, it's nice to meet you too."

Quinn laughed. An authentic, untainted-by-the-crap-of-the-world guffaw.

Something like peace settled inside Penny. A tingle. Was this happiness? It had been so long she couldn't even remember how it felt.

"Shit." Quinn shuffled backward, looking skyward. "You hear that?"

A rhythmic pulsing cut through the air, and Penny stiffened. A military chopper hovered somewhere beyond the fog. Stupid idiot. How had she been so careless? The peacemakers had no love for curfew breakers. If she and Quinn were caught, they'd be thrown into a displacement camp and processed for unruly behavior. Rumors of cruel and unusual punishments were rife in those places, the stuff of nightmares. The ripping off of fingernails, plucking out of eyes, scalping of heads. Yet the truth of it all was irrelevant. Gossip or not, Penny's trick was simple enough—to not get caught and to never find out.

Chapter Two

THE CHOPPER WAS upon them like a hurricane. Its blades whipped up a storm of noise and dust, picking up Penny's short hair and flicking it wildly about.

A column of light caught them in its grip. Penny looked to Quinn, the shock on her face mirrored her own.

"Run!" Quinn grabbed Penny's hand and jolted her forward with such muscle that whiplash disoriented her vision.

Quinn yanked Penny from the beam of light that tracked their movements. A searing pain shot down her bicep and exploded at the elbow. Shoulder stretched to the edge of popping. No time to focus on it. Above her, a pair of peacemakers slid down a rope at mesmerizing speed.

Quinn sprang onto a rusty service ladder and shot Penny a message with no words, eyes black with fear. Capture would not be an option. Then she was gone. Penny followed, pounced onto the ladder, its mottled rungs creaking under her weight, and down she went, into the inky abyss. There was no choice. It was go or be caught.

Penny slipped down the ladder as fast as she could, her feet missing and twisting as she struggled to find the crossbars. Panic culminated in fear, step by step, until she finally hit solid ground.

"Hurry," said Quinn, a whisper in the darkness. No time for a breath.

Quinn grabbed Penny by the shirt and ran, dragging her deep into the shadows of the underpass, navigating blindly over potholes and abandoned junk.

The peacemakers followed, silent and swift, flashlights bouncing off pylons, a patter of footsteps, like wild dogs, fervently seeking their prey.

The girls popped onto the road at Water Street, buoyed by the moonlight, yet as they rounded a corner, Quinn skidded on a patch of gravel and fell to her knees. Penny, trailing by seconds, hoisted Quinn up by the waist with a strength she had no idea she possessed. Snatching

Quinn's hand, she pulled in any direction; she didn't care as long as it was away from the peacemakers, those shadows, those black ghosts.

The pain of breathlessness sent ripples of lightning through Penny's lungs, chest explosion imminent. Yet the peacemakers still chased, closer and with a confidence so cool and calm Penny was sure the fight was over. With less than five yards between them and as an impending sense of gloom swept over her, one of the peacemakers slipped on the same patch of gravel that had taken Quinn down, and the other ran so close behind they collided in a tangle of arms and screams.

This was all the girls needed to slip their grip, and they zigzagged silently through a maze of alleyways, stopping only when they hit the Pearl Street Triangle.

Penny had been in this area once for the flea markets back when she was younger, but there was nothing left of the landmark except a few painted cobblestones. The miniature trees that used to border its perimeter were long since dead and lay rotting in broken pots.

Quinn ushered Penny toward a graffitied roller door, which was covered in Division propaganda.

AMERICANS SERVE AMERICA!

YOU'RE THE DISEASE. YOU'RE THE PROBLEM!

DIVISION IS THE FUTURE!

PEACEMAKERS UNITE!

Quinn rolled the door up a notch and disappeared beneath it. The chopper pulsed in the sky above them, its floodlight frisking the sidewalk nearby. Penny froze in fear.

"Come on," whispered Quinn, popping her head out from under the roller door. "You got a death wish?'

Penny grabbed Quinn's outstretched hand and followed her new friend under the door. A flash of pain seared her knee as it slammed shut and a protruding wire hooked itself in the fold of her leg and scooped out a chunk of flesh.

Quinn's voice came so quietly in the darkness that it felt like a dream.

"You okay?"

"I think so," said Penny, her voice raspy and sharp, and her breath faltered to catch up. It was pitch-black in this place and smelled of gas and coffee. Her lungs ached, her knee throbbed, and her legs quivered, but she was alive. She was free. She was lost.

Chapter Three

PENNY'S KNEE SEARED with pain, and when she reached for it in the darkness, she found a tear in her sweatpants and a cut in her flesh. She rubbed the blood between her fingers. It was warm, slippery. The smell of earth and rust.

"Do you see me? I'm right here." Quinn's voice echoed so close to Penny's ear she could almost feel the weight of her words.

Penny rolled onto her side and swept her arm through the oily darkness. Relief washed over her when she gripped the fabric of Quinn's cold jacket sleeve.

"Gotcha," said Quinn as they searched out each other's hands, fingers fumbling to right their grip. Found each other. Held on tight. A magnetic spark rippled through Penny, rushing into her throat and forcing her to gulp stale air. Was it nausea or nerves? She couldn't tell.

"This way." Quinn pulled Penny to her feet and ushered her through the darkness.

Penny's knee thumped as if it had its own heartbeat, and her legs shook so hard she could barely walk straight. A tear pushed at the corner of her eye, but she resisted the urge to fall to the ground and bawl her eyes out. Quinn released Penny's hand and lit a lantern, which she placed on a pedestal by the door.

Relief came instantly as the darkness gave way to a small room awash in an orange glow, which, despite the sparse furnishings, was warm and homey. A single mattress and a stack of boxes sat on one side. A chair, a desk, and a wireframe trash can on the other. There was a poster, where a window should have been, of the Central Park Boathouse from its prettiest angle—all ducks and sunshine and more than a little old-fashioned. Why the boathouse, wondered Penny, when the window could take her anywhere in the world?

"Well, that was quite the caper," said Quinn, placing a freshly lit candle on the bedside table.

"Yeah, you sure know how to show a lady a good time." Instant regret followed heat in her cheeks, and Penny silently thanked the room for being dim enough that Quinn couldn't see her embarrassment and self-loathing.

Quinn smiled and lit another candle. "It's not for romance. It's a practical thing. You know. With the limited electricity and all."

Penny smiled but looked away, returning the favor of embarrassment without an audience. She looked at the ceiling, walls, floor, candles. Candles everywhere. She plonked herself on the floor, beneath the boat-house poster. "So, you live here?"

"Sure do. It's my loft, overlooking Central Park." Quinn continued lighting candles until the room twinkled like a Christmas party.

"It's nice. Cozy."

"Cozy, yeah. That's very glass half-full."

"I'm a glass-half-full kind of girl," said Penny and smiled because she was exactly the opposite, and in fact, she was becoming decidedly more glass-half-empty every day.

She remembered Aruba then and put her hand in her pocket, relieved to find she'd carried the picture of her favorite beach along with her. She squeezed the corners of the well-worn paper. Comfort, home, safety.

Penny pulled her knee toward her chest and pressed the edge of her wound. It was thick with blood, a gelatinous pink goop, like pudding or days-old milk.

"What happened? Is that blood? Are you bleeding?" asked Quinn.

"It's fine. It's just a cut."

Quinn hopped over Penny's good leg and rummaged through a box before pulling out a white first aid kit emblazoned with a red cross.

"Today's a beautiful day to save lives," said Quinn as she held the kit over her head. A hero in the making.

"I'm not sure saving my life is entirely necessary. At this stage anyway."

"Did you ever watch *Gray's Anatomy* reruns?" asked Quinn.

"Not really."

"I used to love that show." Quinn bounced toward Penny and sat cross-legged beside her bad knee. "That was the catchphrase of Dr. Shepherd. You know, McDreamy. Handsome dude, fluffy hair, and a sexy eye thing. Ring any bells?"

Penny stared at Quinn, wishing like crazy she had a single clue what she was rambling on about. She loved the way Quinn's eyes glistened as she spoke and how she bit her bottom lip, smiled at the floor, and flushed red at even the smallest of embarrassments.

"Shit-talk rule," said Quinn, "I'll shut up now."

"I didn't know there was such a thing?"

"What? McDreamy or shit-talk rule?"

"Both."

"One day, I'll educate you thoroughly on both topics, but for now, let's patch you up." Quinn pulled a bunch of cotton swabs from a sealed bag.

"Honestly, it's fine," said Penny, but Quinn went about fixing her up, patting the wound so gently she was barely touching it.

"Is that bone?" asked Quinn. "Or a bit of sweatpants? I'm not great with blood."

"Me neither," said Penny. "I mean, I know I'm okay, but I also kind of think I'm dying right now."

"Like you're just going to bleed out right here."

"Or pass out, one or the other."

"Here, hold this," said Quinn, placing a fresh swab over her knee.

Penny obeyed and watched curiously as Quinn ferreted through the first aid kit. Her hair, dark and unruly, framed a sharp jaw, paired with hazel-colored eyes. Her skin, a rich olive tone, bronze, was unfazed by the recent sunless days. Penny wondered if the peacemakers saw her as an immigration question or if she breezed through the roving checkpoints on good looks and charm.

"This stuff"—Quinn pulled out a spray bottle—"might hurt, but I think it will do the trick."

"Sure thing, Doc." Penny removed the bloodstained cotton swab, and Quinn held the spray to her knee. "Just gentle, okay?" Penny added, pumping her hand as if to quell any gung-ho attitude Quinn might have.

Quinn nodded and pumped the nozzle three times in quick succession.

"Ouch and fuck! Ow, ow, ow!" said Penny.

Quinn sucked in a gulp of air as if it were her own wounds she was tending. "Sorry! Does that hurt?'

"Yes! It stings like hell."

Quinn fell back with laughter.

"It's not funny!" said Penny, trying to repress a smile.

"I know, I know; I'm sorry. It's not funny." Quinn put a fist to her mouth and continued to laugh despite Penny's objections.

"Stop it." But Penny couldn't contain her own laughter, and when the undeniable joy took hold, she couldn't resist its power, allowing the feeling to stay with her until tears streamed down her face.

"I'm really sorry," said Quinn as her laughter wound down. "I don't even really know why I'm laughing anymore. Is your knee okay?"

"Well, I'm not dead, so that's good news." Penny rustled through Quinn's kit and found a square bandage with which to dress the gash on her knee. "Perfect," she said before shuffling backward along the floor and hoisting herself into the chair.

The chair was innerspring with ugly floral fabric, but it was most comfortable, and she stroked her fingers along its elegant wooden arms— smooth and shiny, a fancy relic of a time long ago. She looked around the room and spotted a pile of paper planes on the floor next to Quinn's bed.

"What's with all the origami?" asked Penny.

Quinn rifled through the pile and picked one out. She straightened its wings and sent it sailing across the room. It landed on Penny's lap.

"I guess I make them when I'm bored," said Quinn. "And I'm bored a lot, obviously."

Penny picked up the plane and admired the exact creases and complicated detail of each fold. "Can you make anything else?"

"Just planes."

"Just planes?"

"Yep."

Penny laughed. "That's so weird." She blushed because it actually wasn't that weird; it was entirely charming.

"That's me, weirdo all the way," said Quinn.

"Well, A-plus for construction." Penny sent the plane sailing back toward its home in the pile on the floor.

"Thanks. My dad taught me when I was a kid. Every Sunday, we used to go up the Empire State and fly them off the top. He told me the wind blew south on Sundays, and if we got the right breeze, it would take my planes all the way to Brazil, all the way to my mom. I used to write notes in each plane and number them so that when she received them, she could read them in the right order. In the end, I think Dad even believed it was true."

Penny bit her lip to stop a plethora of inappropriate questions from rolling off her tongue.

"Where's your dad now?" she said and instantly regretted it. "Sorry, that's really nosy. You don't have to answer."

"He's lost." Quinn shrugged off the awkwardness. "He was in Croatia for a funeral when they shut the borders and wouldn't let him back in."

"They didn't let him back in? But I thought they shut the borders to stop people leaving. Didn't they need him?"

"Not the old ones. The old ones are a burden."

"So, he's just out there, in the world? And you're here."

"I'm here."

"All by yourself?" said Penny.

"Pretty much."

"What about your mom?"

"I don't know, really." Quinn picked at her thumbnail. "She left three months after I was born. My dad never stopped waiting for her to come back." She flicked the corner of her eye with her little finger and sat up. "So, what about you? I bet the porcelain-white skin is working for you?"

"Somewhat, I guess, but it doesn't mean I haven't come across my fair share of peacemaking assholes."

"And you're not from this side of the bridge." She pushed her hand through her unruly mop of hair.

"No, ma'am."

"And I'm assuming, by the way you roam the streets after curfew, that you probably don't have a pair of amazing parents who tuck you into bed every night. You might even be an orphan like me?"

Penny laughed. "Your powers of deduction are mind-blowing."

"So, I'm right?"

"Not at all," said Penny with a smile. "Well, my mom died when I was six. It's just me and my dad now. He used to be a science professor at Cooper Union before the Division, but they ended up firing him for teaching climate-change facts."

"You mean the real facts or fake ones?"

"Real ones, of course. He completely ignored the New American Curriculum when they rolled it out. So, boom, gone. I could be living the high life in a fancy Haven right now if he'd just complied. Now he has a new passion for the procurement of potato vodka. He's supposed to sell it so we can live, but he drinks most of it."

"What?" said Quinn. "That's amazing."

"It's disgusting. No wonder I'm out sleepwalking every night. I'm high on the fumes."

"So that's what you were doing past curfew?"

"More or less."

"And the brick I saw tied to your foot?"

"Don't ask me," said Penny. "I was fast asleep. My subconscious can't be trusted to make good choices. That's all I can say on the matter."

Penny swallowed the dry lump in her throat. Just one more thing to add to the list of things that sucked about her life. She closed her eyes, only for a moment, only to clear her head.

Chapter Four

IT WAS THE view of the boathouse that confused her when she woke. The day and time had stopped being important to her a few months back, so location and situation were the big questions that needed answering upon waking. Penny blinked, and her body groaned with the events of the night before, but the arms of the chair anchored her memory in what had passed. She curled her fingers around its smooth wood, as warm and soft as the wrist of a human. She dipped a hand into her pocket and sat up with a start. Quinn sat on the edge of the bed with her prized possession gripped between her fingers, curiously pondering the picture of the beach scene with its torn edge and dark crease lines.

"Hawaii, isn't it?" asked Quinn.

"It's private, is what it is." Penny snatched the magazine clipping with no resistance from Quinn. She folded it and stuffed it back into her pocket.

"How's the knee feeling?" Quinn seemed either unaffected or unaware of Penny's churlish attitude.

"It's okay." She glanced at her sweatpants, streaked with dirt and blood, and the humiliation crept in. "It looks kind of gross but doesn't hurt too much. Anyone would think we lived in a war zone to look at me."

"And they would be right." Quinn dug into one of her boxes, pulled out a box of Pop-Tarts, and tossed one in Penny's direction.

Penny tore off the wrapper and tucked in without pause, relishing its sickly-sweet taste, unbearably tart, a dry slice of sugar-coated cardboard. But it had been a long time since she'd eaten anything with such a kick, and it made her feel terribly happy. "It's so good. You have to tell me where I can get these."

"You have to know people who know people," said Quinn.

"I know you. Does that count?"

"I guess it does."

Penny demolished her Pop-Tart in a few swift bites, then brushed the crumbs into her hand and put them in the wastepaper basket beside her. "I'd better go," she said. "Make sure my dad eats something before he starts on the vodka. How do I get out of here?"

"This way, mademoiselle." Quinn slipped on a green bomber jacket and draped a leather satchel over her shoulder.

"She speaks French," said Penny.

"Nope, that's the only word I know."

Penny laughed, but her smile quickly turned as she stood and remembered her knee. It was stiff and achy, and each bend and stretch cracked open the scab that had started to form. The urge to get home was suddenly rife, but confusion clouded her mind. She stood between two doors, one on each side of the room, looking from one to the other.

"Front door." Quinn pointed to the door on the left. "And back door. That's where we came in last night."

"So this is literally a cupboard?" Penny gazed at the space with a new perspective of curiosity and awe.

"Literally," Quinn repeated as she led Penny through the front exit and into a commercial kitchen. It was quiet but messy. A dough hook lay on the bench. Footprints that weren't theirs showed in a scatter of flour across the floor. The oven emanated warmth. A generator ground out power, humming from somewhere in the next room, behind a door with a porthole.

Quinn grabbed a neatly folded apron off the bench. It was lightly dusted in flour and embroidered with the initials *JJ*. She wrapped the apron string around her waist and smiled at Penny.

"What are you doing?" Penny asked as Quinn leaned against the door with the porthole. A wisp of music filtered into the kitchen.

"Cool as a cucumber, right?" Quinn swung her way through the exit.

Penny caught the door on the backswing and was struck with both fear and excitement. This was a fully functioning bakery with music and coffee and pastries just like before the Division. She hadn't been in such a place in many years, and if one even existed in her borough, it would not have been a place she could afford to frequent. While the virus had killed a small chunk of the population, most of the damage had been in the utter decimation of the economy. Jobs and business had been lost for good and resulted in a huge division between the rich and poor. She was one of the latter.

Penny followed Quinn through the door, but her joy was short-lived. The place was full of peacemakers in their tailored navy uniforms and with their vulgar sense of entitlement. They slurped coffee and yelled across the tables to one another. Penny surveyed the scene before her, stunned. She had no idea the perks of peacemaking extended to coffee and donuts; it was no wonder there were so many new members.

The man behind the counter, with his rounded eyes and salt-and-pepper hair, raised an eyebrow at Quinn, and then smiled at Penny as she passed him by.

Quinn dropped back a step and cupped Penny in the middle of her back. "Just keep walking. I'll meet you outside," she whispered.

Penny watched Quinn grab a paper cup and fill it with coffee. She hoped Quinn might share it with her. It had been many months since she'd tasted coffee from a bean. She walked toward the door and was almost outside when a voice boomed above the din.

"Oi! Get over here!"

Penny turned toward the peacemaker who had spoken but quickly discovered he hadn't summoned her.

It was meant for Quinn.

Penny watched as she strolled toward the peacemaker, cool as a cucumber, just like she'd said. Penny slipped behind the door and made herself invisible. A man behind the counter looked on with eyes as hardened steel.

The peacemaker, jockish and riding a power high, slammed his fist on the table, making his buddies jump and stare at the table in submission. "Damn these donuts are good today, girl!" he said as he slapped Quinn hard on the ass, making her coffee slosh onto the floor. "What's the secret?"

Quinn put her hand over her heart and grinned at the guy. "It's love, of course!"

The whole table erupted with laughter.

"Ah, get outta here!" The peacemaker gave Quinn a final brief feel up before rejoining his buddies in conversation.

Quinn slipped away from the table, coolly, silently. She tossed the empty cup into the garbage and walked past Penny as if she didn't exist at all.

"Go," Quinn whispered as she passed through the door.

Penny shuffled behind Quinn and let her walk ahead for half a block until Quinn stopped and waited for her to catch up.

"I thought those bastards were going to load you up and pop you on the next Numbers-bus to some backwater Haven," said Penny.

"More like a reconditioning camp for me." Quinn gave Penny a quick sideward glance. "Not ladylike enough."

Penny smiled and blushed. She'd heard about the new technology that claimed to be able to recondition what they called "sexually confused" individuals and heralded a 99 percent success rate. She swallowed at the horror of it and didn't want to think about it.

"So, do the peacemakers think you're the baker?" Penny asked, desperate to change the subject.

"The apron says it all, don't you think?" Quinn untied the strings and pulled it over her head, then rolled it into a log and stuffed the end of it into her back pocket.

"What does *JJ* stand for?"

"Jonah Jakob. My dad."

Penny bit her lip. She should just keep her mouth shut in the future.

"He worked in the bakery for eighteen years. As long as I've been alive anyway. I'm lucky to have Ron looking out for me."

"Is he the guy behind the counter?"

Quinn nodded. "Jesus, those guys are assholes."

"Agreed."

Penny took at least five steps before she realized Quinn had stopped abruptly. She retraced her steps and followed Quinn's gaze into an alley shrouded in shadow. The dreary lane was barely wide enough for a small car to drive down. Along one side, toward the back and deep in the shadows, Penny could make out a row of laundry hung in perfect order. Jeans mostly, from what she could tell, but it struck her as an odd place to hang a rack of clothes to dry.

A row of dumpsters lay at awkward angles beneath the clothes, teeming with squalid garbage. Penny covered her nose and looked up at Quinn, whose eyes were dark and hollow. Quinn slipped her arm through the crook of Penny's elbow and tugged her away from the alley, marching along the sidewalk at a brisk pace.

"What did you see?" An impending sense of dread washed over Penny. "Shit. Not laundry?" She looked over her shoulder as fear crept in, then scurried to get as far away from the alley as possible.

"Not laundry. People. Dead people."

They hustled shoulder to shoulder for at least a block before the shock of what they'd seen diminished.

Quinn said, "I hear the peacemakers are cutting numbers into their chests and staging the dead according to their sins."

"Jesus, that's grim. So, it wasn't enough to divide us economically, now they're pushing a moral authority on us?"

"Well they have to, I guess," said Quinn. "If they need us to serve the Havens, they want to make sure we're submissive. You know, they don't want their street cleaners to have murderous tendencies."

"Wow, whose side are you on?"

"Definitely not theirs," said Quinn. "But I can see why they do it. It's a textbook dictator move. But if you understand the beast, you can fight the beast, right?"

"Not if the beast carves numbers in your chest and cuts your head off."

Quinn shook her head, and although Penny had only just met her, she recognized the fear on her face. "I don't know what it's like on your side of the bridge, but it's pretty fucked up over here."

Penny focused on long deep breaths. She leaned into Quinn, their arms still intertwined, their feet striding in unison. She felt safe under her wing. She felt like she'd known Quinn forever. "But why the numbers? Why would they do that?"

"It's because they want to take your name and your soul. You're nobody if you're just a number. And Numbers are useful in the Haven. Numbers clean toilets and serve the Haven assholes in their mansions."

"I don't know if that's entirely true."

"Think about it. The Havens can't operate without Numbers to do the shitty jobs they refuse to do, but they're so paranoid that we all have the virus that they need to give us these numbers to track our coming and going. What's paradise without someone to serve and clean? But it's the peacemakers we need to watch, misogynist assholes—racist misogynist assholes with power to punish. And they do it regularly, and they do it well."

Penny swallowed. She felt sick to her stomach.

"You just gotta go to your happy place," said Quinn.

"If I went to my happy place every time something bad happened, I'd be living there full time."

"Sounds good to me." Quinn shot her a sideways glance.

Penny stared into the distance as they ploughed forward with false purpose. She'd said too much. Her happy place was hers alone and not up for further discussion.

Penny suddenly felt awkward, strolling arm in arm with a girl she barely knew, and sighed quietly as she untangled her arm from Quinn's elbow.

"Okay, ma'am?" asked Quinn.

"Yup, you?"

"I'm about as good it gets, considering all things."

"All things." Penny involuntarily mimicked her as her mind raced to consider all the things they'd been through together in the last twelve hours. She thought of her new friend, swanning through the bakery earlier in her father's apron. It had seemed strange at the time, but now, considering *all things*, it seemed perfectly reasonable that Quinn would want to do her best to blend into the background.

"Do you do have to keep up that charade every day?" asked Penny. "Back in the bakery, I mean."

"Most days, I'll sweep through like nobody's business. It's usually smooth sailing."

"I guess it's all fun and games until someone pokes an eye out."

Quinn stopped and laughed. "What?"

"What?"

"That kooky saying?"

"It's not kooky. It's a legit phrase," said Penny.

"I've never heard it before."

"You've never heard it? Ever in your life?"

"Never," said Quinn. "And furthermore, I believe you just made it up."

Penny laughed. "I swear I didn't make it up."

"Either way, it's the craziest saying."

"Sure, but it's still a saying. And there's some good advice in it."

"Well," said Quinn, "if you're playing a game that involves any kind of poking near the eye area, I guarantee it's not fun."

Penny took a breath and sighed, but it came out as a laugh. She'd been doing a lot of that in the last twelve hours.

Chapter Five

THE LEFTOVER STATE of Brooklyn was much worse than the Leftover State of the Lower East Side where Penny lived. Boarded-up windows ran the length of quiet streets. There were only a few shops still in operation—bakery, grocer, newsagent—but they sold not much more than black-market cigarettes and censored papers filled with fake news.

As Penny and Quinn walked past a pair of junior peacemakers painting black over a graffitied wall, Quinn slipped her arm through Penny's and pulled her close.

"These ones are just babies," Penny whispered.

"Babies with guns. Just be as cool as a—"

"Cucumber?" said Penny. "Gotcha."

Quinn smiled, but her eyes were steely and her smile merely painted on.

The peacemakers didn't even notice them as they walked by, but Penny held her breath until they'd turned the corner.

Quinn dropped her arm, and Penny allowed herself a breath.

"It's tense on this side of the bridge," said Penny.

"Things are ramping up. Every day, there's a new idiot in a uniform."

Penny stopped suddenly in front of a graffitied wall and traced her finger over the text. The paint was pink and fresh, smooth beneath her fingers. "Triumph over hate," she read aloud. "Love is all around. I am not a number."

"Wiser words have never been spoken." Quinn's cunning smile lit her face.

"And I suspect I might know who the culprit of these astute musings might be."

"Just doing my bit for the, ah, for the cause."

"I didn't know there was a cause," said Penny.

"Well, there's not really. I just like seeing those assholes sweat."

Penny's laugh was drowned out by a surge of cheering that rolled down the alley. "What now?" she said.

"I know what it is. Tech burn-off. Come on." Quinn grinned and scooped up Penny's hand. She pulled her down the alley and into the street beyond.

A bunch of hooligans hollered around a bonfire singing, "You are just a Number! You are just a Number!"

A pile of iPads, phones, cords, and laptops lay in a pile, and the people were throwing them on the fire as cheers erupted from the crowd.

"Are they burning iPads?" Penny asked.

"And the rest."

"What for?"

"It keeps the Numbers from mobilizing," said Quinn.

"Mobilizing?"

"You know, on social media. They don't want us congregating online."

"But they're a Number too," said Penny. "Don't they realize that? And how are we supposed to congregate online if we don't have transmission access?"

"It's all for drama." She stared at the surging crowd. "I mean, that's what I assume. Supporters of the Division are not typically the sharpest knives in the block, especially the ones inhabiting the Leftovers."

"So, it's entirely possible these cretins think they're actually preventing a revolution."

"It's totally possible; in fact, I think it's certain." said Quinn as she touched Penny on the shoulder and guided her beyond the frothing crowd. "Keep walking toward the bridge. I'll meet you on the other side of this muppet fest."

Quinn then spun on her heels, raised a fist, and pumped enthusiastically in the air. "You are just a Number! You are just a Number!"

She was pushing her luck, Penny thought. What exactly did she think she was doing?

Penny watched Quinn swipe an iPad from the edge of the pile and skip into the crowd, chanting as she held it high above her head. She then tossed it into the flames. Penny averted her eyes, unimpressed. She picked up her pace. She knew the way home from here.

Penny had walked a quarter of a mile before Quinn finally caught up to her.

"Wait up," Quinn said as she sidled up to her. "You walk fast; you know that?"

"Only when I'm being chased by undesirables."

"Oh! Ouch," said Quinn with a smile. "And by undesirable, you mean me?"

Penny raised an eyebrow, trying her best to convey disgust. "If that's what you do for fun, then yes, you're worse than undesirable. You're an idiot."

Quinn clutched her heart and spun to a stop in front of her. "Ouch, my heart."

Penny tried not to smile, pursing her lips as they began to curl upward.

"I think I'm having a heart attack," Quinn said as she slipped her hand into the depths of her jacket and pulled out a smartphone. "Who's the idiot now? It's even charged up."

"You stole that?"

"I prefer the term 'found it a new and loving home.' Rescued from the flames of hell. Gifted life where death was imminent."

"You know it's useless, don't you?"

"Only to those who lack imagination," said Quinn.

"Put that thing away." Penny pushed it back into Quinn's jacket. "They'll think we're in cahoots."

"Cahoots! How old are you? Like, ninety-five?"

"Something like that," Penny said.

"Come on then, Grandma, let's get you home."

THEY WERE THE only couple on the bridge, and they walked without speaking until Quinn finally broke the silence at the halfway mark.

"I'm going to stop here," she said. "It gets a little hot under the collar past this point, you know, with a skin tone that's not bright white."

"What are you saying? I'm not glowing or anything." Penny held out her wrist as proof.

"You're pretty white. Not quite ghostly, but getting there."

"Ghostly! There are so many better adjectives you could have used. Like porcelain, luminous, um, resplendent."

"Incandescent," Quinn said.

"Well that's going a tad too far, but you're on the right track."

Quinn stuck her hands deep in her pockets, her shoulders lifting into a shrug.

"Well," Quinn said as she tapped her toe against the tip of Penny's shoe, "it's been a hoot, Grandma."

"Back at ya. I guess I'll see you around." Penny felt a twinge of regret. She didn't have many friends, and she truly hoped this wouldn't be the last time they met.

"I'm at the carousel most nights if you're ever bored," said Quinn, "or out sleepwalking."

"Like, the actual carousel? The one across the bay?" Penny pointed toward the barracks that ran along the waterfront.

"The one and only."

Penny had been to Jane's Carousel as a child only once, and it was a memory she cherished, not for the actual events of the day but for the melancholy sentiment. The touch of her mother's hand. Her smile. The way her mother's dress blew in the wind and swept across her face. Single fleeting moments of love.

Penny squinted out across the bay in the direction of the carousel. "It's all boarded up though. What happens there? Discos, vintage reruns of cheesy medical dramas?"

"You'll find out."

"You're confident I'll be back."

"How could you not?" said Quinn. "Didn't I show you a good time?"

"Not really."

Quinn laughed. "Well it's all fun and games at the carousel. I even have a no eye-poking guarantee."

"No eye-poking? Isn't that half the fun?" Penny fished around in her sweatpants pocket and her heart sank. "Oh, no. My ID."

"I didn't think there were checkpoints off the bridge." Quinn squinted her eyes into the distance as if she could see that far.

"There weren't until a few weeks ago. Now they're everywhere. I guess they have to keep all the new recruits busy somehow. I just wish they'd stay in one place. You can't go anywhere without being surprised by a new checkpoint these days."

"Why would they put a checkpoint off the Bridge?" She opened her arms to the world as if she were addressing the nation." It doesn't make sense. It's not like they need to protect a flourishing Haven."

"Actually, my side of the bridge is totally amazing." She outstretched her arms and spun in a circle. "It's all rainbows and butterflies; it's even summer there right now. We've even got unicorns. No wonder they want to keep riffraff like yourself out."

Quinn laughed. "I would have believed you if you hadn't gone overboard with the unicorns."

"Easily fooled." Penny pretended to scribble notes on the palm of her hand with an imaginary pen. "Noted."

Quinn held up her own imaginary notepad and paused to look at Penny before she scribbled her own notes. "Cheeky, forgetful, snore-y."

"Snore-y?" said Penny. "I'm not snore-y. What does that even mean?"

"Snore-y. You totally snore."

"I do not snore." Penny's cheeks flushed hot.

"I beg to differ."

"How can I snore if I don't even sleep?"

"Oh, you sleep. You sleep like a log," said Quinn. "A big old snore-y, log."

Penny couldn't help but laugh. She held her palm up in front of her face and scribbled madly with her imaginary pen. "Insolent, audacious, petulant."

"Okay, okay." Quinn gently grabbed her palm and pulled it downward. "I get the message."

She flipped Penny's palm over and gave her a sideways glance. "Feisty." She threw her hands up in defeat. "I'm done, no more."

Penny smiled. So good was the company she'd forgotten she was stranded on a dreary bridge with no ID and headed for a surefire run-in with checkpoint guards. Leaving the vicinity of your Leftover zone was a foolish feat. The Haven states had practically wiped out the virus thanks to excellent medical facilities that only money could buy. Penny turned from her new friend's smiling face to the bridge walk, now empty of people, always a bad sign.

"You'll be fine," said Quinn, seeming to read her mind. "You were here for the tech burn-off, and you lost it."

"Tech burn-off—that's good. That's a good excuse." Penny nodded in the guise of convincing herself she'd be fine. "Can you take this?" She pulled out her folded-up beach picture. "It's Aruba by the way. In the picture. Aruba, not Hawaii. It's kinda special, but it's also paraphernalia." Hearing the words come out of her mouth made her smile at the absurdity of it.

"I'll look after it," Quinn said with touching sincerity.

Penny took a deep breath and started walking backward.

"Cool as a cucumber,' Quinn said. "You're an entitled, white chick. You got this."

"Cool and entitled. Got it," said Penny. "See you around, rabble-rouser."

"Back at ya, ghosty."

The urge to laugh overcame Penny once more, and she turned and walked toward an uncertain future with a smile on her face. How odd, she thought, to feel such hope in such a hopeless time.

Chapter Six

PENNY USED THE sleeve of her shirt to wipe the beads of sweat off her nose, gathered there despite the chill fall air, then tucked her hands deep into the pockets of her pants. She didn't want trouble with the checkpoint peacemakers, who were nothing more than hired bullies and low-level street recruits, gifted with power well beyond their rank.

Up ahead, two guards lounged on the black-and-white striped barrier, smoking authentic-brand cigarettes and looking bored. Their sharp navy-blue uniforms, slim-cut pants, and tailored coats complemented their lithe bodies. Boys, enjoying a fancy night on the town in swanky outfits and shiny leather brogues. Diamond-shaped peacemaker badges crowned their lapels, popping off in gold and black. Confirmation of their power.

The lanky one stubbed his cigarette on the ground as Penny approached and arranged himself in front of the checkpoint in a practiced pose, legs spread wide, hand resting on his gun clip. Clean-cut, with hair short at back and sides, he was handsome in a burly, college-jock way. Eighteen, perhaps, and only a couple of years older than herself, his defining difference was the rifle that dangled at his side, the handgun in a holster, and a swagger well beyond his reach.

"What have we got here, then?' said the peacemaker, following up with a wolf whistle.

Penny said nothing and concentrated on keeping her breath at an even keel.

"Cat got your tongue, honey?"

Penny swallowed and sought out her voice, which finally came to her, raspy and broken.

"I'm just, I just, um, I live nearby." She pointed in the general direction of the twelve brownstone tenements that polluted the skyline just south of the bridge.

"Do you now, darling?" said the Lanky One as he unlatched the handgun from his holster. "And your ID can verify this?"

"I lost it. I mean, it was stolen," said Penny.

The Lanky One pulled his handgun from its holster and held it up to Penny's forehead.

She lifted her hands, fingers stretched wide.

"I see," he said. "So was it lost, or was it stolen?"

"Stolen. It was stolen."

Penny's breath caught in her chest. She was floating, yet her limbs were heavy, filled with lead.

"You got a weapon?" A smile spread across his face.

Penny shook her head in fast but microscopically small movements out of fear he might decide to blow her brains out if she dared to move. She blinked back tears that threatened to fall, but as her brain raced to gather her thoughts, a man approached in full Division military dress with navy fatigues and a don't-fuck-with-me, ankle-length coat littered with medals and regalia. He moved with swift strides and came upon the peacemaker like a southern wind, deftly whipping the gun from the kid's hand.

"Put the safety on, you idiot," said the man, releasing the magazine clip and offering the lame gun back to the peacemaker.

"Yes, Lieutenant." He shuffled in behind his buddy, making himself small.

The lieutenant looked Penny up and down, barely hiding the disdain he obviously felt for people like her, who made his life difficult. "ID?" he said.

"I lost it, sir. I mean, it was stolen."

The instant the lieutenant sighed, Penny knew her lies were not fooling him. She dropped her eyes, and every mark and stain that ran the length of her sweatpants made her face flush with unbearable humiliation. This powerful man saw her as nothing more than an annoying fly to be swatted away. She curved into her shoulders, making herself small, making herself invisible.

"If I catch you without ID again," said the lieutenant, "I'll have to process you at a displacement center. Do you understand what that means?"

"A Numbers camp? But I'm not—"

"A displacement center is a term used by the dignified among us," said the lieutenant. "For displaced citizens, to gather their bearings. It is not a *Numbers camp* as you so inelegantly put it."

"But I'm not displaced. I just live—"

"How do I know you're not displaced if you don't carry your ID?"

Penny bit her lip, putting a stop any other words that wanted to dribble out her mouth. Arguing with this man would clearly get her nowhere.

"Check her for weapons," said the lieutenant, and then he immersed himself in his clipboard and wandered off.

Penny stepped toward the barrier, and the Lanky One smirked.

"Arms to the side," he said.

Penny obeyed and braced herself as he groped her, pinching her breasts and buttocks. She clenched her jaw and accepted his greedy hands until, finally, he pushed her aside.

"She's clean," said the Lanky One to the lieutenant, who wasn't paying any attention. "But she's a dirty bitch." He then lifted the barrier arm with one hand and pushed her forcefully with the other. "Now fuck off back to your slums, you faggot lover."

Penny staggered through the checkpoint, nimble enough to not fall, but smart enough to make sure she wasn't being further pursued. She turned to see the beady eyes of the Lanky One staring with contempt, and the tremble of infuriation rattled her bones. To see him drink her in like that made her want to spit in his face.

The lieutenant, still immersed in his clipboard, spun on his heels so swiftly his regal coat ballooned at his ankles like a tutu in the wind. He strode away, clearly with somewhere more important to be. Penny smiled, an idea blooming. She clutched her fists to her chest, shuffled slowly backward, toward safety, toward home. One last look, straight in the eye, broad smile, toothy grin. And then swiftly, with the momentum of a punch, she flicked up her middle fingers in unison.

"Fuck you," she whispered, mouthing the words carefully so he wouldn't misinterpret them as anything other than an insult.

The Lanky One slammed his hands on the barrier, and Penny almost screamed in fright. A rush of delight and fear swept through her. Message received loud and clear.

"You little fucking bitch!"

Penny took off at a sprint and didn't stop until she got to Confucius Plaza, where she collapsed outside the Jade Paradise shopfront, with its boarded-up windows and wonky purple awning.

She was winded and gasping for air, but the thrill of the chase left her smiling. When Penny was sure she hadn't been followed, she burst into laughter, exhilarated, buzzing.

"You little motherfucker," she whispered with a grin that wouldn't fade.

This feeling, not quite happiness but something between peace and delirium, filled her with undeniable hope. Slowly, her breath returned, and Penny picked herself up and jogged all the way home.

Chapter Seven

THE HOUSING ESTATE wasn't such a grim place to live in on a sunny day, but on days like this one, when the clouds hung low and the fall frost nipped at your lungs, it was a dismal place to call home. The weeds that filled the garden beds and often flowered during summer were now scraggly and limp, and the brownstone tenement, a relatively short building at only eight levels high, was a squat and domineering presence in the landscape.

Penny used the last of her energy to tug on the entrance door handle. It was locked, and she was without a key, so she ran her finger along a line of buttons, buzzing a whole row of residences in the process.

She waited, shivered, and considered the pavement, which was covered in Division propaganda. The flyers were delivered every Sunday, and every Sunday, left unread by the tenants. She picked up a poster with a picture of a kid on it, just a few years younger than herself and decked out in military regalia. The title read *Junior Peacemakers, Americas Heroes*. She ripped the poster in half and let the pieces fall to the ground. Penny felt lucky to have dropped out of school before the Division took over the education system. The peacemaker movement was gaining momentum, and the rising trend of treating the uninitiated as nothing more than traitors worried her. There was no tolerance for difference in this regime, and although it went unsaid, the majority of the peacemaker "heroes" were white, heterosexual youngsters. Penny had been able to slip through her world relatively unscathed up till now, but this surge in checkpoints manned with youthful thugs was deeply unsettling. There was a change afoot; she could feel it in the air. How much longer would she be able to roam her own streets without coming to serious harm?

The cold trickled in beneath her clothes. With her patience all but depleted, she thumped on the button board and pulled her fingers downward, buzzing every single apartment in the block.

"What?!" an angry voice rang out from the speaker, some random inhabitant filled with static and rage.

"Hi, it's, um, it's Penny from 3C. I've forgotten my key. Can you—"

The door buzzed and unlatched.

Penny let herself in and was struck with the smell of piss and stale smokes. She covered her nose with her sleeve and skirted through the pockets of rubbish that littered the tiles before starting her ascent to the third floor.

The level three sign hung askew at the top of the stairwell. Penny swung at it, then continued down the corridor with row upon row of identical blue doors. She stopped when she reached her door and rested her head upon it. Her breath was short from the hike up the stairs, and she stared at the floor while indifference swept across her like a wind. She lifted her arm and let her fingers trace a path across the ridge above the door in search of the spare key. She took it from its hiding place and let herself in.

The light from the day tried without success to pierce through the curtains, which in turn draped everything in a blue hue. Uncle Benny slept on the kitchen floor, apparently manning the two pots boiling on the stove. Plumes of steam curled toward the ceiling, where they lingered as little clouds and occasionally pooled into a drop that splattered onto the floor. Penny considered the batch of vodka on the go and noted her father's absence, pondering his luck at not having burned the whole tenement to the ground. He was probably passed out somewhere and more than likely snoring.

Behind the potatoes, another pot whistled madly. A copper pipe, wrapped entirely in a thick layer of duct tape, extruded crudely from the lid. The piping routed up the wall, over the top of the fridge, through a coat hanger suspended from the ceiling, and down to the bench. From there, it dropped into the sink where pure alcohol dripped into a flask.

Penny switched off the stove at the wall, and the smell of yeast and tobacco filled the room. She made haste in pulling back the curtains and punching open the windows. While the once-busy courtyard below used to teem with activity, it was now eerily quiet. The smart ones had long since moved north or west to California where Leftover towns bordered the ocean and the state governance was less rigid. At least, that was what she imagined. It was difficult to get any reliable news and even more difficult to move from a Leftover zone without money or status. Right now, Penny was destined for a life as a Number, a dreary life of servitude in one of the many Havens of New York. That, or join the peacemakers.

Penny turned her back on the view as a growing sense of dread trickled down her spine. She nudged open the door to her father's bedroom. He lay sprawled on the floor in his underwear, the air rich with the scent of alcohol, and beside him sat the empty container labeled in her own handwriting. *FORESHOTS! DON'T DRINK IT LARRY!!*

"Christ, Larry. This shit will kill you. You can't drink the fucking foreshots!"

Penny had warned him about drinking the ethanol extract from the first pour of the final stage of the fermenting vodka. It was so high in alcohol content that it could potentially blind a person or, at worse, kill them. Naturally, he hadn't listened.

"Idiot." Penny dragged a blanket from his bed and tossed it more or less on top of him. Larry didn't budge, not even when she kicked his foot free of the door before slamming it shut.

A frisson of hope piqued Penny's senses as she entered her own room. Her personal haven wasn't quite like the Havens that existed north of the bridge, but it was escape enough for her to simply close her eyes and shut the world out.

Her bedroom was simple and practical. Double bed, side table, chair, cushion, window, lamp, retro tape deck. The only flair was the pinboard on the back of the wardrobe door, covered in photos and magazine clippings of various beaches and summer scenes. A pair of sunglasses with orange lenses hung from a pin. She took the glasses carefully off the board and replaced the pin. She flicked up the corner of the magazine clipping and let her fingers run over a photo of her mother's face. The one remaining image of her mother that her father hadn't destroyed.

The genetic similarities that she and her mother shared were uncanny. Penny was a mini version of the graceful woman in the photo: large blue eyes, innocent yet brimming with sorrow; her hair a dusty-blonde bob, cut to the jawline. Yet who could have ever foretold that her beauty would be her eventual downfall? Melancholy, mistaken for grace. Despair, mistaken for elegance. A woman this strikingly beautiful wasn't allowed to experience suffering. Yet Penny could see it so clearly. Clearly enough that she recognized in herself the same fatal genetic predisposition to enjoy the feeling of wallowing in gloom.

Penny grabbed a pair of fresh sweatpants from the closet floor. Gray, comfy. She put on her headphones and melted into her chair. The sunglasses transformed the room from a dull fall day to a Sunday in summer, and she pressed Play on her mother's tape deck and stared at her pinboard with unwavering concentration.

Her mother's favorite music took Penny to a beach in Aruba and asked her repeatedly if she was fond of sand dunes and salty air. Her answer was always the same. Yes, yes, yes. The family had holidayed there once, when she was five and her parents were still in love and her homeland hadn't yet caved in on itself. It was beautiful there, on that beach with the swaying palm trees. She could feel the sand in her toes and the sun on her face, the waves lapping on the shore. If she concentrated hard enough, she was usually able to conjure up the face of her mother, who smiled at her behind wisps of blonde hair.

Penny was so invested in her daydream she ignored the first rock that smashed through her window and rolled to a stop at her feet. She blinked and refused to leave the dimension her dead mother's music had taken her to. The second rock, though, came faster, harder, and hurled into the wall on the other side of her bedroom. Penny tore off her head-phones, stomped over to the window, despite the broken shards of glass, heaved up the shattered pane, and leaned out.

"What the fuck?!" she yelled. "If there's no happy face, there's no business! Do you see an emoji here anywhere? Huh? Do you?"

The teenagers on the ground looked up at Penny. A boy and a girl. The boy held a rock in his hand. The girl stood one step behind him, clasping his free hand between hers.

"Yeah, I, um, I kind of do," said the boy. He dropped the rock and pointed to the happy face emoji stuck to the wall on the left side of her window.

"Fuck!" Penny ripped the laminated sign off the brick wall. "Well, you can't just throw boulders at windows and not expect them to break."

"Sorry. I've got money; I can pay," said the boy as he pulled out a rolled-up wad of cash from his pocket and waved it above his head.

"Put that away," said Penny, shaking her head at his idiocy.

The kids must have been no older than fourteen, and they both wore expensive-looking jeans, adorned with flashes of colored cotton here, an extra pocket there, a carefully manicured rip on the knee. The girl wore a plain white tee, and the boy's polo shirt was ironed to a crisp with the shoulders creased sharply on the top edge. Someone, probably his mother, had pressed it for him.

"So, are you holding?" asked the boy.

She sighed and felt both sorry and envious of these kids, buffered from the kind of life that a majority of the Leftover citizens were subjected to, ever since the military had been given voluntary control of the Division regime under the premise of brokering civil peace between the rich and poor. It was only supposed to be a temporary hold, but the apparent consensus was the military had done so well at protecting the country from the insular oblivion that they were now the best-suited candidates to broker peace and productivity in a newer, bolder, better

America, which included dividing the people into two clear camps. The privileged and the rest.

The Havens had started quite by accident. As the virus struck in those early days, the wealthy instinctively sheltered themselves in pockets of like-minded communities. They drove out the riffraff by hoisting prices and creating actual borders around the districts. This kept the inhabitants protected from the discomforts and drama created by the virus and forced the military to step in and manage the Haven states run by the people with the money. The ones who continued to bolster the community while the rest of the country succumbed to illness and strife. These divisions were so successful in the eyes of those privileged few that it soon became the accepted rule. A new way of life encouraged by the presidency in order to maintain some economic stability.

Penny sighed as she looked at the pair of rich kids and felt at least grateful they'd chosen partying over peacemaking; although, what there was to celebrate, she had no idea.

"Hurry up," Penny said. "Go around the front. I'll buzz you in."

Penny watched the pair from the doorway of her apartment as they swaggered down the corridor seemingly without a care in the world. The boy was younger and scrawnier close-up, and his girlfriend shuffled behind him like a shadow.

"Hi," the kids said in unison as if they hadn't just smashed her window to pieces.

Penny curled her lips upward in what felt like a smile. "Got a bottle?"

"Oh, yeah, yes. Yes, ma'am," said the boy as he pulled an empty Coke bottle from his bag.

"And a hundred bucks," said Penny.

"A hundred? My buddy told me it was only fifty," said the boy.

"Well, it's gone up this week. It's a gold batch. Double strength."

"Oh, gold batch," said the boy and exchanged a knowing glance with his girlfriend. "Double strength, huh? Perfect. The guys will be happy. Party, party, and all that, you know?"

"Yeah, party, party, and all that." Penny tried hard to keep her sarcasm at bay.

She held out her hand and waited as the boy counted five twenties into her palm. "Plus, a hundred for the window."

"Of course. Yeah, sorry about that." The boy planted another hundred in her hand and pocketed the remaining bundle of cash in his pocket.

"All good." Penny smiled. "Just do me a favor, okay?"

"Sure," said the boy.

"Stop waving that wad of cash around. You'll get cut open just for fun around here."

The boy shuffled nervously, glanced over his shoulder. His girlfriend sidled closer and intertwined her fingers in his, the blood draining from her hands with the tightness of her grip.

"Sure, sure," he said. "Thanks for the tip."

"This is not a Haven. You know that, right? It's a Leftover district. This is the wrong side of the tracks, okay? Very wrong."

"Wrong, got it."

The boy looked nervous enough now, and Penny was satisfied they'd make it home in one piece.

She smiled—a genuine one this time. "I'll be back in a sec. Wait here, okay?"

"Um, can't we wait inside?" asked the girl.

"No one is going to knife you on my doorstep," Penny said. "Just out there in the big bad world, you know? Relax, I'll be two seconds."

In the kitchen, Penny poured an inch of potato vodka from one of her father's bottles and topped it off with water. The less alcohol these kids imbibed, the better.

The boy grinned stupidly when Penny handed over the watery vodka, her words of wisdom seemingly already forgotten.

"Just be careful, okay?' said Penny.

"Sure, sure," he said, "watch out for baddies and all."

The girl giggled and nuzzled her face into the boy's shoulder as they retreated.

"Hey," said Penny. "Why are you buying bootleg? You could get the real thing for less than a hundred Uptown."

"Where's the fun in that?" said the boy, and then he waved and disappeared down the stairs.

"Fun?" said Penny, but the pair had already traipsed out of earshot. "Idiots."

Penny shut the door and made her way to the fridge. She took half the money from the wad the boy had given her and placed it in a battered-looking, frozen-stiff paper envelope, which she stuffed back in the side door of the freezer. Nausea rushed through her, the precursor to her spiral of withdrawal. The floor tilted beneath her feet as if she were perched on the keel of a boat. The wall steadied her, and she pressed her eyelids shut until the motion subsided. She made her way to her room, one step at a time, where she dropped to her knees and rifled through the shadows under her bed. She retrieved a shoebox, covered in a fine layer of dust, with *ARUBA FUND* written across the lid in capital letters. She tossed in the money and stuffed the box carelessly back into its hiding spot.

Her hands shook, and a giant hiccup threw her shoulders forward. The box of sleeping pills awaited her on the bedside table. Penny hoisted herself onto her bed and stared at the packet shaking in her hands. The words marched around the perimeter of the pack, taking a different form with every blink of her eyes. Ambien, Amoeba, Am-I-a-bee, Be-I-am. She'd been warned against upping her dose of sleeping pills, but what other solution did she have once they'd stopped working? Penny swallowed the pills dry, two at once, and waited for the nausea to subside. A deep breath, count down from a hundred until her eyes became so heavy she had no choice but to let them close, and finally, finally, the black rolled in.

Chapter Eight

A CRACK RAN the length of the wall, and Penny traced her finger along its crevasse, panic slowly subsiding. The knife in her hand, small and sharp, was clean of blood, and by the look of the handle, one from her father's collection. Shame and fear overwhelmed her. How long had she been standing there, staring at the wall?

"Breathe, breathe," she whispered. Safety check, she wasn't hurt—fearful but not in pain. As far as sleepwalking escapades went, this was a good outcome, but her goal to stay out of trouble's way was significantly hindered by these nightly expeditions.

The parking garage, lit by a succession of faulty bulbs that flickered in fits, pulled ghostly shadows from grottos in the darkness and filled Penny with a terror to make her knees tremble. "Basement 1" stamped itself intermittently across the walls amidst graffiti that was typical of the hateful vitriol she'd become accustomed to over the last few years. Hostile propaganda, the wallpaper in the background of her life.

The exit sign hung askew a metal door, open and balancing on a corner, off a single hinge. Lights buzzed overhead like a swarm of mosquitoes; the smell of rot repulsed her to the point of gagging. It was dark beyond the broken door, and the stairs leading upward filled her with dread. She gripped the handle of her knife with sweaty fingers. Without another thought, she made a forward rush up the stairwell, her footsteps fueled by adrenaline, step after step, the stale wind on her shoulder like the breath of a ghost. Her steps, pounding in her ears, echoed behind her like a killer on the loose, or a rabid dog hungry for the flesh of a damsel in distress. Her imaginary enemy chased her out the exit at level four and onto the street, on high alert, knife held high, eyes blinking under the harsh light of dawn.

The smell of wafting coffee filled her with both longing and dread, and she knew she was in trouble even before she spotted the grand arch of Washington Square Park. Greenwich Village was one of the more exclusive Havens. Leftover scum from the Two Bridges district, where she resided, were not welcome unless, of course, they'd been trucked in to do some menial labor for the privileged who lived there.

Penny tucked the knife blade up into her sleeve; the cool steel tap-tapped against her wrist as she skirted along the edge of the park. All around, people swished by in suits or activewear, exercising themselves and their dogs. The hustle-bustle of life in this Haven depressed her to the core of her soul. Was the virus nonexistent in the Haven districts, or did their five-star healthcare afford the citizens such enviable freedoms?

The Leftover states still struggled to control the spread of the virus due to a broken healthcare system. Paranoia kept everyone locked inside their apartments, but who could afford the gas even if they wanted to travel somewhere, and where would they go anyway?

In the Leftover states, cars were practically a thing of the past, but here, in this beautiful clean Haven state, the traffic jostled along like no big thing. Penny stared in awe until a man in a taxi slowed to eye her suspiciously. She dropped her head, accelerated her stride, and was off at a brisk pace, suddenly aware of just how visible she was in her scruffy sweatpants and sockless sneakers. The organic grocer at the corner of Bleecker and Sullivan stopped her in her tracks. Row upon row of perfectly stacked fruit beckoned her like a pile of diamonds. When was the last time she'd seen a real mandarin? She dared not touch a single piece, but stared with envy, inhaling the sweet tropical scent of a once-familiar life. What a world this Haven was, where bananas sold for one hundred dollars a bunch and life ticked along as if the Division had never happened at all.

The fruit vendor, peeking out from behind the safety of his cash register, glared at Penny with such ferocity she felt his eyes like a slap to the face. She spun on her heels and continued down Bleecker Street, past the Starbucks whose offerings included mocha and donut combos for only sixty-five dollars. A peel of saliva wet the corner of her lips. Just a bite, a single sugary bite. Crisp yet soft, sweet yet tart, she could almost taste it as she barreled around the corner, pondering the luxury of a donut only to discover she was beelining her way toward a checkpoint. She missed a step. Her breath caught in her throat.

"Shit," she whispered and stopped briefly to search out the nearest trash can, across the street, on the diagonal, forcing her to jaywalk. Pausing at the corner, attempting to look nonchalant, she was relieved to find not a soul cared about her existence. At least that much hadn't changed, even in the Havens. New Yorkers were still New Yorkers. Clear plastic lined the shiny green garbage can, and nothing lay within. Even the trash was immaculate on this side of the city. She nervously scanned the vicinity for onlookers, and when she was finally satisfied no one was watching, she let the knife slip from her fingers and flinched as it clanged into its new home.

The checkpoint was manned by yet another pair of peacemaking idiots. Their boyish peacocking would have been funny if it weren't so serious. Whose idea was it, anyway, to give these idiots guns?

Penny tugged at the hem of her sweatshirt and approached Idiot-One cautiously. She'd have to come up with some more distinctive names if she was going to label all the assholes she came upon.

Idiot-One looked at his buddy, Idiot-Two, and they exchanged knowing smirks.

"This one looks like she might have a weapon, Corporal," said Idiot-One.

"A gun, Corporal?" said Idiot-Two. "Definitely a gun."

Idiot-One sauntered toward Penny and promptly grabbed her under the chin, turning her face upward. She was so close to his face she could see the tiny hairs up his nose.

"Little bitch got a gun, huh?" said Idiot-One.

He came at her, nose to nose, and squeezed her jaw in a vise grip. His breath smelled like oats and ash. Dewy hair and acne littered his face. A face only a mother could love.

"Got a gun under there, babyface?" he said, letting his free hand slide down her neck and grab at her body, pulling her breasts and pinching her crotch. His laughter was shrouded in the fog of her mind, and she suppressed the urge to fight back.

"What's the holdup?" said a distant voice, booming with authority.

Idiot-One released Penny and stood to attention. "We, um, we think she's got a gun."

Penny didn't move. Not an inch.

The voice let out an audible sigh; footsteps followed, heavy and swift.

"Where is she hiding it? In her shoes?" said the voice with such scathing sarcasm Penny would have laughed had she not been so petrified—but then was surprised to see her own fear mirrored in the teen soldier's face. Being chastened by this man was a serious thing. Her brief relief turned to shock as she turned to see the lieutenant from the bridge checkpoint. His authority radiated from the crisp cut of his uniform and the hint of gray that washed through a receding hairline. Deep creases around his eyes foretold the story of trauma and perseverance.

The lieutenant raised his eyebrows in recognition, made no attempt to hide that he knew exactly who she was. "This is not your district," he said. "Why are you here?"

Penny could ask him the same question, but she bit her lip to stop from speaking it out loud and presumed he could see the guilt oozing out of her every pore.

"Cleaning shift," she said. "At Starbucks up on Fifth."

"There are buses for your type. Why aren't you on one?"

Why? Why? Why? Think.

"Because I'm not one of them," Penny said with a sniff and a toss of her chin. "I'm not a dirty Number, so why should I travel with them?" She crossed her arms in front of her chest, unfolded them, and tugged at a strand of hair that fell just below her earlobe. Swallowed. Turned a deep shade of red.

The man rolled his eyes. He was clearly no fool and obviously suffered them lightly. "And your paperwork? I need to see your numbers."

"Numbers?"

"For your job. Your cleaning job, at Starbucks."

Penny heard the sarcasm.

"Didn't think so," said the lieutenant. A smirk spread across his face as he pulled a pair of handcuffs from his back pocket. "I've got no choice but to send you to a displacement center on order of identification processing. Hands in front."

"But I'm a citizen," said Penny desperately. "I don't belong in a Numbers camp."

The lieutenant clicked his fingers at her impatiently. "Your rights as a citizen of the United States have been automatically waived under article two-fifty of the new code of compliance by military decree. If you do no—"

"It's not fair," said Penny. "I haven't done anything."

"Your rights as a citizen of the United States have been—"

"No," said Penny, shuffling backward. "They haven't!"

"I don't have time for this," said the lieutenant. "Corporal, cuff her and prep her for transport."

Without a beat, Penny's arms were yanked from behind and cuffed at the wrist. Too tight. Sharp edges dug into skin. Idiot-Two dragged her backward, and she staggered to keep up. The incessant beeping of a car horn only added to the drama of Penny's arrest, and it wasn't until it stopped that they all took notice. The corporal paused, allowing Penny to find stable footing.

In the middle of the street, holding up traffic, was a large pink four-wheel-drive vehicle. The door opened and out hopped a pear-shaped woman with a head of perfectly puffy bright-red hair. She wore a crisp white sweatsuit with yellow stripes and spotless pink Nikes. The woman slammed the door and faced the line of cars stretching back down the street.

"Oh, for goodness' sake, drive around, you imbeciles." She tossed back a lock of hair and strode toward the checkpoint.

Penny almost cried with hope. Rita, local do-gooder, wealthy upper east-sider, queen of the Two Bridges borough, and long-time friend of Penny's mother. Rita's dedication to the families of her Leftover district was commendable, including but not limited to setting up a soup kitchen paid for out of her own pocket. Rita was a distant but significant contributor to the welfare of Penny's family. She was connected somehow on her mother's side, loyal to her family, yet Penny wasn't entirely sure what warranted the loyalty and struggled to imagine a friendship between such polar opposites. Where Rita was brash, Penny's mother was soft. Rita strode toward her with a confidence so excessive it was almost vulgar to see, yet in that moment, Penny had never been so grateful to know her. With a fierce look and a nod in Penny's direction, Penny knew well enough to keep her mouth firmly shut. *Not another word, girl.*

"Morning, Lieutenant!" said Rita, waving her arm in broad strokes above her head. "Lovely day for it."

The lieutenant clenched his jaw, sinewy veins coiling down his neck like dragon tails.

"Lovely day for what, Rita?"

"For catching stray Numbers, of course." Rita laughed and slapped him on the back. Hard.

The lieutenant tripped forward but quickly righted himself and tossed his head back, glancing at his subordinates, who had politely turned their eyes upward, busying their gazes in the Manhattan skyline.

Penny took the chance to run from her distracted captor and into the arms of Rita.

"I see you've gotten a wee bit mixed up with this one," said Rita, throwing a protective arm around Penny's shoulders. "Cuffed her up and all, Lieutenant. Goodness me, this *is* a mistake."

"I'm just doing my job, Rita."

"Well, if you were doing your job properly, you wouldn't have my little blonde, American friend here, cuffed up to the eyeballs, now would you? Look at her. She's skin and bones. What's she going to do? Raise an army? She's barely able to raise herself."

"She's not cuffed up to the eyeballs, Rita."

"No, you're right, because you're going to uncuff her before I can count the little beads of sweat forming on your forehead," Rita said and poked the lieutenant right in the middle of his furrowed brow.

Penny froze in awe and delight. This was a side of Rita she'd never seen, and she could barely believe it when the lieutenant spun her around and released the restraints.

Penny massaged her wrists where the metal had dug in but was immensely grateful to have been saved by Rita, yet again.

"There's a good boy," said Rita in such a condescending fashion even Penny felt the need to turn away to preserve the remaining ounce of dignity that was all the man had left.

Rita gasped and cradled her cheeks between her hands. "Oh, my goodness, listen to that angry traffic. I hope I'm not holding everyone up," she said in mock dismay. "Thank you, Lieutenant. And don't forget—You-Know-Who is always watching."

Rita pointed skyward and winked at Penny before grabbing her by the shoulders and ushering her toward to the pink truck.

Penny hopped into the passenger side, ignoring the furious honking that trailed off in the line of cars behind them. Rita wriggled comfortably into the driver's seat and fussed with her makeup in the rearview mirror before turning the engine over.

Penny, fascinated by Rita's coolness, heard her throwaway catchphrase as if for the first time. As if it hadn't been heard a million times before at every social occasion. It wasn't actually a casual attempt to keep the stray flock morally in line. For the first time, Penny suspected "You-Know-Who" wasn't God after all. You-Know-Who was a threat—a serious threat. An actual, living, breathing, always-watching person.

THE INTERIOR OF Rita's car was the most luxurious thing Penny had been privy to in a long time. The seat, warm and soft, enveloped her in a leathery hug. Even the air inside the SUV was as fresh as a spring day. If she'd had a choice in that moment, she would have happily spent the rest of her life living in that vehicle. She glanced at Rita, who shot Penny disapproving glances every few seconds.

"Thanks, Rita," said Penny.

"Don't you thank me, young lady."

"So who do I thank? You-Know-Who?"

"I hope you're not being brassy."

Penny smiled. She loved the way Rita peppered her sentences with old-timey language, and she always promised herself to try to remember each quaint word she learned from Rita and bring it back, kicking and screaming into the present. "Brassy? That's the best word."

Penny was still considering the joy of her newly acquired jargon when she flew forward in her seat as the car came to an abrupt and screeching halt. A chorus of horns filed off down the street behind them. "What the fuck, Rita?" she said as her head jolted back against the head-rest.

"You want to know 'what the fuck' is, my darling?" said Rita as she pointed a serious and frightening finger in Penny's face. "The fuck is you wandering around in sectors you have no business wandering around in. The fuck is you underestimating the power of this administration. The fuck is you being brassy with the good Lieutenant Dixon. The fuck is you getting your shit together. That's the fuck. Understand?"

Penny nodded. While she had a few of her own counterpoint fucks— such as referring to the military leaders of America as an "administration" and the framing of Lieutenant Dickhead as "good"—she dared not raise them. And she was still in mild shock to hear a fully grown adult say the word "fuck" so many times in a row, especially an apparently deeply religious fully-grown adult with an apparently deeply respectable life and finely tuned moral compass.

Penny grew anxious. Who was this woman she thought she knew so well? It made Penny nervous to think there were other complicated and angry sides to this woman that she had no idea existed.

Rita sighed, flicked a lock of flaming hair over her shoulder, and calmly restarted the car. They drove in silence for at least ten blocks, and Penny lost herself in the streets as they made their way from gold-gilded shopfronts full of pricey consumer wares to boarded-up brownstones and empty streets.

The subway entrances and parking garages had been nicely paved over in brick and stone up into Greenwich, but farther south, broken boards and patchwork steel seemed to be the material of choice. How dark would it be beneath streets in the deserted subway system, and what horrors lay in there? Murderers and zombies and gray ghosts.

"Are you even listening to me?" Rita clicked her fingers at Penny's face.

Penny shuddered and left the imaginary subway zombies chasing the car behind them. "What?"

Rita rolled her eyes. "Your father? I asked how he was holding up. He's got a full plate, my dear."

"We've all got full plates, Rita."

"Yes, but some of us have stronger arms to hold our plates, don't we?" Rita reached out and stroked Penny's cheek gently.

Penny eyes filled with tears. She was unaccustomed to such tenderness. "Sometimes, they're really heavy plates." She let the tears roll down her cheek without wiping them away.

"I know, honey."

"And Larry has totally lost his plates."

Rita was silent for a minute and then rested her palm on the armrest between the seats, just behind the handbrake. She slapped the back of her hand twice on the armrest, and Penny placed her hand on Rita's, instinctively intertwining their fingers. Instant calm.

"Iron sharpens iron, my dear. So one man—"

"—sharpens another," said Penny. "You've told me that one already. It didn't help then, and it doesn't help now." She tore her fingers free from Rita's grip.

Penny thought Rita understood her struggle, understood her fight, but nothing was less authentic than tossing around neatly packaged quotable titbits in her general direction.

"I know what will help," said Rita, completely unfazed by Penny's outburst. "A night at the Church of Rita. I haven't seen you at the soup kitchen in so long, my dear, and I could do with the extra help. We're so busy nowadays, and you know better than anyone that idle hands are the devil's work."

Penny nodded as Rita pulled to a stop outside Penny's tenement. This wasn't a suggestion; this was an order. As Penny hopped out the car, a sense of freedom engulfed her. She slammed the door shut, and the cold air hit her cheeks like a slap. She waved to Rita, feigned a smile, and ran.

Chapter Nine

PENNY SHUT HER bedroom door and leaned against the frame, shaken by the events of the morning. The dull light of the dreary fall day splintered through the hole in the broken window, and a restlessness boiled up from deep inside her, starting small, like wind tossing a leaf but growing in fervor until a mounting discomfort took control of her mind. The window, still broken and long since forgotten, only served to make her sink deeper to a place of despair, the problem of fixing it almost unbearable.

She paced around the edges of her room, counting down from one hundred, and finally stopped in front of her Aruba-dreaming pinboard. With a sliver of shame, she pondered how silly she had been to think that things would get better. There was no goodness left in the world, and her future was bleak, if indeed she had one. The pinboard, plastered with pictures of happy moments, sunshine and rainbows, no longer gave her any joy, so she hoisted it off the wall and placed it over the shattered window. Problem solved, but no weight lifted. In fact, her soul was so burdened her legs could barely hold her up. She looked at her bed and fell forward into a comforting sanctuary of blankets, which embraced her in a warm grip of cotton and feather. She curled into a ball, sank her face in her hands, and surrendered.

Footsteps and muffled words drifted into her room from behind closed doors. Her father, drunk or sober, she didn't really care as long as he let her be.

Bang! Bang! Bang!

The knock on her door startled her like a bolt of lightning.

"Get out here, Penn. Benny's hungry," said her father.

Deep breath. Patience depleted.

"For fucks' sake, I'm not your maid," said Penny.

"As long as you're living under my roof, you're my fucking maid. Open this damned door."

"It's not even locked."

Larry stumbled through the door, shoulder first. Clearly drunk; and she had no fight left in her.

"Darling," he said. "I just miss you, that's all. You're my baby, my beautiful baby."

"Jesus, Larry, sober up."

Tears pooled in his eyes, and Penny's stomach lurched with nerves, fear, sadness. It all felt the same these days. This broken man was a heart-breaking sight, desolate and rocking from foot to foot, with his drunk eyes, rolling and blinking, unable to focus on a single solid object.

This sight was doing nothing to lift her mood. What was the point of eking out this crappy existence in a horrid Leftover borough at the ass end of nowhere? She was fed up.

"While I've got your attention, Larry," said Penny, picking up the happy face sign off the floor. "I quit. I'm not doing this shit for you any-more."

She slammed the sign into his stomach, where it fell instantly to the floor and bounced off his toes. Larry wrapped his arms around his waist, a late reaction before he stumbled forward, caught his footing again, and laughed.

"Taxi!" he said as he shot an arm into the air and waved it about like a fool.

Penny suppressed an unusual urge to slap him. Her anxieties had never culminated in a desire toward violence. Instead, she shook her head and paced into the kitchen, where she found Benny standing by the door staring at the floor. His pain of simply existing seeped out of every pore. Sometimes she forgot how sensitive he was. He'd lost a sister when Penny's mother died, and he had taken the loss very hard, every step, labored, every word out of his mouth, forced. He'd showed up at their apartment a day after the funeral and never left. Penny knew she re-minded him of his sister and that it both hurt him and gave him joy. In turn, she felt responsible for his wellbeing.

"Hey, Uncle Ben," she said. "Hungry?"

He nodded, smiled.

"Sit down. I'll make you an egg."

Precious eggs. A rare treat. She'd spent ten whole dollars on one sin-gle egg and had been saving it for a special occasion, but there would be no special occasions, and what did she want with such luxuries anyway?

The fry pan was dusty from underuse, and she blew the cobwebs out and set it upon a hot element. The refrigerator was mostly bare, filled only with a scattering of long-expired condiments. She carefully removed the one egg from its compartment and cradled it in two hands. Careful, careful. A smile broke from her lips as she cracked the egg into the pan and watched it bubble and spit. It surprised her how much pleasure this gave her. Sunny-side up, with a split yoke. You didn't really know someone until you knew exactly how they liked their eggs. This was a subject she had thought long and hard about and, according to her research, had discovered a list of attributes that were common among certain egg-eating types. Over easy—optimistic. Scrambled—complicated and tormented. Fried—sad. Omelet—well, omelet people were a breed of their own. Peacemakers, she imagined, would be big on the eating of the omelet.

She slipped the egg onto a plate—fried, of course—and grabbed a fork from the drawer before ushering the food over to Benny, who sat at the table waiting patiently, as if he could wait forever and ever. They smiled at each other, and she helped him wrap his shaking fingers around the fork. The hands of an alcoholic in withdrawal.

Penny went back to the kitchen and poured Benny a glass of vodka, tamped down with a fair bit of water, just enough to stop the shaking. He looked like he was going to cry when she handed it to him. She sat next to him and rested her head on his shoulder.

"We're a broken lot, aren't we, Ben?"

"Nah, we're okay, girl." Benny curled his arm up around her head and stroked her hair. "We need a bit of oil in the tank to get going sometimes."

"Oil? Is that what you're calling it now?"

Penny's father shuffled into the room; his tearstained face belied the smile he wore. "The party started without me? No way," he said as he poured himself a vodka.

Penny lifted her head from Benny's shoulder. She clenched her jaw, annoyed beyond belief that Larry had cut short her tender moment with Benny. She'd felt a great sense of peace wash over her. Just for a moment, a single second, a single blissful second.

The room felt suddenly small and devoid of air, giving the sensation of being slowly suffocated. Penny needed out. She certainly couldn't be around Larry anymore. He wasn't the same man she'd grown up with, and after her mother's death, she'd watched him shrink from a quirky and intelligent professor to a bleary-eyed fool. Although she occasionally pondered the disabling guilt he must invariably harbor, it wasn't something she could consider for long, for it made her own guilt rise to the surface, spiraling her into a state of bewildered contemplation that couldn't be conquered by bootleg vodka. Ultimately, she'd been abandoned twice. First by her mother and then by this man who called himself her father.

She kissed Benny on the cheek. "Take it easy, okay?"

"Always, Penn."

She managed to make it to her room without starting another fight with her father, but her restless sense of defeat hadn't left her. She lay on her bed and stared at the ceiling, mind racing from one thought to the next but never settling for long enough to catch a stable idea. With the black monster of anxiety rumbling around her chest, she finally rolled off the side of her bed and rested her head in her hands.

Her brush with the lieutenant raised a lot of questions about Rita and how she had so much power in this new world order. Penny had been summoned to the soup kitchen, and her instincts told her she'd be foolish to ignore the demand. Rita was clearly not a woman whose bad side you wanted to be on. Besides, it seemed a small payment for being rescued, and Penny could get a free meal. She was absolutely starving. She scoured the floor of her closet for some cleanish clothes—jeans, tee, hoodie, coat—retrieved her ID from the side table, and pulled on some trainers, already feeling better.

It was quiet in the kitchen. Penny pulled out two pieces of bread from the freezer, threw them on the counter and splashed water on her face. In the living room, her father had fallen asleep with his head resting on the table, and Benny stared out the window, oblivious to her existence.

She turned the stove off at the wall and dumped the pot of smoking potatoes in the sink. The pan spat and sizzled as she doused it under the running faucet. She was amazed they hadn't burned the apartment down yet.

"Larry," she said as she scraped the bottom of the potato pot. "Dad!"

"What?" He shuddered out of his slumber.

"You're gonna burn this fucking place down one day."

He sighed and put his head back on the table.

"Enough of this shit, Larry."

Her father snored in answer.

Penny let her frustration settle before she grabbed the semi-defrosted slices of bread off the counter and made her way out the door. Without a single glance over her shoulder, she yelled her usual farewell line.

"And stop drinking the fucking foreshots!"

Chapter Ten

PENNY'S RELIEF UPON leaving the apartment was palpable, like a heavy cloak slipping off her shoulders. Bread already consumed, she brushed the crumbs from her hands and made her way down South Street. It wasn't the most straightforward route, though she was less likely to come across rogue peacemakers looking for trouble.

The fall wind nipped at her cheeks but was offset by the ambience of the season. It was her favorite time of year, with all the dropping leaves in their copper shades and the promise of change thick in the air.

Penny turned onto Rutgers Street and walked past an array of Chinese and European fast-food joints, punctuated by a liquor store at the end of the row, now with recently boarded-up windows and shut down for business. It was a shocking contrast to the thriving bustle she'd witnessed in Greenwich Village. How did those elite few exist like that when so many others were merely surviving just on the other side of town? Did they even know?

The queue along Madison Avenue Promenade extended at least one hundred yards. A bleak mood overcame her as she strolled past hundreds of hungry citizens waiting patiently for their chance to sip a cup of hot soup, perhaps their only meal of the day. She stopped at the single-level brownstone, which had a large sign above its entrance proclaiming: Kingdom Hall of Jehovah's Witness. Penny noticed for the first time that the whole wall was untouched by graffiti. The good citizens of the Lower East Side were hedging their bets on the existence of God, and any God would do at this stage, especially one who drove a pink SUV and gave away free meals.

The people at the front of the queue eyed Penny suspiciously as she made her way to the top of the line.

"I'm a volunteer," she said, hands held up as if being accosted by a bunch of gun-wielding maniacs. She tried her best to smile, felt her lips curl upward. She put her hand on the door and pushed but was stopped by a man at the front, dreadlocked and barefoot, who gripped her wrist tightly.

"You're cutting," said the man. "Back of the line."

"Me?" said Penny. "But I work here."

"You're not on Rita's list."

Penny looked the man up and down. Scruffy, certainly no doorman. Certainly, no security guard.

"What list?" said Penny. "Your imaginary list, for imaginary doormen?"

"The list is in my head." He tapped the side of his temple and puffed out his chest in pride.

"You don't even know my name. Who the hell do you think you are?" Penny tried to shake her wrist free, but the man's grip only tightened.

"No one goes in until someone comes out. That's the rule."

The man's eyes were hardened and hollow like someone who had suffered. She knew these eyes well for they reflected her own trauma, but she also knew that trauma was nothing to fear in others, and in fact, it made them weak. She saw his weakness for she suffered the same affliction. No, she wasn't afraid, and how dare he try to intimidate her. Penny squashed down the rising sense of exhilaration, an opportunity to unleash her growing disdain for the world.

"If you don't let go of me right now, I'll scream blue murder and have you shipped off to a numbers camp faster than you can drink the cup of soup I'm about to serve you."

The man tightened his grip momentarily, squeezed harder as he stared directly into her eyes. She stared directly back.

"I can vouch for her," said a boy standing in the queue a few people down.

Penny looked at the kid, handsome, with immaculately styled dirty-blond hair. His face was friendly but not one she recognized, and surely a face this beautiful she'd not forget. She stared at him curiously, struggling to place him, but nothing came.

"I've seen her before—working, I mean—in Rita's Church," said the boy before looking suddenly self-conscious due to the attention he was garnering.

The dreadlocked man, without taking his eyes off Penny for a second, lifted his chin, released his grip slowly, and cocked an imaginary gun at her forehead, pressing his dirty finger hard against bridge of her nose, cold and seething.

Penny swatted his hand away and smiled. "You're welcome in advance," she said with a sarcastic tone that reminded her of her brush with the lieutenant. She pushed her way through the door but not before taking a last look behind her at the handsome boy who'd risked his own spot in line for her. She couldn't wait to see him again.

THE CHURCH WAS warm, welcoming, and full of life, with its fluorescent lights and bustling volunteers. It was the change Penny had been seeking. The chaos had a semblance of normality, and the people here seemed comparatively happy. They sat in groups, talking and occasionally laughing, forgetting about their troubles outside Jehovah's sanctuary.

Penny made her way through the rows of foldout tables, toward the serving lane where six flush-faced volunteers ladled soup into bowls.

"Look what the cat dragged in!" Rita paused her ladling duties in order to fetch an apron from under the bench and toss it in Penny's direction.

Penny caught the apron with one hand and clutched it to her chest, feeling a rush of pride to be part of something bigger than herself. It was honorable that Rita manned the front line with her crew when she could just as easily hole up in her luxurious Upper West Side apartment and forget about the mess in Two Bridges.

"Hey, boys." Penny greeted Rita's twins, Robert and Drew, who were only a year younger than Penny but acted like a pair of ten-year-olds on a sugar bender. She could easily ignore them, but she loved to see them blush. Today was no different, and Penny was satisfied only after both of them flushed a deep beet-red and mumbled greetings into their chests.

"Get to work, my darling!" said Rita. "You can help Sam on biscuits, down the end."

Sam smiled and raised his eyebrows at Penny.

"No tomfoolery today, you two," said Rita from the bottom of the line. "I know what you're like when you get together." She peered at Penny from behind the giant soup pot and threw her a trademark Rita wink. "And don't forget"—she pointed at the ceiling—"You-Know-Who is watching, and he tells me everything!"

Rita shrieked with laughter and greeted her next guest in the queue as if they were family coming home for Thanksgiving.

Penny discreetly scanned each ceiling corner for a hidden camera and felt a shameful rush of paranoia overcome her.

"She's crazy," whispered Sam.

"Careful," said Penny. "You-Know-Who is taking notes. He'll be reporting your insolent soul to the lady at the top."

Sam brushed his hand through his thick dark hair. It curled lazily across his forehead and swept the edge of his big almond-shaped eyes, which glistened as if he was always on the verge of tears. She'd known Sam since they were children and was familiar with every expression that washed across his face as if it were her own. She could see his worry loud and clear. How she loved her sweet friend.

"Take it easy," she said, wrapping her arm around his shoulder. "I promise you, no one is tattling. You're too boring to be tattled on anyway."

"Penny." Sam looked exasperated.

"I'm kidding. You know I love you. You are a bit boring, though. Even you have to admit that. You got nothing to hide. Unless you do... Oh my god, you're keeping secrets from me now. What are you not telling me? Come clean, boy, this instant."

Sam laughed. "No secrets. Ever."

"No secrets." Penny glanced at her best friend, kind and innocent and completely in the dark about just how out of control her life was spiraling. She really needed to make more time for him. He was a good influence in her life.

Sam shoved the tongs into Penny's hand. "Take over," he said. "I'll have Rita's wrath to face if I burn the rest of the biscuits."

Penny raised her eyebrow at Sam and tried to think of a witty quip.

"Don't even," he said, walking toward a beeping oven. "You're trouble, Penelope Ann Carter."

Rita's hungry guests smiled curiously in response to Penny's laughter as she placed the remaining biscuits into the napkins in their hands as they shuffled by. She usually tried to avoid too much eye contact—unless she was dealing with kids, and then she would always offer a smile.

Sam charged up from behind Penny with a tray of steaming biscuits and dumped them on the table.

Their doughy smell, sweet and sour, wafted through the air, homey and full of comfort, reminding Penny she was starving. But her hunger pangs merged into nerves as the handsome boy from the front of the queue meandered down the line. She kept her eyes firmly planted on the pile of biscuits before her.

When the boy finally reached her station, he stopped and smiled sheepishly. "I'm Mark," he said and blushed.

"Penny." She offered her hand, which Mark graciously shook. They looked into each other's eyes and laughed. A meeting of new friends, a reconnection of old souls.

"What's the holdup?" said Rita, peering nosily down the line and frowning at Penny. "Chop-chop, kiddies. These biscuits won't serve themselves."

"I'll see you around, right?" said Penny to Mark.

"No question."

She smiled without even trying.

Sam raised his eyebrows at her, questioning the interaction with Mark, his face a combination of amusement and envy.

Penny shrugged her shoulders and shook her head. "No big deal."

"If you say so." Sam thrust a pair of long tongs with wooden handles in Penny's direction, while simultaneously snatching the short metal pair from her hands. "Trade with me, would you? I have a thing about touching the wooden handles; it gives me the shivers."

"You're so weird," said Penny.

"Why, thank you. I'll take that as a compliment."

Sam took a deep breath and sighed. "It's been so boring here without you. Where've you been anyway?"

"I've been around."

"Around?" said Sam, with a cheeky grin. "What kind of answer is that from one best friend to another?"

Penny wondered how she could fit the details of the past month into one sentence while hungry people stopped by expecting her to serve them hot biscuits. "I'm just tired," she said.

"Still sleepwalking?"

"Mm-hmm. I've been doing some crazy shit at night."

"Now we're talking! Fill me in."

"Well, I ended up in Brooklyn one night," she said, ignoring Sam's gasp. "And then I went to Greenwich the next. I've been getting around."

"Holy shit, across the bridge? It's lucky you didn't get murdered."

"And I met a girl called Quinn."

Sam stopped and turned to look at Penny with a serious face. "I see. Quinn, huh?" He grinned from ear to ear.

"Stop it," said Penny, simultaneously delighted and embarrassed. "She's just a friend."

"Right. A friend, okay."

"Of course she is. I'm not even sure if I'm, you know, into, you know—"

"Girls," said Sam nonchalantly. "Into girls."

"Shhh! Christ, Sam, keep your voice down. They'll take me in for reconditioning before I've even kissed one."

Sam suddenly stiffened and became serious. "That's not funny, Penn."

"I wasn't joking," she said, taken back by his defensiveness. "Take it easy."

"You know it's real, don't you? They're taking people—forcefully, I might add—and literally frying parts of their brains. You know, they walk out the other side like straight zombies."

Penny shook her head. "I don't believe it. It's just like conversion therapy gossip gotten out of control."

"Penn." Sam put his tongs down and looked seriously at her. "It's real. I've seen it. I've seen what happens to them." A tear escaped the corner of Sam's eye.

Penny thrust her tongs into the hands of the woman who was waiting for a biscuit. "Help yourself," she said, then grabbed Sam by the elbow and ushered him through the door behind the serving table.

The small, dirty kitchen had pots and pans piled up in almost every free space. Bench, floor, windowsill. A cool blue light washed the room, emanating from a single fluorescent bulb flickering and buzzing from the ceiling.

Penny plonked Sam into a chair at the table in the corner and crouched in front of him, resting her hands on his knees. She reached up and wiped away a tear with her thumb, swallowing the lump in her throat and struggling with everything inside her not to break down alongside him with the horror of everything, the horror of this life.

"Sam," she said as her voice broke, "what's happened? What's wrong?"

"They reconditioned Simon," said Sam, shaking his head and letting the tears roll out. "They just took him, just barged the door down and took him out of his bed."

Deeply saddened by how fearful Sam had become, Penny spoke as softly as she could, trying to make sense of what he was telling her. "Hang on, who is Simon?"

"Simon," said Sam, incredulous that Penny didn't know. "Simon, the doorman from my apartment."

Penny felt sick. She'd known Simon almost as long as she'd know Sam. He wasn't just a doorman; he was a friend, a happy face they'd taken for granted since childhood. A giver of cuddles and high fives, and sound advice and candy and, sometimes, a simple smile that came from such a gentle place in his soul it warmed like a blanket.

"They can't do that," said Penny. "They can't just take people as they sleep."

"Well, they did." Sam put his hand on his heart as if trying to still the pain in his chest. "And when he came back, he was just a shell. A zombie. He couldn't talk for two weeks, Penn. Two weeks. He's broken. He's just broken."

Penny froze and tried to keep control of her breath. "Who ordered it?"

Sam stiffened. "What do you mean, who ordered it?"

"You know what I mean. There are people in that building who never accepted him as he is, including your dad. They don't just take people for reconditioning because they have a kink in their wrist."

"A kink in their wrist? What the hell is that supposed to mean?

"I'm just saying, you can't take someone for reconditioning because you think they might be queer. You take them when you know for sure. When a worried parent...well, you know?"

"Oh my god, open your eyes." Sam abruptly stood and strode toward the door, knocking Penny onto the floor in the process. "Not that you deserve my warning, but think carefully about who you are. It's not safe, you know, for different kinds."

"Different kinds?" Untapped fury stirred deep inside Penny. "I'm no 'different kind.' I'm not a *kind*. I'm me. I'm just me."

Sam shook his head and paused at the door, half in, half out, and turned slowly to face her. Tears streaked his face, but he now seemed completely at peace. "Calm down. You know what I mean. You always twist my words into something dramatic. Not everything in the world is about you."

"I never made this about me. *You* made this about me. *You* dragged me into this."

"See, drama. Good luck with that." And then Sam was gone before she could even respond.

She and Sam had fought like brother and sister forever and knew damn well how to push each other's buttons, but this was out of line. She scooped up a gravy pot stacked on top of a pile next to her and hurled it with all her strength at the door.

"Fuck you! Just fuck off!"

The tears came instantly, pouring out in huge gulps, and she curled up into her knees, letting her head come to rest on the gritty floor where she sobbed until she was too weak to sob any more.

Chapter Eleven

PENNY WAS STILL curled up on the kitchen floor, spent from crying when the door creaked open and a dish rag landed on her head.

"I'll wash, you dry," said Rita. "It's just a few pots today, darling."

Penny pulled the tea towel off her face and laid her eyes upon Rita who towered over her with an outstretched hand. She sighed and pushed herself onto her knees before taking Rita's hand and allowing the woman to hoist her to her feet.

Penny's body ached from lying on the floor for so long. How long, she wasn't sure. She looked around the room and took in the mess. There were at least twelve large commercial pans caked in a variety of gunk and piles of small trays and pots and utensils to clean.

"Just a few," said Penny with the hint of a smile.

Rita wrapped an arm around her shoulder and gave her squeeze. "Hard work betrays none, my darling. So get scrubbing."

As they worked together in silence, peace drifted back into Penny's soul, and as she took in deep slow breaths, a sense of balance returned. She was going to be okay, and she knew it, but Sam had a point. She knew she had to be careful, but she didn't believe for a second that Sam's father hadn't called in the peacemakers to take Simon for gender therapy reconditioning. His father had never liked Simon based purely on his sexual orientation. It hurt Penny to think of lovely, cheerful Simon in pain and fear. She could only hope the rumors of torture and humiliation were untrue.

Penny watched Rita scrub the pots with aggressive determination, but her sparkling eyes contradicted her delight in the challenge of cleaning a burned-bottomed pot. This woman, elbows deep in caked-on grease, clearly had power well beyond what she allowed them all to see.

"So how did you get him to do it today?" said Penny.

Rita stopped scrubbing and looked at Penny as innocently as a kid caught with a hand in the cookie jar. "How did I get whom to do what?"

"Lieutenant Dickhead," said Penny. "How did you get him to let me go?"

Rita laughed in that way she did, head tossed skyward, a shrill cackle emanating from the shallow place in her throat. "Oh, that silly little man, we go way back. He was an asshole when he was five, and he's an asshole now."

"You've known him since you were five?"

"Sure. I guess he's almost like a brother. A shitty asshole brother that everyone hates."

"So, less a brother and more a cave-dwelling Neanderthal?" said Penny.

Rita chuckled quietly, a laugh Penny had never heard. A laugh that was real.

"Very perceptive, my dear," said Rita. "But we have a professional relationship that has mutual benefits and an agreement that he stays out of my business and I stay out of his. If we keep to the rules of the game, everything rolls along hunky-dory. Sometimes he just needs a wee reminder; that's all."

"So that's why this place hasn't been raided by the peacemakers. You've got a lot of disillusioned people congregating here. How do they know you're not organizing an uprising?"

"Uprising?" said Rita, arms deep in a pot. "I should think not, my darling. They know who they're dealing with."

"Who's 'they'? The evil associates known as the Division?"

"More or less."

"And they're scared of the Cupcake Queen of the Upper West Side?"

Rita laughed. She always loved it when Penny mentioned her infamous Martha-Stewart-wannabe-You-Tube channel that had an inexplicable viral following before the Division. Penny suspected its infamy was born out of mockery, but either way, that had been history since the demise of the cellular network to citizens outside of a Haven.

"I prefer Sweetheart," said Rita.

"America's Cupcake Sweetheart."

"Although, I might be pushing it in the age department to be anyone's sweetheart."

"Don't be so sure. I heard our dear and mighty military leader has a soft spot for Martha Stewart types?"

"Does he now?" Rita blushed and pushed her hair back off her face. "But"—she held up a finger with a sly look on her face—"is it the Cupcake

Queen he's after or the powerful man she married, who lurks beneath her shadow?"

"Oh, it's like that? They want the big money, so they chase the frilly pink apron to get it."

"You got it, darling, and someone's gotta fund this war."

"War? I've never heard anyone call it that."

"Well, that's exactly what it is. Don't let anyone tell you otherwise."

"So whose side are you on? You're feeding the hungry down here, but you just basically told me that your husband is fueling a war against his own people."

"Not his own people, my darling," said Rita, whipping off her rubber washing gloves. "It's all about education and offering a better life to those, how do you say, less privileged. The Numbers, the poor, the gays, the sex addicted, all those fringe-dwelling types who make our society ugly. Oh, and the junkies, can't forget the junkies; we do a lot of good work for them." She cast a swift sideways look at Penny.

Sick to her stomach, Penny hesitated. "Education?" It was all she could finally say.

"Exactly. We have programs for all problem types. It's about straightening them out." Rita held up a finger in Penny's direction before continuing. "In *all* ways. We give them life. A new perfect, proper life. A good life, a Christian life."

"That's so wrong."

"Oh, darling," said Rita, utterly nonplussed by Penny's accusations. "Just remember who saved you from having to join the junior peacemakers."

Penny nodded. It was true Rita had authorized her permanent departure from the New American Education Regime. Her father had refused to sign the papers, insisting that a bad education was better than none at all. Penny thought he was awfully hypocritical considering his own exit from the business of education, and she'd sought out the Rita's help as she'd been a long-time teaching assistant at the local high school. Seeing how things had turned out, Penny was grateful for that.

"I wonder, my darling," said Rita, "if the peacemakers wouldn't be a good fit for you after all?"

"The peacemakers? Seriously?"

"Why not? You could turn all that passion into a real fire and make the change we desperately need."

Penny bit her lip and picked up a small packet of leftover dinner rolls, which she shoved into her satchel. "The peacemakers are a nasty business, and I'm happy to have no part in it, and that's all thanks to you."

"You're welcome, my darling. I'll do anything to help the needy."

"Wow." Penny walked to the door, paused, and knew in that second she would never again step foot into this crazy Church of Rita. "Just do me one last favor," she said.

"What's that, my darling?"

"Open your fucking eyes."

The exhilaration of speaking up felt like a slap across the face as Penny strode down the promenade, making a beeline for the Hudson River. Dusk was at its peak, and the red sky that framed the brownstone low-rise buildings lit up like fire. Penny took a breath, and something close to serenity washed over her, just for a second, a fleeting moment that almost instantly slipped away. The urge to look back upon the Church of Rita was hard to resist, and she could feel the gaze of Rita's beady eyes piercing into her shoulder blades. But Penny would give Rita no satisfaction in seeing any glimpse of regret. She lengthened her stride, threw her shoulders back, and hoped it hurt to watch her leave.

Penny stopped when she hit the South Street junction and watched a single car pass slowly by. Both she and the driver stared at each other curiously before she stepped onto the four-lane street, hopped over the barrier, strolled across, and perched herself on the lip of the river that overlooked the Brooklyn borough. The water sloshed a few feet below her, murky and dark. What treasures and horrors lay beneath? Penny's gaze drifted across the bay to a plume of smoke as it chugged from the Hudson Power Station and curled into the night. The thud of a military chopper droned away in the distance, and she searched the sky to find it. Enemy unseen. Panic rising. She stood and surveyed her surroundings. Darkness had fallen more quickly than expected, and curfew was only minutes away.

Penny headed toward her tenement block but was struck with an itch to keep moving. With barely a thought for her actions, she cautiously made for the Brooklyn Bridge. The peacemakers patrolled farther uptown most nights because there was a lifestyle to protect up that way, and having seen it with her own eyes, she understood why.

As predicted, the checkpoint was clear, and she strolled across the bridge feeling surprisingly buoyant, fearless even, her mood brightening with every step. At the midpoint on the bridge, she paused to take in the view, the silhouette of the old carousel just visible at a squint. It had once stood as a landmark of joy, but now, boarded up and scuffed with graffiti, it imitated a forgotten Christmas gift. A dusty old box just missing its bow. Penny smiled and continued with a skip in her step. She made her way down the service exit she and Quinn had used to escape the peacemakers, but as she descended beneath the bridge, a quiver of uncertainty washed over her. The tide lapped at the shore, and the smell of seaweed and gasoline filled her nostrils. Her footsteps, crunching in the damp gravel, sounded as loud as a freight train in a tunnel. At Plymouth Street, she cut through the Main Street Park and paced carefully along the walking paths, once reclaimed and gentrified but now broken and unstable.

The carousel, surrounded by knee-high weeds and broken glass, had no clear entry point, so Penny paced around the perimeter while trying to ignore the messages of hate scrawled on every empty patch of wall. A dull ache grew in her chest, fear looking for a home. Had she misunderstood the invitation from her new friend? Was there another carousel? She stood before the desolate boarded-up box and sighed with disappointment. What was she even doing there?

The darkness that moments earlier hadn't bothered her now filled her with a sense of gloom, and her confidence faded swiftly into angst.

A footstep? She froze and squinted into the night, but before she could move, a rolling shadow loomed out of the dark and grabbed her by the shoulder. A scream left her lips and broke the silence, sending an eerie echo across the bay and bouncing back into her chest with a gasp of air.

Chapter Twelve

"PENNY?" SAID A voice she immediately recognized, despite having known it for less than twenty-four hours.

"Quinn? You scared the shit out of me."

"Sorry. Didn't you hear me whispering to you?"

"What do you think?"

"I'm thinking not."

"And you'd be right." Penny put her hand over her heart as if holding it might stop it exploding—from fear or joy, she couldn't really tell.

"So, you came for the grand tour?" Quinn grabbed Penny's hand and paced off toward the boxed-up carousel. Quinn lifted a piece of the wall which hung loose on a single hinge, and a beam of light sprawled out across the ground, illuminating her smile. Penny had forgotten how beautiful she was and, indeed, how out of her league with her catlike eyes and her unruly mop of hair bouncing around her face, a complete mess of perfection. Penny's heart slowed its beat.

"Is your knee okay?" asked Quinn. "You'll have to crawl a bit."

"It's fine," said Penny as she made her way over to the hatch. "I'm not too above my station in life that I can't crawl around in the dirt every now and then."

Penny stuffed herself through the porthole and clambered to her feet on the other side. Quinn entered the hatch behind her and skipped over to the carousel, arms stretched wide.

"Wow," said Penny, taking in the sight of the reclaimed carousel.

"And it's all mine."

"You look like the cat that got the cream."

"See. I've only known you for forty-eight hours, and I already miss you and your granny-isms."

Penny smiled for the compliment hidden in the mockery but mostly for the carousel which was lit up like a Christmas tree. Rows and rows of white bulbs dotted the awning and framed the hand-painted seascape portraits that adorned its grand perimeter. The horses, frozen in gallop, wore dazzling bridles, while cherubs, draped in white robes and framed with flowers and lace, embellished the carts.

Penny hadn't seen anything so beautiful in a long time. She stepped onto the platform, and a deep-rooted melancholy overcame her as she walked among the horses, letting her fingers glide across their cold plastic bodies. "My mom used to bring me here," she said, "and the horses used to scare me."

"They are freaky-looking. It's kind of like they're screaming. I never noticed that before."

"I think they're supposed to be smiling."

"Well, it's not a good look for a horse."

Penny laughed and hopped into one of the carts. The memories flooded back. "I puked in here too."

"In the cart?"

"Yep, right about here." Penny tapped her foot on the brushed metal floor of the cart. "I'm probably the reason they got rid of all the carpet. This is a much better option. Imagine how many kids puked in these things over the years."

"Like, one," said Quinn.

"No way. There would have been thousands. Especially with the ice cream van that was right next door. You don't give a kid a double scoop and spin them around for ten minutes."

"Ew," said Quinn, brushing her hands on her pants. "I'm looking at this place in a whole new light."

"Speaking of light, how did you get this thing to work? Surely there's no power down here."

"It's generator run," said Quinn. "A bit of gas, and you're smoking. Not literally—I hope."

"So, where do you get the gas from?"

"Listen, lady. You're on a need-to-know basis."

"Got it. It's obviously not something I need to know."

"Exactly. Just sit back and enjoy the ride."

"Come on, then, I want the whole experience. Entertain me."

"She's only a little bit demanding, ladies and gentlemen." Quinn zigzagged through the horses and disappeared into the center console. She emerged a moment later, just as the carousel lurched into action and threw Penny forward.

"Hey!" said Penny, grabbing the dashboard of the cart. "Precious cargo here."

"Sorry, learner driver at the wheel." Quinn hopped into the cart alongside Penny. "Wait for it." She smiled as she held her finger in the air, seconds before the quiet was broken with the sound of a distant harpsichord, whispering an alpine folk tune. "It's coming from an old gramophone I found out back. You have to be really quiet to hear it."

Penny had no idea what a gramophone was but assumed some kind of terribly ancient device for playing terribly ancient music. The tune peaked and troughed in elegant waves as the carousel began a slow turn, picking up speed until it was spinning at a quick walking pace.

"Amazing, right?" said Quinn.

It certainly had an undeniable charm, enchanting even, and Penny couldn't help but smile. "A rollicking ole time, that's for sure."

Quinn laughed at Penny's old-timey expression, and Penny blushed. She felt so comfortable around Quinn, and it surprised her that she wasn't afraid to be a dork. It had been so long since she'd had anyone to laugh with. It had been a long time since she'd been silly.

"Pretty great, huh?" asked Quinn.

"Well, I'm definitely entertained."

"And! I'm glad you came because I have something for you." Quinn pulled a small paper plane from her pocket, then handed it to Penny.

"It's an F-15 Eagle."

"For me?"

"Of course."

Penny held the tiny plane in the palm of her hand. Its folds were neat and sharp, and every end matched at perfect angles, the care that had gone into its creation evident. "It's amazing." She couldn't remember the last time anyone had given her anything. "Is there a message inside?"

"Of course, there's always a message."

Penny stared at the fighter jet in her hand and admired the perfection of Quinn's handiwork. "I don't want to open it up. I won't be able to fold it back together."

Quinn smiled and tilted her head at her, looking amused.

"Oh, all right," said Penny, unfolding the tiny plane. "But you have to put it back, okay?"

"Deal."

Penny smoothed the paper between her fingers as she carefully dismantled the F-15 Eagle. Her voice broke as she whispered, "Aruba or bust," fighting back the tears that threatened to come. She handed the paper to back to Quinn to refold, couldn't speak for fear of tears, and bit her lip instead.

"I didn't mean to upset you," said Quinn, making quick work of folding the plane back into its shape.

Penny shook her head and waited until the tears stopped pressing against her eyeballs. "It's just really thoughtful. A rare thing in these times." The slow spin of the carousel suddenly made her queasy.

"You okay? Not gonna be sick again, are you?"

"Maybe."

"I'll shut it down."

Quinn disappeared into the bowels of the carousel, and the fair ride wound down.

Penny got out of the cart and sat on the edge of the carousel, holding her feet off the ground as the ride came to stop. Quinn sat next to her.

"This wasn't really the outcome I was going for," said Quinn.

"No, it's not this. This is great. It's amazing."

Quinn sighed and ran a hand through her hair. "You're not the only one doing this life, Penny. It's tough now. It's tough for everyone. I get it."

Penny nodded in response, trying hard not to cry. "I should probably get home," she said, realizing she had about an hour before the dry retching would begin. The length of time between her need for Ambien was becoming shorter by the day, and her dosage was becoming larger. The first pill usually took away the withdrawals; the second one sent her off to sleep.

"Well, I'm walking you all the way," said Quinn.

"No, you're not. I'm a big girl."

"You're an insignificant ant when it comes to those assholes out there."

"The other day, you told me I was white and entitled, that I didn't have anything to worry about."

"I was lying. Those idiot peacemakers are fucking mongrels; you have everything to worry about."

"Well, thanks for the uplifting speech just before I walk for forty-five minutes in the dark by myself."

"Isn't it lucky, then, that you have a courageous warrior princess to escort you through the fires of hell?"

"Fires of hell? I wouldn't go that far."

"Well, maniacal, blood-chilling streets of Brooklyn. Better?"

"Worse. Let's go before you freak me out too much and I end up living in this box for the rest of the occupation."

"Sounds like the perfect solution to me. What more could we need?"

"Um, food, water, and sunlight for starters."

"We'll just survive on love," said Quinn, her cheeks flushing a deep shade of pink. "Come on, then, my lady." Quinn outstretched her hand yet kept her eyes averted to the floor.

Penny took Quinn's hand and allowed her to pull her to her feet. Quinn's grip was soft but firm and sent shivers down Penny's spine as if actual electricity flowed between them. Their eyes connected, and Penny's breath caught in her throat. Quinn pulled her close, a smile on her face, and under the lights of the carousel, she kissed her, softly but with an undeniable intensity as if words were being spoken. As they retreated from each other's lips, trancelike, in need of relief from the pleasure yet regret for the wanting, Quinn trailed a finger softly along Penny's tear-stained cheek. A smile, a laugh.

"Let's get you home," Quinn whispered.

Unable to speak for the pounding of her heart, Penny intertwined her fingers in Quinn's and waited for her to guide her home.

Chapter Thirteen

PENNY AND QUINN didn't speak a word to each other until they stood before the door of Penny's apartment. The walk across the bridge had been dark and full of tension, and they both looked relieved to have made it across without any complications.

Penny ran her hand along the ridge at the top of the door. Took the key. Stuck it in the lock and said, "Just, be—"

"Cool as a cucumber?"

"No. More like as open-minded as something that's really open."

Quinn smiled. "Like a can? That's been opened?"

"What?"

"Nothing," said Quinn. "I'm open. My mind is fully open."

"Just. Oh, just come in," said Penny as she escorted Quinn through the door and closed it quietly behind her. Benny was snoring on the couch, while her father lay in the doorway of his bedroom. The *drip-drip* of the distilling vodka echoed like a ticking clock.

Quinn raised her eyebrows and smiled when Penny grabbed her hand, dragged her to her bedroom, and shut the door quietly behind them. "Do you sneak all your girls in like this?" she asked.

"You're the only one that's laid a complaint."

Quinn looked the room up and down and walked over to the Aruba dream board, which didn't fully cover the shattered window behind it. "Have you been picking fights with windows?" Quinn pulled a corner of the board toward her and peeked at the broken window, then shoved it back into place. "Shattered dreams."

"Something like that," said Penny as she plonked herself on the bed. She was tired, and her hands were cold and twitchy. She lay her head on the pillow. Equilibrium be damned. "So, you never told me what exactly you do at the carousel every night? Is it just the joyriding around on horses?"

"Yes, yes, it is," said Quinn. "I like to spend my spare time riding plastic horses and listening to German folk music."

"Really?"

"No, of course not!" Quinn laughed and sprawled herself out on the bed next to Penny. "Oh my god, your pillows are so good." She bunched one up under her head. "And you have, like, a hundred of them."

"They're good pillows."

"They're great pillows. They're like little marshmallow puffs."

"What's a marshmallow puff?"

"It's like a little marshmallow in a puff shape."

"If you say so."

"I do say so, and what else was I saying?"

"The horses. You like riding them, along with folky music and marshmallows."

"Oh, yeah. The horses," said Quinn. "They're just a bonus, but I'm actually trying to hack through the system."

"The system?"

Quinn looked coy. "Yeah, there's a Wi-Fi pocket at the carousel, but it's password protected. I think it's a leak from the financial district, just across the Hudson. I haven't found any other Wi-Fi breaks in the whole of Brooklyn. They've pretty much locked it down."

"So you're trying to get online?"

"Sure am, just like the olden days."

"Well, that's noble."

"Ahh, not so much noble. Selfish. I miss porn."

"Oh my god, you do not watch porn."

"I do, and I also miss the TikToks."

"Are you kidding me?"

Quinn draped her arm across Penny's waist and closed her eyes. "Of course I am."

"So why, then?"

"Well, two reasons. One, I'm bored out of my mind, and two, for the uprising."

"What uprising?"

"There's always an uprising in these situations. Someone just has to start one."

"Someone like you?"

"Sure, why not? They took our voices when they shut down the cell towers, and I want mine back."

"So what would your first words be?" asked Penny. "If you hacked the system and all those useless devices out there suddenly flicked into life?"

"I don't know, haven't thought that far. Penn for president, maybe?"

Penny smiled, admiring her casual attempt to overthrow the powers that be. "So how do you know how to do that stuff?"

"Not a clue. I just sit there and type in password-guess after password-guess. I've got a little book, and I write them all down so I don't double up."

"That sounds really time-consuming."

"Stupid, huh?"

"Not stupid. Just time-consuming."

"Lucky I've got so much time on my hands, then. I figure I'll have to hit the mark at some point."

"Can't you find someone to help you? There must be professional hackers out there."

"I do have a friend guiding me on it, but he's got too much to lose to get involved. A family, kids. Everyone's scared."

"We're all scared."

"Not me," said Quinn.

"Why not you?"

"I've got nothing to lose."

"You've got your life."

"If you say so."

"I do."

Quinn traced her finger over a scar that ran the length of Penny's forearm. "Nasty paper cut?"

Penny ran her finger alongside the scar in unison with her. "Not so much a paper cut."

"Did you do it to yourself?"

"Of course not. Well, not really. It's my sleepwalking issue. Sometimes I get hurt."

"And sometimes you try to jump off a bridge with a brick tied to your ankle?"

"Exactly. Or sometimes I wake up on the edge of a window, three stories up, with a knife in my hand. It's happened a few times now."

"Jesus, really?"

"What can I say? My subconscious wants me dead."

"But *you* don't want you dead, right?"

"No way; I'd never do that," said Penny as her eyes welled up. "I'd rather be miserable and have everyone see me constantly cry than fake a smile and off myself while my kid is in math class."

Quinn sat up and twisted her fingers in Penny's. "Is that what your mom did? I thought it was cancer or something."

Penny shook her head. "People think it's my fault."

"Of course they don't, Penn. Don't think that. You were just a kid."

"I was so angry with her for so long, and now I just have this fury that's always bubbling below the surface."

Quinn lay back down and snuggled in. "Get in here," she said, pulling Penny into a tight embrace.

Penny buried her face into Quinn's neck and tried not to cry. She felt safe in this girl's arms, like she'd known her forever. Like she'd come home. Home to a place that was both familiar and foreign. A place she hadn't known for a very long time yet that was overwhelming in its warmth. The two of them stayed snuggled in each other's arms until Quinn's grip softened as she fell into a deep sleep.

Penny maneuvered herself gently from Quinn's embrace, and as soon as she sat up, the room began to tilt. She took a few long breaths before grabbing the pack of pills off her side table and popping one into her mouth. She lay back down, curled up next to Quinn, and watched her as she waited for the shaking to subside. Quinn's presence was so comforting that she felt confident there would be no sleepwalking on this night, and she closed her eyes and let the black take over.

Chapter Fourteen

IT WAS THE morning frost that pulled her out of her slumber. She felt it in her toes, and it crept up through her body as if she'd inhaled a cool wind. She stood on the corner of Madison and Grand staring into an empty street. A traffic light swung from its wires and flashed in an endless cycle of red, orange, green. A tide of panic rolled in, and she surveyed her immediate surroundings. No blood, no weapons, and apart from the fact that she couldn't feel her toes, she seemed to be okay. She looked left and right, gained her bearings, and began the brisk walk of shame.

She scuttled among the shadows of the buildings, nerves creeping to the surface, on the lookout for checkpoints and roving peacemakers. The bridge leading south onto Pike Street was usually quiet and clear of danger, but it wasn't till she cut onto Monroe Street that a sinister thought clarified itself. While she hadn't seen any peacemakers, she also hadn't come across another single being since she'd woken to find herself standing on a street corner.

"Shit," she whispered and searched the length of the street. Dead quiet. Too quiet. Her tenement was less than five blocks away, so she started to jog, her footsteps pounding in her ears. Panic rising in her chest. The Jefferson Alley shortcut would take minutes off her journey, so she ducked off the street and into the squalid one-way alley without a second thought. Eyes on the clearing at the other end, she sprinted, too fast and quick-witted for capture. Yet as the shadows slithered into view, so did the reality. A pair of kids were stuck, halfway up a fire escape, hanging over the ledge and into the alley.

She moved cautiously, ignoring the nausea and alarm that surged below the surface of her clouded thoughts. The jeans on the boy seemed familiar. It looked like her idiot lovebird friends; the pair with a fondness for bootleg vodka were unmoving. Something was very wrong with this scene.

"Hey," she said, "are you okay?"

No response as they hung motionless. Unable to look away, she took in the angle of their hands jutting out like claws. They weren't holding on to the fire escape; they were tied to it, and as she got even closer, she saw the blood that trickled down the girl's face from the numbers deeply etched into her forehead.

The boy's shirt was ripped down the front, and scratched into his chest were the words "Number Lover," followed by a final exclamation of a knife that had been thrust deep into his abdomen. The blood that dripped from his wound trickled down his pant leg and pooled, gelatinous and brown, in a gruesome shadow beneath him. His skin was blue, his eyes clouded over. Lifeless.

A surge of air rushed up Penny's gullet, and she fell to her knees, choking on her breath. She crawled along the pavement until a surge of adrenaline lifted her off her feet. As she stumbled to gain her footing, a glance over her shoulder revealed the silhouette of a man, a peacemaker with a rifle dangling from his side. He took a step toward her, and Penny shot off down the alley, racing home faster than her legs had ever taken her.

PENNY PAUSED AT the door to the apartment and wiped her face with the sleeve of her shirt, suddenly feverish despite the cold. A layer of sweat unfurled from her brow and dripped down her hairline. She took a deep breath and thought of Quinn, wondered if she was still there, hoped she wasn't. She traced her finger along the ridge above the door and collected the key, relieved to find it was still in place.

The kitchen was humid with potato steam, curtains drawn, the usual sight. Quinn sat at the table with her father, a glass of vodka in front of her. Penny knew it wasn't water because the water that ran from their faucet was usually gray and needed to be boiled twice before it could be drunk.

Penny stood at the door, fists tight, jaw clenched. "You're not drinking that shit, are you?"

Quinn looked up, relief on her face, then sat back, pushing her fingers through her hair. "God no. I mean, no offense, sir."

Penny's father sat upright in his chair and pulled Quinn's drink happily toward him. "Sir Larry, that's me," he said, slurring his words. "Good manners this one; she's a keeper." Larry kept his eyes fixed firmly on his two glasses of potato vodka.

"Did you sleepwalk?" asked Quinn.

"No. I just went to Starbucks for coffee and donuts."

"Really?"

"What do you think?" Penny held her arms out in question, a scowl set hard on her face.

"Cheeky tart," said Larry. "It's the drugs she's on. Think I have a problem? At least I'm not trying to end myself every night."

"I'm not trying to end myself," said Penny, clenching her fists tighter and digging her nails into the soft flesh of her palms. Her father knew how to push her buttons, and it took everything she had not to give him the satisfaction of seeing her cry, scream, erupt.

"Whatever helps you sleep at night," Larry said. "Oh, that's right. You got drugs for that."

Larry's drunk laughter sent her over the edge. Penny charged for her room, slammed the door behind her, and screamed as loud as she could, releasing all her pent-up frustration. "You're a fucking asshole!"

Penny collapsed on her bed, a broken mess of tears and anxiety. She buried her head under a pillow. Exhausted. Traumatized.

The door opened slowly, and she knew it was Quinn when she sat on the bed. Penny's body rolled involuntarily toward her with her weight. Quinn rested a hand on her shoulder, and calm seeped into Penny.

"I'm glad you're okay," said Quinn. "We were really worried."

Penny tossed the pillow off her head and sat up. "No, you weren't."

"Don't tell me how I feel," Quinn said. "Just let me worry about you, okay?"

Penny lay back on the pillow and tried with all her might not to cry. She watched Quinn pick up a packet of pills from her side table, stare at them, turn them over in her hands, inspect every inch of their branding.

"They're not real drugs," said Penny, snatching them from her, anxious she might take them away. Without them, she would be all alone in the night, wide awake with monsters and men. Quinn didn't know what it was like to suffer the agony of insomnia. It was frightening and lonely. "They're just sleeping pills. I can't go down without them."

"That shit is really addictive, Penn. How long have you been on them?"

"They're prescribed to me by a college-educated doctor who knows a fuck load more about it than you do." That was an outright lie.

"Okay, calm down."

Penny threw her pillow at the wall in exclamation and rolled off the bed on the opposite side to Quinn.

"Doctors don't know everything," said Quinn.

"Oh my god, just drop it."

"How long have you been taking them?"

"Long enough that I can get some sleep."

"How long's that? Six months? A year?"

"Yep, about a year," said Penny.

"A year? Holy shit, no wonder you're going crazy at night. You gotta stop it, Penn."

"You can't just stop it. You can't just throw away the pack, and that's it."

"You can," said Quinn.

"Actually, you can't. Not without suffering through traumatizing withdrawals. The withdrawal can kill you."

"No, it can't."

"It can so," said Penny, but she didn't actually know either way.

"Well, you're gonna die one of these nights anyway."

"Harsh," said Penny.

"Where did you go last night?"

"I didn't go anywhere."

"Penn, you went somewhere."

"It's none of your fucking business what I do."

"I just want to help," said Quinn.

"Just go."

"Penn, please."

"Just—if you really want to help, you'll just leave me the fuck alone."

"Come on, Penn. Don't be like that."

"Just go," she said. "Just fucking go. I don't want you here."

From her periphery, Penny saw Quinn's shoulders drop as if her words had physically attacked her. Penny lowered her eyes to the floor and willed Quinn not to leave, not really. She closed her eyes, and when she opened them again, Quinn was gone.

Penny slid down the wall and let her emotions come pouring out in a heavy stream of tears. She was broken beyond repair, and she'd just tossed away a lifeline because she was too proud to be helped. Well, she didn't need Quinn, did she? She didn't need anyone.

She crawled into her bed and curled up like a kitten. The tears came easily, and she stared at the wall for a long time until the spot under her pillow was as damp as if it had been left in the rain. The room got dark after a while, and she didn't know if she was asleep or awake. She only moved when the shaking turned into tremors. She reached out to the side table and grabbed three pills, popped them in her mouth, swallowed, and waited for the black to free her.

Chapter Fifteen

PENNY FOUND HERSELF perched on the windowsill of her bedroom three stories high when she shivered into consciousness. Her hands gripped the windowpane, and shards of glass cut into her thighs from the panel that was still broken. She gasped for a breath and surveyed her surroundings. The sky burned pink. Dawn or dusk? The view was familiar. Home. At least and she hadn't fallen or jumped. She shimmied backward and tumbled to the floor.

"Fuck."

Penny was dressed in nothing but a long T-shirt, and her toes were so cold they'd turned blue, the color of death. She closed her eyes and used a corner of the bed to prop herself up, taking a moment to shake her head and smash her thoughts to pieces. In a daze, she shuffled into the living room where Benny and her father—drink still in hand—were fast asleep, one on the couch, one on the floor. She envied their slumber, alcohol-induced or not. She suppressed the urge to scream.

The light in the bathroom, a single bulb, was unflattering and dreary and did little to help her mood. She undressed and watched the faucet choke and splutter, then jumped into the tub and let the water fill around her. The warmth arrived in spurts and dashes and stung her toes. The wound on her knee was red at the edge of the bandage, and she picked a corner until she had grip enough to rip it off in one swift move. A crust covered the white, spongy flesh beneath, starting in its center and creeping outward. It reminded Penny of the skin that formed atop the undistilled potato vodka.

Penny pulled her knees into her chest and wrapped herself in a hug, allowing a moment to indulge in her utter hopelessness. Big fat tears rolled down her face as she thought about the two rich kids who'd been murdered. They'd been stupid, yes, naive, most definitely. But what kind of sadist would do that to a pair of children? The Division leadership was a bunch of far-right politicians and military elites, but surely, they had laws to abide by. Were they murderers now?

Too restless to wallow in the bath, Penny turned off the faucet, stepped out, and without a towel in sight, stood before the mirror with no option but to drip-dry. The dark circles that shadowed her eye sockets were as purple as a bruise, and her cheeks had all but disappeared, bones protruding in their place. Penny cupped a hand to her face but found no comfort, only pity. Her eyes filled with tears, an unbearable sight, even to herself, and she walked away before she broke her heart any further.

Penny found some relatively clean sweatpants on her bedroom floor. While the act of washing and dressing had made her feel better, it had done nothing to quell the deep shame that pressed at her temples. She sat on the end of her bed, staring at the Aruba dream board, which now lay upturned at her feet. Who was she to think she was special? Who was she to think she would ever make it to the shores of Aruba? And even if she did, going there wouldn't magically bring her mother back. She picked up the dream board, took a breath, and smashed it on the floor.

"Idiot!"

THE NIGHT HAD fallen swiftly and, along with it, a strictly enforced curfew, which Penny once again disregarded in order to make her apology. She'd stalked the perimeter of the carousel twice before she found the loose board that led inside. She crawled through the hatch, and then she was standing in darkness. Shadows slid around her like gray ghosts, every one of them coming for her.

"Quinn?"

No reply but for a faint echo that may or may not have been her own. This was a mistake.

She reached for the loose board she'd just entered through and pushed at the wall, attempting to repress the image of an attacker creeping toward her with arms outstretched. Her breath came in short and hard until the wall finally gave way, and she fell through the hatch into freedom. Penny scrambled to her feet and raced along the broken promenade toward the bridge. She was too old to be afraid of the dark, and she stopped to take a breath and assess her next move. Home was no option. She wandered back to the bridge underpass and began retracing the steps to Quinn's loft. Before Penny knew it, she was standing before the heavily graffitied service door to the bakery.

The roller door felt like a block of ice beneath her fingers, and she paused mid-lift to wonder if knocking was an option. Surely, she had no choice but to break in? With frozen hands, she struggled to hoist the door upward. Her grip slipped, causing the door to slam to the ground with a crash that echoed down the alley. She crouched and searched the area for onlookers. Once she was sure she hadn't attracted any unwanted attention, she tried again.

Carefully this time, she lifted with slow precision. As the door reached eye height, a patch of gray fabric hanging from a protruding wire caught her attention. The missing puzzle piece to her ripped sweatpants. The memory of the night they'd outrun the peacemakers made Penny smile. With one hand holding the door open, she shimmied awkwardly beneath it and rapidly rolled into the middle of the room as the door slammed shut in a cacophony of metal against concrete. With all the racket, Penny half expected Quinn to be waiting for her yet managed a smile despite the disappointment. She was comically bad at breaking and entering and would really have to work on her skills

The fluorescent bulb hanging from a hook in the ceiling draped the room in an ugly yellow hue. Huge sacks of flour lay in a pile on one side of the room, and on the other, a rack full of baking equipment, dough hooks, bowls, and large bottles of oil stood in neat rows on tidy shelves. Penny opened the door to Quinn's loft with a rush of guilt.

"Quinn?" she whispered. No reply. "Quinn? It's me, Penny."

Quinn's bedside lamp lit the room, lending an extreme coziness as if a fire were burning in a hearth. Everything was perfectly tidy, the bed made, sheets tucked, and pillows neatly arranged. Not a thing littered the floor, a stark contrast to Penny's own bedroom.

The old-fashioned chair with the wooden arms invited her into its floral embrace. She fell into its fold, threw her satchel to the floor, and sank into its comfort. How she envied this independent life and dared for a moment to wish it were her own. The stash of boxes in a pile next to the chair taunted her with their mysterious contents. She poked a finger into the top box, casually flicking the lid back. Wedged on one side was the first aid kit Quinn had used on her. The rest of the box held a plethora of goodies. Tylenol, Advil, NyQuil, Ding Dongs, Pop-Tarts, jerky. How Quinn hadn't consumed everything all in one go, she had no idea.

Penny, unable to resist, removed a Twinkie from the box and toyed with the wrapper before simply ripping it open and stuffing it in her mouth. The sweet taste clenched at the edges of her jaw, and she shivered till it passed. She almost cried with the flavor. Almost cried at the guilt. Almost cried with all the boundaries she'd crossed in one night. Yet another thing she would have to apologize for.

She was on the last bite when Quinn opened the door. Caught in the act, she wasn't even sure if she'd be welcome or not—a total modern-day Goldilocks. Nosey, thieving, make-herself-at-home interloper.

"Quinn?" she said.

"Shit! Penny?"

"In the flesh."

"You scared me."

"Sorry. I hope it's okay that I'm here."

"It's just a surprise, that's all."

Penny still didn't know if she was entirely welcome or if Quinn was being polite. Dammit, why did she have to go through her stuff and eat her out of house and home?

Quinn tossed a shopping bag onto the floor. It clanked as it hit. Spray cans. Graffiti night.

"Created any masterpieces tonight?" asked Penny.

"Everything I create is a masterpiece," Quinn said with a smile. She crouched in front of the chair and placed a hand on each of Penny's knees. "So what brings you to this neck of the woods?"

"Um, I just wanted to say sorry, you know, about being such a bitch."

"Don't say that. You weren't a bitch—"

"I was. I was a total bitch to you, and you didn't deserve it."

"Stop it, Penn, seriously. Let's just forget about it."

"Forget about what?"

"Everything. Every shitty, tiny thing in the world."

Penny smiled and bit her lip. "Can I just come clean about something first? I snooped through your loot while you were out."

"I know. I can see the wrapper."

"I'd make a shit intruder."

"A cute intruder, at least. I'm glad you came back. I missed you."

"It's only been, like, a day."

"A really, really long day." Quinn fell onto the bed and scrunched a pillow up under her head. "And I'm ruined forever from enjoying my pillows again after experiencing the joy of your marshmallow puffs."

Penny laughed and crawled onto the bed. She cuddled up alongside Quinn, looking into her eyes.

Quinn stroked Penny's cheek gently. "Are you going to stay with me tonight?" asked Quinn.

Penny nodded, and they slowly intertwined fingers and legs and arms, like tree roots twisting together. The rush of comfort was so good it was almost unbearable. How could she say no?

"You know I might never let you leave," said Quinn as if reading Penny's mind.

"I'm counting on it."

"Oh! Speaking of death wishes—" Quinn pulled a piece of twine from her pocket, about twenty inches in length, and let it dangle between the two of them. She proceeded to tie their wrists together.

"Kinky," said Penny, somewhat amused. "But I'm not sure ropes are my thing."

"Not for fun. For safety," said Quinn with a grin.

"So, I'm your prisoner now?"

"For the hours of sleep, yes. You are officially not going anywhere without me. This is a no-sleepwalking zone."

"Nice, I like that. "Penny snuggled her face into the nook of Quinn's neck, dizzy with pleasure.

Quinn kissed her forehead, and the warmth of that kiss dripped down Penny's face and into her bones. Every kiss from Quinn was as intense as if it were a solid object.

Penny listened to Quinn's breathing slow until, minutes later, she'd fallen asleep right where she was. Penny was both awed and envious that such a thing was possible. But with every second that passed, she began to feel decidedly less amazing, and the room seemed as though it was rocking ever so slightly.

Penny lifted her free hand to her face and watched a tremor start up. It wouldn't be long before the dry heaving would begin. She sat up and leaned toward her satchel, careful not to wake Quinn. She managed to snag the corner of the bag with her little finger and drag it close. Relief.

"Please, please," she whispered as she ferreted around inside it, one-handed, until finally, frustrated, she just upended the bag onto the floor, shaking it vigorously. Out tumbled her ID card, a twenty-dollar bill, a handful of quarters, four stale biscuits wrapped in napkins—she'd forgotten about those—a pen, a lip balm squeezed to an inch of its life, and finally, there it was. The Ambien packet had been rustling around the bottom of her bag for so long the seal was broken, and the contents of the few remaining pills lay scattered on the floor crushed into shards, interspersed with lint and other bits of unidentifiable crumbs.

"Yes, yes."

Penny licked her fingers, then pressed them down on the pill snippets and inserted them into her mouth. When the floor was suitably clean of pill residue, she rolled back into bed and hoped it would be enough to get her through the night.

Chapter Sixteen

PENNY'S BARE LEGS were numb and cold when she slithered back into her skin, but the cold creeping in from the floorboards replaced the mental discomfort at having to puzzle together who and where she was. Her arm was tucked behind her at an awkward angle and tethered to Quinn, and one anxiety replaced itself with another as she crawled back into bed and warmed herself up against Quinn, a human heater, safe and soothing.

"You're still here," Quinn whispered.

"Still here."

"Hungry?"

"Mm-hmm."

Quinn opened her eyes and smiled. "I think there might be a market for me in kidnapping."

"Most definitely. Kudos to you, my lady."

"I'll get started on the business plan immediately." Quinn untethered herself from Penny and hopped out of bed. A new intimacy had opened up overnight and declared it okay to see each other, sleepy and with morning breath.

"Let's see if my man Ron has got anything good today," said Quinn. "Don't go anywhere."

She disappeared through the left-side door and returned less than two minutes later with a flask of coffee. The aroma of happier-days-past filled the room, the smell of life before the Division, the smell of Penny's mom, the smell of a normal world.

"Please, don't be teasing me," said Penny.

"It's coffee."

"I know it's coffee, but is it real coffee?"

"It's real coffee." Quinn dumped a handful of creamer and sugar packets onto the bedside table before pouring the coffee into two cups and handing one to Penny.

Penny emptied four packets of sugar into her cup. She didn't so much like the taste of coffee; it was the smell she adored. It took her to the edge of a memory, one she couldn't quite bring into full color, but it involved her mother and a warm blanket and a newspaper. It was homey. It was love.

"It's like Christmas," said Penny.

"Minus the presents, the tree, the turkey, the family, Santa."

"All the unimportant bits." Penny laughed and emptied two packets of white powder into her coffee. Quinn handed her a spoon, and Penny held the cup close to her nose while she slowly spun the contents. The coffee was strong and rich and jolted her awake.

"Good?" asked Quinn.

"You don't even know," said Penny as the two of them immersed themselves fully in their coffee drinking, the quiet only broken by their enthusiastic slurps.

"Guess what time it is?" asked Quinn with a cheeky smile.

Penny shook her head, shrugged. She had no idea. "Ten thirty?"

"Nope."

"Midday."

"Nope."

"Then I have no idea. It could be nighttime for all I know."

"Yup."

"What?"

Quinn laughed. "Well not quite, but close. It's four in the afternoon."

"Jesus." Penny drained her cup in a few short gulps. "I've really got to go."

"Noooooo. Don't go."

"I have to. The boys can't be trusted not to burn the place down. If they haven't already."

"They've got a pretty impressive setup going on with the vodka," said Quinn.

"Imagine what they could do if they weren't the world's most useless alcoholics."

Penny stood up and felt Quinn's hand slide around her waist.

"Don't leave me."

"I'll be back." Penny removed Quinn's hand from her waist and searched the floor for her belongings.

"Like the Terminator?" asked Quinn.

"The what?"

"Oh my god. Please tell me you've seen *The Terminator*."

"I have no idea what you're talking about."

"It's a super old movie about a revenge-seeking robot from the future," said Quinn, with a heft of enthusiasm Penny found intriguing. "And his catchphrase was, 'I'll be back.'"

"What? That sounds really stupid."

"Get out. Get out right now, and never darken my door again." Quinn pointed at the door with a grin, and Penny reciprocated with her own smile.

"If you say so," she said as she picked up various items of clothing, including the twine, which she stuffed into her back pocket.

Quinn was by her side in two quick hops. "Just kidding."

"I know."

"But you're going to need some educating in the field of moving-image entertainment. Lucky for you, a space just became available on my bucket list."

"Very lucky for me," said Penny as she slipped on her sweatpants and then hopped in crooked circles as she tried to pull on her raggedy, fake name-brand sneakers.

"Wait," said Quinn. "I'll walk you to the bridge."

"It's a nice gesture, but I really feel like going solo. Regroup my headspace before I have to deal with the Larry situation."

"You sure?"

"Totally."

"Just promise you'll be careful."

"Always."

"Uh, not really."

Penny laughed. "Always when I'm awake."

"Okay, you can go."

"That's generous of you," said Penny as she smiled and opened the door.

"Now get outta here, Granny," said Quinn.

Penny blew Quinn a kiss from the door and exited through the storage room. The roller door was already open to halfway, and she was surprised to see a delivery underway. Piles of large flour sacks had been dumped around the room at random. Penny traced a path between them, ducked beneath the door, and was suddenly struck by the brightness of the day. A man sidled around the side of the delivery truck and brushed by her with a full sack. He looked at her sideways, and she raised her eyebrows before strolling off down the alley.

She rounded onto the Pearl Street Triangle and stopped. Everywhere, on every space of wall, were the words painted in fresh pink spray paint: I am not a number.

"Wow," she whispered and continued her walk toward the bridge. She let her fingers trail over the freshly graffitied walls, and her smile couldn't be contained. It took all she had in her to suppress the urge to laugh.

Penny stopped abruptly at the top of the Water Street alley. It teemed with peacemakers, but taking a new route was out of the question. A sudden about-face would appear as an admission of guilt.

"I am not a number," she whispered. "I am not a number."

She lifted her chin, feigned confidence, and as she began her march straight through the middle of them, her fear subsided. These soldiers were children, barely thirteen years old at a guess. Penny smiled, lengthened her stride, shoulders back, and made sure every junior peacemaker down that strip knew she was the boss of them. At the end of the alley, she paused to read the graffiti the peacemakers were scrubbing.

"Penn for President," said Penny and laughed as the peacemakers looked her up and down suspiciously. She felt exhilarated by the time she got to the end of the lane, so much so that she wanted to go back around and give it another go.

PENNY'S BUOYANT MOOD propelled her over the bridge, the skip in her step powered by the coffee in her system. The sun setting in the horizon filled the sky with brushstrokes of fire, and the world almost felt like the normal, relatively well-functioning place it had once been, when the main job of the powers-that-be was to protect, not destroy.

That thought had barely dripped from her brain before she found herself trotting down the bridge stairs and straight into a checkpoint. Worse still, the Lanky One was on patrol, along with his brain-dead sidekick. Penny recalled the incident where she'd flipped him the bird. In hindsight, it hadn't been her smartest decision.

The gangly peacemaker grimaced at her, his ugly stare stopping her in her tracks.

"It's my favorite little slut," he said.

His colleague, Mr. Brain-Dead, laughed like it was the funniest thing anyone had ever said.

"Take a break," said the Lanky One to his buddy, who didn't hesitate to roll off his stool and meander into the shadows under the bridge.

The instinct to run consumed her, but Penny's pride didn't let her. Backtracking to cross at Manhattan Bridge would eventually lead to a similar outcome. She had no choice but to push ahead, shoulders back, and brace for a fight.

"I am not number," she whispered and descended the stairs slowly, keeping the Lanky One locked in her sights.

She was wholly unprepared for his attack, which came in, swift and vicious. He sprang at her, grabbing the scruff of her T-shirt so forcibly that the fabric of her shirt constricted her breath. He dragged her to the bridge pylon by the neck of her shirt and threw her against it, then grabbed a fistful of hair and sniffed her, mouth to her ear, his breath like stale ash.

"Spread your legs, bitch!" he yelled into her ear as the words popped and fell away to static.

She froze, stunned with panic, as the Lanky One's hands smothered her body, gripped her flesh, tugged at her sweatpants in an attempt to loosen them until, finally, alarm bells rang. Protect yourself.

"Don't fucking touch me," she whispered. "Don't you dare."

The Lanky One laughed and cupped his hand to his ear. "What, dollface, you want me to fuck you?"

Penny clenched her teeth and let her head fall back onto the pillar, the stone rough beneath her hair. She took a deep breath, looked her attacker in the eye, and threw her forehead forward with as much force as she could muster. His nose crunched beneath her skull as a dull thud rocked her mind. Pain blasted like lightning. A scream filled the air—hers or his, she didn't know. His grip loosened. She was free, and she ran, ran, ran.

"You fucking whore! I'm going to cut your tits off! You hear me!"

The world was a mess of zigzags, black creeping in at the corners, but beneath the haze, she could see her tenement building looming in the distance, a shifting blur. Blood trickled from the end of her nose, leaving a red trail on the front of her T-shirt. Her blood or his? She didn't know.

The tremors kicked in as she approached the apartment block entrance. Her breath came in gasps as she caressed the aching bump on her forehead that protruded like a golf ball. Penny let her body melt down the side of the building and counted down from one hundred, waiting for the black edges to subside.

Chapter Seventeen

PENNY IGNORED THE white sneakers at the door of the apartment and made a direct beeline for the refrigerator. She ripped a tray of ice cubes from the freezer and dumped them unceremoniously on the counter. The throbbing in her head was unbearable, and everything was draped in a blurry halo. A dish towel for the ice would be a fat chance. With the pain really kicking in, she picked up a cube with bare hands and ran it across her forehead. Instant relief.

"You're safe," said Sam. "Thank god."

Penny concentrated on the soothing ice, the earth on a tilt while all three of them sat there watching her when all she needed was peace.

"Penn?" said Sam.

If she did nothing, would they just disappear? Growing dread trickled through her veins.

Sam, Benny, and Larry, at the table, stared uncomfortably into their potato vodkas.

Tears stained Sam's face. He pushed himself up from the table and walked toward the kitchen counter. The concern on his face deepened when she saw Penny's blood-streaked cheeks. "Are you okay?" he asked.

Penny nodded and continued to run the ice across her forehead. "What's going on?"

"They've taken Dad," said Sam.

"Who? Who's taken him?"

"They just walked right in. Just knocked the door down, off its hinges, and walked right in. Dragged him out of his bed, all the way to the street, and then he was gone. Just—just gone. Just like that." Sam sobbed into his hands.

"Who? Who dragged him?"

"The peacemakers. They went through the entire building, just grabbing random people out of their beds and taking them away in buses."

Penny couldn't think properly, thoughts swirling, shooting hot spikes into her head. "They can't just take people," she said. "What do they want with him?"

"I think they're going to revoke his citizenship?" said Sam.

"They can't revoke his citizenship; he was born here."

"They can if you're the offspring of immigrants."

"No, they can't. There's nothing to revoke. If you're American, you're American."

"It must be a new law," said Sam. "Mom is freaking out because everyone's been saying—"

"They can't revoke something that's irrevocable."

"Well, he's gone anyway, and I don't know how to find him."

"Why would they take him but leave your mom? It doesn't make sense."

"How would I know? How the heck would I know what's going on?"

"Okay, okay, calm down." Penny couldn't seem to hold on to a single thought for longer than a second. "Well, they can't just drag someone out of their home. It's totally against the law."

"What isn't against the law these days?" said Benny with slurred words. "The whole place has gone to shit. It's martial law out there."

"You're not helping," said Penny, although she thought Benny had a relatively valid point. "Do you know where they took him?" she asked Sam, suppressing an urge to scream.

Sam shook his head. A tear ran down his cheek.

"Were they proper peacemakers?" asked Penny. "Did they wear uniforms?"

"Some of them. They were pretty young, and they all had guns. Loads of guns. What do I do?"

Penny was in no state to help. She wanted to yell at Sam that she didn't have a clue. She was clueless, helpless, and broken. She couldn't help Sam any more than she could help herself.

"Okay. Come with me."

Penny took Sam's hand, led him to her bedroom, and shut the door behind them. "I don't want you to worry," she said. "I know he'll be fine. The peacemakers are idiots, but they have to work within the law." The lies were just flowing off her tongue.

"They're going to torture him," said Sam with tears welling in his eyes. "They're going to fry his brain and turn him into a fucking zombie."

"They're not going to torture him, Sam. Stop freaking out."

"I'm scared."

"We're all scared," said Penny, swallowing her fear. This was too much for her to cope with. Her mind was unhinging itself from her head and floating into the sky.

She dropped to her knees, slipped her hand under her bed, and searched for her Aruba fund box. She pulled out ten fifty-dollar bills and handed them to her friend. "Take your mom and get out of the city."

"Where will we go?"

"I don't know. Go to Queens. Don't you have family there?"

"Yes, but—"

"So go there."

"I can't take your money," said Sam, handing the bills back.

Penny pushed his hand away. "They're ill-gotten gains anyway. Just take it, and go. Promise me you'll get out."

"I don't know if I can do this."

"Of course, you can. You got this."

"I got this," he whispered.

"And you're American," said Penny. "Don't ever let them tell you you're a number."

Sam walked to the door and froze. "I'm scared. Can you come?"

Penny looked to her hands trembling in her lap. She knew he couldn't walk alone; he never could. As she got to her feet, she felt curiously untouchable, as if she were watching herself in a movie.

"Let me get my jacket."

PENNY LED THE way, north of the underbridge passage and along Gold Street toward Battery Park. The streets were pitch-black and full of whispers. Imagined or real, they crept around them like ghosts. The pavement seemed to tilt and sway, and every step was a wonky one that threatened to topple her. She took short, sharp breaths and focused on each footfall, one after the other.

"I feel like I can hear footsteps," said Sam.

"You can. Ours."

"Not ours. Extra ones."

"There are no extra footsteps. There are just ours."

Penny hung off Sam's arm like an old man being helped across the road. Her eyes flicked back and forth, and every which way, alert for predators.

"Why are we taking the long way?" Sam said, shivering. "We should have taken the FDR Parkway."

"It's safer up here. No peacemakers."

"How do you know?"

Penny stopped, and the pavement swayed beneath her feet. She wondered for a second if she was sleepwalking and tucked her hand discreetly into her coat to pinch her arm. "Nope."

"What?"

"Look, if you're happy to walk down the FDR without me, be my guest. I'm not feeling amazing right now, so I need to get you home. Will you just work with me, Sam?"

"Wow." He dropped Penny's arm and walked ahead. "Sorry for the inconvenience. It's only my life at risk."

Penny's world spun a little faster now that Sam had set her free. She pinched the bridge of her nose. "Wait," she said, "just give me a second." Her legs gave way, and she knelt on the pavement and stared at the dirty cement, pancaked with gum and spit and muck. "We can cut through DeLury Square and onto Fulton if you want?"

"Through the park? Are you crazy?" Sam hovered over Penny, balancing from foot to foot and scanning the area for signs of danger. "What's wrong? I think we should keep moving if we can."

"I just don't feel well. Help me up." She stretched her hand toward Sam, and he hoisted her to her feet without hesitation.

"It's the pills, isn't it?" he asked.

"What?"

"You've got a problem. You're so fucking sick-looking, Penn. Like you can barely hold yourself up."

"What? That's bullshit."

"I know you have a problem. It's those sleeping pills."

"It's not the sleeping pills. In case you didn't notice, I have a lump on my head the size of an egg after being attacked, and now here I am escorting you home because you're too much of a baby to handle the darkness."

"Whatever. Rather scared than a junkie."

"Junkie? Are you fucking kidding? I'm helping you, and you're accusing me of being a pill-popping junkie."

"If the shoe fits."

Penny's world spun even harder as if she were floating. Then a shadow fell upon her, looming and quick.

"Looks like we've got a pair of damsels in distress, here," said a voice drifting out from the depths of the alley across the street. The voice morphed into a shadow and then into a peacemaker. He had a wiry frame and a gray beard. A smaller figure followed him, a son perhaps or a loyal recruit. Peacemakers after curfew were never the law-abiding types. They were the rogue creeps, hunters looking for prey.

"Shit," said Penny. "Run."

Sam grabbed Penny's hand in an attempt to pull her to her feet, but Penny's body was lead. The sky was low and crooked, and she didn't know which way was up or down or sideways. Her feet lifted from the ground but struggled to find a place to fall, and then, as if the cement reached up and slapped her across the face, she was lying on the ground again.

"Get up!" Sam screamed as he dragged Penny along the ground.

She struggled to place her feet and hands. If only Sam would stop dragging her, just for a second, just for a chance to find her feet. Her whole body shook and shuddered. She needed to be home.

The peacemakers walked slowly behind them, laughing and pointing. Enjoying the fear they'd incited in their prey.

"Move!" screamed Sam. "Get up!"

The older peacemaker unsheathed a knife from a holster in his belt and continued to walk closer.

"Please," Sam, stopped. "She needs help; we're just trying to get home."

"You know what we do to curfew breakers?" said the man.

"We're not curfew breakers," said Sam. "We're just trying to get home."

"Look like curfew breakers to me," said the old man, and then he sniffed the air for drama. "Smell like curfew breakers to me."

"Fee-fi-fo-fum," said the boy before looking to the man for approval.

"That's right, my boy!" The man ruffled the boy's hair and laughed. "Fee-fi-fo-fum. I smell the blood of a traitor wooh-man."

Penny couldn't move. She retched onto the pavement, but nothing came out but air and saliva. But it took all her wind, leaving her panting with the energy it had taken. Her body shook, and she watched, helpless, as the peacemakers moved in slowly on them.

Then another presence emerged. Swift and silent. Like a shadow-wind. It took a moment for Penny to recognize the dreadlocked man from the soup kitchen. His feet were bare, and his hair, long and tangled, swung about his waist as he deftly disarmed the old peacemaker in one fell swoop, finishing with the knife under the man's chin.

The boy squealed like a frightened piggy.

"Walk away," said the dreadlocked man. "I'll slice you up with this pretty little knife, understand."

The peacemaker nodded frantically beneath his grip. Once Mr. Dreadlock was satisfied, he unfurled him from his grip and kicked him, foot to face. The peacemaker tumbled along the road, staggered to his feet, and ran off after his boy, their footsteps echoing long after they disappeared.

Penny closed her eyes as a rush of nausea washed over her like a wave. She was lifted then and cocooned in a blanket of sweat and whispers until she woke up in her own bed, shivering but alive.

Sam handed her three tablets and a cup of water, his face stern, unapproving. "This is what you need, right?"

Penny swallowed and felt his discontent.

"You almost got me killed tonight," Sam said.

"What do you even mean?"

"I mean that creepy old peacemaker with the machete. You couldn't even move. If it wasn't for Aaron, we'd be dead."

Penny's thoughts were moving so fast she couldn't keep tabs on them. "Mr. Dreadlock's name is Aaron? He doesn't look like an Aaron."

"So, it's all just a joke to you?"

Penny shook her head. She was feeling much better, relaxed, but the black would come soon, and she wanted Sam gone before that happened. "I'm not the bad guy here," she said. "And don't you think it was a bit convenient that Mr. Dreadlock happened to save the day? He was following us. I'm sure of it."

"He wasn't following us," said Sam. "He's one of Rita's guys."

"Rita has guys?"

"Rita has a lot of things that you don't know about."

"And you do?"

"I know a lot more than you."

"So, do you know why one of Rita's guys was following you?"

"Not me. He was following you."

"Me?"

"I told her you were sleepwalking," said Sam. "And about all the drugs too."

"Jesus, Sam. They're not even drugs. They just help me sleep." Penny's eyelids felt so heavy that, once again, all that anxiety just slipped away in a little puff of smoke.

"First of all, they are drugs. And second, when I told Rita how worried I was about you getting murdered on your nightly escapades, she asked Aaron to watch over you."

"Wow, there are so many things wrong with this I just don't know where to start," said Penny.

The black edges were curling in, and Sam's face was drifting farther and farther away, his voice floating on the wind. "Rita is not your friend," she whispered. "She's bad."

Sam shook his head, his mouth opening and closing, his words dull, slow drumbeats, and warped. The last thing Penny saw before the black took hold was Mr. Dreadlock walking through the door and hovering over her bed.

"If you're so special to Rita, why doesn't she buy you some fucking shoes? No one invited you, Footloose," said Penny with a cynical laugh, proud of the wit she could still muster despite the black cloud of Ambien, wrapping around her brain like a woolen blanket.

She had some more mean quips up her sleeve she needed to get out before sleep stole her away; she wanted to tell Mr Dreadlock how much she despised him. But the shadow of her mother beckoned her into the fog, a temptation to difficult to resist, and she found peace at last in the dreamy arms of her dead mother's love.

Chapter Eighteen

PENNY SAT CROSS-LEGGED on the street opposite the squat brownstone building that had been dubbed the Church of Rita. It was a place as familiar as her own habitat, yet it took her a few moments before she realized she'd sleepwalked here. Chilled to the bone, she must have been sitting there for a while. She rubbed her pale hands together, and steam exited her mouth with every breath as she looked left and right, panic rising to the surface.

The streets were quiet, and she wondered if Mr. Dreadlock had followed her. If he'd always been following her. If he was the reason she'd remained safe despite her dangerous night wandering. She thought back to the morning in the Greenwich Haven parking when Rita had conveniently rescued her from Lieutenant Dixon's hands. It had been no coincidence after all. But why? Why did Rita care so much?

Rita's church sat short and squat before her, staring at her with accusatory mocking. Although the building was dwarfed by a pair of skyscrapers on either side, it screamed of a domineering stubborn presence that would lure one in and then spit them out half-chewed. Maybe, that was more likely to be the woman who ran the place.

Penny's shame reached a new level, and she allowed the tears to fall. She really was going to die, or worse, get someone else killed. Her body craved the pills that allowed her to sleep, but when had she allowed them to dictate the course of her life? She crossed the street to the front door of the Church of Rita. She knew that Rita was in there, due to the pink Range Rover that sat conspicuously at the curb. Penny took a deep breath and pushed her way through the door.

The Church of Rita left no shadow unturned, lit corner to corner with stark fluorescent bulbs. Penny walked directly to the kitchen where a hubbub of activity radiated from beyond the double swing doors. A stream of yellow light crept out below the crack in the doors and stretched across the cracked vinyl flooring. The hum and whistle of Rita's singsong voice as she clanged and banged a variety of pots and pans was almost intoxicating. Penny took a moment to remember herself as she entered the kitchen, and a flutter of nerves asked just what she was doing there.

Rita, styled to perfection with her red curls and pink lips, was the complete opposite to the sensitive, tortured soul that Penny's mother had been.

"My momma always told me crying was for wimps," said Rita as she dumped a box of onions on the table in front of Penny. "And wimps had no place in the Pettigrew family, no ma'am. If there was one thing you didn't want to do in the Pettigrew family, it was cry." Rita laughed and rifled through a small box on the counter.

"Three lashes of Daddy's belt for every single tear. Even worse for the boys. Aha!" Rita whipped a sharp paring knife from the box and held it high as if it were a trophy, then handed it to Penny. Rita pulled out the chair that sat next to the box of onions. "But we never got lashed for onion tears." She picked a large brown onion from the box and rolled it between her hands. "No ma'am, can't help them onion tears. Heck, even Mama cried her fair share of onion tears."

Rita placed the onion in front of Penny, who, without question, began to cut it. The effect of its juice was immediate and potent, and within seconds, her eyes burned in response.

"But, of course, I had a workaround," Rita continued. "I've always got a workaround. I used to save up all my tears. I would tuck away every single transgression, every whip, every scolding, every wrong-done thing, and I'd save it in my brain like a little present waiting to be opened. And when Mama had me cut those onions, I would cry and cry and cry."

Penny had chopped half an onion into fine pieces by the time Rita finished her story, tears streaming down her face. She dropped the knife and pushed the box of onions into the middle of the table. Why was she cutting onions?

"I don't need to cry, Rita. I'm not here to cry on your shoulder."

"Oh, I know that, my dear. But maybe some tears would do you good?"

"What would you know about what I need?"

"I know a great deal, my darling, about what you need."

"Oh, do you now? And tell me. Tell me. What exactly does her highness recommend I need?"

"Well," said Rita as she pulled the onions toward her. "The list is long, but it all comes down to one little fact. One fact you're not going to like."

"One fact?"

"One fact," said Rita as she sliced and diced the onion with ease, its fumes having no effect on her whatsoever.

"And this one fact is the start of my path to enlightenment?" Penny said sarcastically.

"Oh yes, darling, well said. The path to enlightenment. I love it. So smart. Totally illustrates my point actually."

"What point is that, Rita?" Penny wished she would just spit it out already.

Rita shrugged, set down her knife, and lunged across the table toward Penny like a rabid dog tethered at the neck. "The fact that you're nothing like your mother. Not a jot."

Something boiled inside Penny, curled up the edges, and slithered up her spine.

"I said you wouldn't like it." Rita picked up a new onion and slowly peeled back its layers with the tip of the paring knife. "You're a daddy's girl, chip off the old block."

"I'm not like him." It was all Penny could say in her defense. "He's a loser."

"And you are?"

"I'm not a loser."

"Well, we're going down a rabbit hole I wasn't intending to visit, but while we're on the subject—no, you're not a loser. But you're on your way to becoming one, my dear."

"What?"

Rita sighed and chopped some more onions, still unaffected by their fumes. "Look, let's keep this spin positive. Your father is many things, but a loser he is not. He's simply been cutting too many onions. His whole life is just one onion after the other. He's wiped out by onions."

"What? What the hell are you talking about?

"He's a strong man who has been felled by his pain, and you are a strong young woman, who is in peril of succumbing to the same fate."

"I'm not like him."

"Well, you're not like *her*, and the faster you realize that, the better off you'll be."

"I am like *her*."

Rita shook her head.

"I am."

"If you think you are anything like that weak-minded sparrow, then you need to take a good hard look in their mirror."

Penny's heart froze. She'd never heard anyone dare utter a bad word against her mother. "Isn't it some kind of rule to not talk ill of the dead?"

"Not a rule in my book, darling."

"Wow. If anyone needs to look in the mirror, it's you. You look in the mirror. You look! You think you're everyone's God-given savior, but you're not. And by the way, how dare you set Mr. Dreadlock on me. How long has he been following me?"

"Long enough to keep you safe." Rita handed the knife back to Penny, who suddenly recognized its brown wooden handle with the silver embossed branding of a lion's head. Distinctive. Rare. It was one of her father's knives.

Penny stood and rushed at the box on the bench. It was full of kitchen utensils, and she rifled through, frantically, pulling out knife after knife until she found seven from the box.

"And those are only the ones you've dropped along the way," said Rita. "Aaron learned pretty early on that extracting them from your fist was an exercise in pain, so he only took the ones you dropped."

Penny couldn't breathe. "I don't need you to keep me safe."

"You needed me last night. And the night before and the night before that and the night before— Penn, darling. Let me help you. There's a place for you here. I can get you in with the peacemakers despite your past indiscretions. I can get you in at a good rank. They'll help you with a fully funded detox."

"Detox? I don't need detox."

"And they'll do the same for your father. We could find him a posting at a sympathetic college. It wouldn't be a top posting, but it would be a job. A good one. And if you both work hard, maybe one day, you'll get into a Haven, a midrange one like...nothing in Manhattan obviously. The starting financial cutoff is more than you will ever accumulate, but well, we can see."

"I'm not joining the peacemakers. I'll never join them. And I won't owe you. I know you like to collect people. I'm not one of your people."

"Are you sure about that?"

"I owe you nothing."

"Well, that's a little ungrateful."

"Just stop following me and call off your fucking dogs."

"I'm not sure Aaron would appreciate being compared to a dog, but are you sure that's what you want, honey? Because once the horses bolt, they ain't never coming back. You understand what I'm saying?"

Rita reached into her handbag and pulled out a paper bag that she threw on the table. "This stuff doesn't grow on trees, you know."

Penny knew exactly what Rita was offering and opened the bag. Inside were boxes of Ambien. The real stuff. The real uncut pharmaceutically made Ambien. Not the cut-up fake shit that she'd had to resort to.

"It's very hard to get a hold of nowadays, isn't it, honey?" said Rita. "Very expensive too. Nothing that a dealer in the Leftovers could afford."

Penny gripped the bag, filled with the urge to take it, but threw it at the wall before it could grow roots.

"Stubborn, like your father," said Rita, "and stupid, like your mother."

"And you're an asshole Pettigrew through and through."

"Thank you, my darling. I'll take that as the compliment it is."

"It's not a compliment,"

"If you say so, darling." Rita picked up an onion and began to cut. "Now, if that's our business completed, then get the fuck out of my church, you ungrateful little bitch."

Chapter Nineteen

PENNY SOBBED HUGE tears from the depths of her soul. She hadn't realized how much she'd come to rely on Rita, how she saw her as the mother she'd never had. Rita had been by her side since the day of her mother's funeral, and Penny had taken every day since then for granted. It frightened her to lose her one ally, despite their differences, and it hurt her to think Rita could so easily throw her away as if she hadn't mattered at all. What had she done? Could she turn back time? Could she apologize? Could she beg to have Rita back in her life? Could she at least beg her not to hate her? Who would save her now?

Benny handed her a damp towel, greasy and probably dirty, but she was grateful for it as she wiped it across her forehead. It cooled and soothed as the dry blood peeled off her skin. The peacemaker blood from two days ago. She took the cloth from Benny's hands and stared at the rust-colored stains that streaked it.

"Thanks, Ben," said Penny. "I needed that."

Benny smiled and dropped to his knees in front of her, attempting to undo her shoelaces. Penny watched as he drunkenly puzzled over the complications of such a task, and despite being completely useless, his presence was a comfort.

"We're a broken lot, huh?" said Penny.

"We just need a bit of oil."

"No more oil for me. I gotta get my head clear. I can't be wandering the streets in a daze anymore. It's going to get me killed."

Benny buried his head in his hands and started crying.

"Don't cry. Please, Benny, I don't need this shit."

Penny had nothing left in the tank. Couldn't these people see she was broken? Why did she have to pick up the pieces of everyone else's lives when her own was falling apart?

Benny nodded, wiped away his tears, then got to his feet and left the room, swaying from wall to wall as he did so.

Penny flicked off her shoes without bothering to untie the laces that were now a knotted mess. She shuffled into her bed and pulled her blanket right up under her chin.

Benny arrived back in her room with a large pot and a glass of water. He placed one on the floor and the other atop the bedside drawers. "Just in case," he said.

"Listen," said Penny. "There's a piece of twine in my pants pocket. Can you grab it and give it to me?"

Benny obeyed and helped her as she placed her wrist against the bed frame before twisting the twine around and around. Penny realized, as she twirled the thread around her arm, how reckless she had allowed herself to become. She could have easily tied herself fast, any night, every night.

"Can you do a knot?" she asked.

Benny shook his head.

"Come on. Please, Ben. I know you can do it? I don't want to walk."

She wanted to scream at him.

He cried as he did as he was told and tied the twine in two tight knots with her help.

"I'm okay," she said, "but I think I'm in for a rough ride."

Benny cried into his hands, but Penny'd had enough.

She put the blanket over her head and whispered, "Leave me alone," from beneath its cocoon. She curled up in its folds and waited for the night before her shaking body turned into shudders, violent and involuntary, limbs lurching in pain. She had to change position every few seconds to find comfort from the pains that struck every muscle in her body.

Flashes of pain slammed into Penny's skull like a sledgehammer, and then she was frozen, all movement sending fresh blows into her skull, ferocious and unbearable. She didn't know she was crying, nausea roiled up from the depths of her bowels, and she tossed the blankets to puke into the pot Benny had left. She rolled back onto the pillow and curled into a ball. Momentary relief came before her headache wound up, worse than before. She wept tears of frustration, frightened, her body out of control. She closed her eyes and shadows lurched out behind them. Imagined faces—Quinn, Sam, Benny, her mother—morphed into various monsters and growling beasts.

And then came the fear from a place so dark just to stay in this space for a moment would leach her of all the happiness she'd ever known, as if she'd broken off from the world, now floating in unending gloom. It hollowed out her insides until she was just a shell, a sliver of paper, a vessel containing nothing but darkness.

She closed her eyes and wallowed in black, unable to differentiate between asleep or awake. At first, the snakes frightened her as they slithered up her walls and into her bed, but when she realized they weren't real, she let them twist around her body. What choice did she have? They bit her ankles, slid around her neck, and shortened her breath. She screamed and cried. She wished for death. The room darkened, and then lightened and darkened again. The snakes disappeared, replaced by paper planes, floating and spinning around her room, a reprieve to focus on while she writhed in her bed until, finally, she stopped shaking and shitting and hallucinating. When the headache subsided to a dull ache, she sat up in her bed, hand untethered with the world teetering on the edge of a spin, dipping this way and that, threatening to throw her off. She lifted the cup from the nightstand and took a small sip, wondered who had put it there. Her cracked lips split open. She pushed herself up off the bed. Her stomach growled, and she wrapped a protective arm around her belly and used the wall to guide her way to the bathroom.

She climbed into the bath and turned the faucet on. The water choked and spluttered before making a continuous stream of rusty water. As the bath filled Penny sipped the water as it came out of the spout, rancid and tasting of blood, but she quickly chided herself. Dehydration was far better than the sickness the unfiltered water could invoke. Lying back, she let the bath fill to the very top until the water lapped at her chin, calm and replenishing. She waited for a single good thought to come, just one at first. She was alive. Then came another and another in single flowing narratives. One at a time, orderly and exact, and before long, a plan began to sprout, perfectly formed, and the void of dire hopelessness was filled with blind hope and love.

THE VIEW ACROSS Brooklyn Bridge used to revive her, but now as she untangled the knots in her shoelaces, Penny felt nothing but claustrophobia. Despite the sky darkening much earlier now that winter was on the way, she was buoyed by the certainty of earlier curfews and longer night hours in which to set her new plan into action. Penny reached under her bed and scooped out her Aruba fund box, grabbed a handful of twenty-dollar bills, and stuffed them in her pocket.

Atop the side table lay two trays of Ambien pills, which stole her attention. She scooped them up and shuffled them like a deck of cards in her hand, longing to keep them as a backup, just in case. But she knew without a doubt that she needed to get rid of her pain—the aching bones, the pounding head, the hallucinations. She took the pills and walked to the kitchen and flushed every one of them down the pipe. "Yes," she whispered. With hunger rolling in, Penny picked up the loaf of bread on the counter and held it up to the single bulb that hung from the ceiling to check for mold. Satisfied, she pulled out four slices. They were soft, fresh. Penny was sure Benny had bought it for her and was thankful. She shoveled down all four and then another six. Her body chugged back into life.

Penny grabbed her satchel, still lying by door. She scratched the dried blood off it, satisfied to watch the bits fall to the floor, little chips of paint, and disappear amidst a year's worth of accumulated dust. She was going to do something about this shit of a life. First stop, Seventh Avenue preschool.

SMASHING HER WAY in wasn't Penny's first option, but she'd thoroughly checked the doors and windows and found no hinge unlatched. She buried her fist deep into her satchel, closed her eyes, and punched through the front door's glass pane. The sound of the smashing glass shattered the silence of the street, and Penny stood under the preschool canopy's shadow, waiting for someone to arrest her, woozy with the adrenaline rush, and tainted with guilt.

There was a reason kindergartens weren't boarded up. They were a respected institution, even now, even when the teachers were forcing the kids to draw their mommies and daddies dressed in peacemaker guard uniforms.

Penny thought about turning and running home to the comfort of her bed. Instead, she pulled herself together. With her sweatshirt over her hand, she poked it through the glass and unlatched the door from the inside.

A trickle of moonlight illuminated the tiny chairs and short tables, and Penny navigated her way to the teacher's desk, where she rummaged through boxes and opened drawers, shuffled through toys and books and puzzles, until she finally came across the treasure trove she was seeking. She tossed the pens into her bag first. Thick red markers, pencils, pens, and a handful of craft knives. She took paintbrushes and paint tubes, in pink, of course. Finally, she grabbed the thick black marker and left a note for the teacher: Sorry! This should cover it.

She took out the wad of twenty-dollar bills and left them in a heap next to her note. Before she left, she picked up the whiteboard marker from its cradle and, starting at the top and in her best and largest scrawl, wrote: *I am not a number.*

"That's a start, then," she whispered.

Penny crept back through the tiny tables and chairs, closed the door gently behind her, and walked to a new future.

Chapter Twenty

PENNY HADN'T BEEN expecting to just breeze in the front door of Sam's tenement. It was in a state much worse than her apartment. At least her door still locked, and there was some semblance of security measures to keep the unwanted out. Penny stood before Sam's door and bit her pinkie fingernail—a brand-new habit, one she could foresee a deep and long-lasting addiction to. The skin around her nail was already chewed, but she nibbled away at it with the single-minded goal of finding a nick to peel away. She pushed her finger hard against a tooth, ignoring the sharp twinges of pain.

A thousand thoughts raced through her mind, and she desperately tried to order them in anticipation of the conversation she was about to have. A flutter of nerves surprised her, followed by a dull sensation of shame. Apologies would need to be traded, especially on her behalf. She dropped her finger from her mouth, then jumped in fright as the door to Sam's apartment swung open. Her friend's eyebrows inclined at such an angle that they appeared to be one furry brow, and Penny was struck with his simple beauty.

"Why are you just standing here?" asked Sam. "I can see your shadow beneath the door, you know?"

Penny bit her lip. "Sorry, I just—I was just building up my courage."

"Well, I thought you might have been Dad, so—"

"So, you're disappointed."

"Pretty much."

Penny took his answer like the punch to the gut it was meant to be. "Can I come in? We need to talk."

Sam shook his head. "Mom's got a headache. She needs her quiet."

Penny saw the lie in her friend's face, in the way his left eyebrow arched; Penny knew all his tells. She'd seen it the first time when they were eight years old. She and Sam had spent a whole afternoon recreating the American Girl hair salon for the Toys "R" Us ads that were relentless at the time. But without an American Girl doll to pamper, they'd lured the neighbor's kid into Sam's room with a handful of stale breath mints. The poor kid's haircut was less than good, and Sam's mother had screamed when she'd seen this child with his hair freshly shorn, patchwork tufts sprouting out at random directions.

At the time, she'd been in awe of Sam as he'd coolly lied, raised an eyebrow with his butter-wouldn't-melt demeanor, scissors hot on the dresser drawer, and clusters of chopped hair beneath his feet. Penny smiled to think about it, yet fearful they were on the brink of losing all that shared history.

"I'm sorry about the other night," said Penny. "I'm off the pills now. Cold turkey. I'm doing great."

Sam looked at his feet, at the wall, at the door handle. Everywhere but at her.

"So, what it's been? Like, two days clean?" He finally met Penny's eyes, emphasizing that this wasn't a question of encouragement but a statement of sarcasm and bile.

Penny hadn't been expecting such animosity. "Um, so, I want to, um, do something about—things." Her face lit red with the heat of her nerves. "And I want you to help." This was not how she'd planned her pitch.

"Things," said Sam, so matter-of-factly that it took Penny's breath away. Sam suddenly had so much power in this relationship, and it seemed to grow with every word. "Things that you need help with."

Sam wasn't asking; he was mimicking, with a hint of incredulity and an obvious skepticism Penny found unnerving.

"Well, Quinn has taken over Jane's Carousel, and we're going to start a—" Penny looked behind her briefly and whispered the last word. "—uprising."

"An uprising. That's the stupidest thing I've ever heard."

"It's not stupid."

"For fuck sakes, Penn. Get serious. This isn't a little game. Real people's lives are at stake."

"I know that," said Penny, sounding a lot more defensive than intended. Sam had always been a better verbal debater. "That's why we're doing it. We need to make a change."

"How noble of you. The ex-junkie thinks she can change the world now."

"I'm not a junkie; I wasn't a junkie."

"Pill head, then. Is that better?" Sam smiled his sweetest smile, white teeth, piercing eyes, out to hurt.

"Why are you being so mean? I said I was sorry."

"Sorry isn't good enough. I thought I could rely on you."

"You could, you can."

"Just go home." Sam slammed the door in her face.

"Wait, Sam. Please."

She stood at the door and stared at the woodgrain, old and full of scratches. Full of their history. Her stomach churned—withdrawal, still? How long would this last? She tried to catch her breath, but a small frisson of discomfort bubbled up inside her, stronger and louder than all her other thoughts until a coherent word formed.

"Toxic," she whispered, carefully sounding out every syllable with growing contempt. "Toxic!" Then she banged on the door with her fist and put her mouth as close to the door as she could, just to be sure Sam would hear her. "You're fucking toxic. I don't need you!"

She didn't need anyone. All she needed was a stack of paper and a dream.

Chapter Twenty-One

PENNY TOSSED THE stolen reams of paper through the carousel hatch and scurried through. Her shoulder ached, and her arms shook after walking so far with the heavy load. She felt like she'd been released from an anchor that had tethered her to a cage, and she smiled as she found Quinn standing at the entrance on the other side of the hatch, holding a bundle of paper.

"Puzzle solved," said Quinn before drawing her into a hug and kissing her gently on the lips.

She was warm, smelled like salt and tasted like candy. She felt like home.

"Are you okay?" asked Quinn.

"I'm fine."

"I was worried about you."

"I'm off the pills."

"I know you are. I came to see you."

"You did?"

"I brought you Pop-Tarts and Wonder Bread."

"That was you?" said Penny. "Benny must have beaten me to the Pop-Tarts. He's got a sweet tooth worse than me, that one."

"I'm just glad you're better. You seemed really sick."

Penny thought of all the vomiting and realized for the first time that someone had cleaned it all away. She flushed red and hoped it was Benny after all.

"I'm okay," she said, trying to ignore the deep sense of dread curling in at the edges, and wondered if the trade-off for being clean would be the black cloud that chased her every thought.

"And you brought me presents." Quinn kissed her on the forehead and ran a thumb down the side of Penny's cheek. Looked into her eyes as if no one else in the world existed.

"I did," said Penny, still feeling contrite about raiding a preschool.

Quinn looked at the bundle in her hands. "Starting an art class?"

"Close. How about an uprising?"

"I'm listening."

"Forget the hacking," said Penny. "Even if you did manage to hack in, no one around here has a working device. Who would access your messages? No one important."

Quinn folded her arms.

"We need to reach the locals," Penny continued. "Make them sit up and listen."

"How? It's easier said than done."

"Paper planes," said Penny, "with notes in them—propaganda about how shit everything is, and that an uprising is on the way."

Quinn smiled.

"Look, I know it sounds crazy," said Penny.

"Crazy, yes."

"We can do it though. We'll just start with something simple."

"'I am not a number,'" said Quinn.

"Exactly. We write it out five hundred times, then scatter it around the streets like busy little postal workers."

"In the least, it sounds fun. Who cares about an uprising? We'll trek to the top of the Williamsburg Tower and toss them off!"

"Now that's a plan," said Penny.

"We're going to need to recruit some artists though. That's a whole lot of scribbling and folding."

"So, I don't have any friends left. That's on you."

Quinn laughed and slipped her am around Penny's waist. "What's with the sudden enthusiasm? You know we'll be shipped off to a reconditioning unit if we're caught."

"I'm just sick of living like this. No one is safe anymore. I just want to do my bit."

"Do your bit by provoking the country's bloodthirsty powers that be?"

"Sure, what else am I going to do with my days? And nights, now that I'm not sleepwalking off bridges."

"Well, when you put it like that," said Quinn. "When do we start?"

"How about right now?"

"THE TRICK WILL be not getting caught, going from here to there," said Quinn.

"So 'here' being the carousel and 'there' being the Williamsburg?" asked Penny as she stuffed two hundred and twenty-three paper planes into her satchel.

"Correct and correct."

"How long did it take us to get them done?"

Quinn looked at her watch and moved it to an angle to read the time through the deep scratches on the glass. "Exactly two hours and fifty-four minutes."

"You know your watch is smashed beyond recognition?" said Penny, grabbing Quinn's arm. "This is so broken."

"Only to the uninitiated."

"Really? Does it have secret laser beams? Convert to a gun?"

"Nope. Better than that, it beeps when it hits a Wi-Fi pocket. I rescued it from a tech-burn, and I've tracked a bunch of hotspots across the city. It's been kind of an obsession."

"Well, this will be your new obsession," said Penny, shuffling the papers in her satchel as she walked toward the exit. "Don't turn off the light till I'm at the hatch. This place gives me the creeps."

"This place?" said Quinn. "With the screaming horses and ghost conductor? Surely not?"

"Ghost conductor? You have ghosts?"

"Did I say ghost conductor? I meant a weird electrics system that just goes on and off by itself."

Penny pushed the hatch open. "You can hit the lights," she said and scuttled through the exit before it went dark.

She waited nervously for Quinn to appear on the other side as a half-moon scattered its blue light across the bay. Soon, Penny's eyes adjusted to the night, but Quinn still managed to frighten her when she finally emerged from the hatch with a small flashlight illuminating the dreary pockets of shadow.

"How dignified," said Penny. "We're traveling by flashlight tonight."

"Just so long as it doesn't get us caught."

"We're just two lovebirds out for a stroll."

"Lovebirds? More like jailbirds with what we've got planned."

"Okay, maybe switch it off, then."

"Wait," said Quinn. "I believe in times of war, there's a little thing called a finders keepers policy."

"Finders keepers? That's a new one. I'll be sure to add it to the rule book."

"Hold still," said Quinn as she shone the flash into Penny's satchel and pulled out a red marker. "Aha!"

She handed the flashlight to Penny. "Shine it on the sign."

Penny searched out the fallen sign and then watched as Quinn righted it. The sign was a vintage-looking thing but wasn't too badly damaged despite its neglect. "Welcome to Jane's Carousel," it read.

Penny watched with a smile as Quinn scribbled Penn's name in the place of "Jane" and then used all her weight to push the sign back into the ground.

Quinn tucked the pen into her back pocket and brushed off her hands. "I hereby decree this carousel to be the property of Penn, next legitimate president-in-waiting of the United States of Brooklyn."

"You're giving me the carousel?" Penny was touched, even though she knew it wasn't Quinn's to give.

"Just don't tell Jane. I mean, if you're going to start an uprising, you're going to need some headquarters."

"And what better place than one with screaming horses and ghost conductors?"

"Precisely," said Quinn. "Now let's go and get this thing started."

Penny laughed, switched off the flashlight, and kept her eyes peeled for roaming peacemakers and swiftly moving shadows. Their footfalls echoed around them, and every sound was the sound of danger.

"It's extra tense out here tonight," said Penny.

"Really? I feel super relaxed, and there hasn't been a single shadow, apart from our own."

"I feel like there are eyes everywhere, just following us. I keep hearing footsteps."

Quinn laughed. "They're ours. Stop freaking out. There's no one around; I promise. I've got bionic ears. If there's anyone out there, I'll hear them before I see them."

Penny took a breath, assured by Quinn and her relaxed attitude. She was still tender from her detox, still managing to find a way to deal with the void in her belly as dark as a black hole that shrank and expanded with every little thing she felt. If a bad thought crossed her mind, the hole started growing, and she was worried it might get so big it would consume her. "Do you really have bionic ears?" she asked.

"Sure do. My dad was deaf in one ear, so he was super protective of my hearing. He used to make me wear earmuffs whenever we went anywhere."

"Earmuffs?"

"Like big fluffy things." Quinn embellished her words with frothy hand movements. "I was always so embarrassed, but thanks to him, I have this amazing hearing."

"That's crazy."

"My dad was super weird. You would have liked him."

Penny interlaced her fingers with Quinn's and let her head fall on her shoulder. In that moment, nothing else mattered.

Chapter Twenty-Two

"THIS IS IT," said Quinn, looking skyward. "The Williamsburg Savings Bank."

"It's beautiful," said Penny, "at least, the bits that aren't burnt to crisp."

It was a gothic-style building with broken scaffolding littered at its base, and pieces of moldy mesh fabric draped over the rusting iron bars. Beyond the scaffolding, the charred building stood proudly, as if the trauma on the lower levels didn't even matter.

"How high does it go?" asked Penny.

"I don't know exactly. All the way to the top, I guess."

Penny laughed. "And we're walking it?"

"Well, we're not using the elevator."

Penny pulled Quinn in for a kiss.

"Let's do this thing, Miss President," said Quinn.

"Lead the way," said Penny. But she waited as Quinn flicked on the flash and surveyed the scaffolding, then pulled at various pieces, checking for strength until she appeared satisfied.

"I think this is going to be our best way in," said Quinn, shining the light upward. "There's a window on the left that hasn't been boarded up. That's what we're aiming for. You go first. I'll catch you if you fall."

"And who will catch you?"

"The ghost conductor, with any luck."

Penny laughed and swung onto the scaffolding with ease.

"Have you been practicing?" asked Quinn.

"I was the queen of the monkey bars in second grade, and if you're good, I'll show you how to do a triple backflip dismount on the way down."

"Please do."

"Meet you at the top."

Penny enjoyed the climb up the side of the building. The scaffolding was reasonably secure, and she was careful to steer clear of rusty patches. The bars cracked and buckled but never threatened to give way. A flurry of nerves hit her when she got to the top and saw the step from the scaffold to the window. It was a big gap, and though she estimated she could do it with one large stride, she didn't feel entirely confident in herself. The space between the building and the scaffold went straight down to the sidewalk in a three-story drop. One mistake, and it would be all over.

Below her, Quinn climbed with nervous movements, which gave away her fear. Penn knew she'd have to be the brave one and lead by example. She gripped the metal pipe, and balanced on her toes. Tipping her weight and without looking down, she stepped.

The stone windowsill was at least a foot wide but slippery with dew, and Penny skidded when her shoe made contact. She managed to balance into the slide, but her heart skipped a few beats. She grabbed the side of the window and looked back to see Quinn staring across, wide-eyed.

"This is kind of higher than it looks," said Quinn.

"Don't look down," said Penny, attempting casual despite the adrenaline.

"Too late."

Penny dried off the window ledge with her sleeve, but the slick of water just slipped across its polished surface. "It's really slippery," she said. "So be careful."

"Holy shit. Look at that drop."

"What did I say about not looking down?"

"Um, to not do it."

"So, don't do it."

"How can I not?"

"Just look at me." Penny reached out her hand.

Quinn looked her straight in the eye, angst obviously bubbling below the surface.

"Take my hand and step. Okay?" said Penny. "Ready? Go."

Quinn grabbed Penny's hand and maneuvered off the scaffold in one step. "Easy-peasy," said Quinn.

"It was smoother than my entrance; that's for sure."

Quinn pulled her flashlight from her jacket pocket and switched it on, then traced a path around the room. In the vast space, baroque chandeliers dropped from an arched ceiling, set upon a crumbling cement facade in varying stages of decay.

"This might be creepier than the carousel," said Penny.

"At least there are no screaming horses."

"That we can see."

Quinn pointed the flash toward the roof and highlighted a sky full of angels, complete with bows, arrows, and feathered wings. "There's an abundance of cherubs on the ceiling."

"Super creepy, and what's with the razor-sharp arrows? Kind of defeats the purpose of being all harmonious and fluffy."

"I've never heard anyone describe an angel as fluffy."

"Just telling it as I see it," said Penny.

"Do you think there are squatters?"

"Well, no, I didn't until you mentioned it, and now, I'm thinking that, yeah, the place is probably full of them."

"Let's go before we talk ourselves out of it." Quinn shined the flashlight on the opposite side of the room and up an arched exit that led the way to a wide set of stairs. "Right there. That's our way to the top."

"Good, let's make this quick."

Penny gripped Quinn's hand and inched forward, eyes opened wide as if it would help her see beyond the reach of the pitiful flashlight. The ascent was motivated by her fear of what lurked in the shadows. With adrenaline coursing through her body, she ignored the burn in her muscles, the lack of breath in her lungs, and solely focused on the horror of someone creeping in their wake.

At level sixteen, a crash from below stopped them in their tracks.

"What the fuck?" said Penny. "Turn off the flashlight."

They stood like statues for minutes and listened closely to the night, but when no other noise came, Quinn whispered in Penny's ear, "Just something breaking off, I think."

"Yep, definitely," said Penny, much too fast and with little thought. The shadows slipped around her like the monsters in her nightmares.

"Let's keep going without the light," said Quinn.

Penny nodded, unseen by Quinn, and tucked Quinn's arm into the nook of her elbow.

"Nice and quiet," said Quinn.

Penny could tell by the lack of confidence in her voice that she was thoroughly spooked. They walked in silence up and up until they could go no farther and finally came upon a sliver of moonlight trickling through a loosely hanging door.

"We're here," said Quinn.

Penny pushed through the door, ecstatic to still be alive, and collapsed to her knees. Relief and pride swept over her as she rolled onto her back and waited for her heart to stop pounding and her breath to find her. She stared up at the clock tower and couldn't believe how big it was now that she was only yards within its reach. She laughed at how silly she'd been to be so scared of the dark.

"We did it," said Penny as she rolled to her feet and joined Quinn at the railing.

"Next time, we'll outsource this part of the job," said Quinn.

"Good idea. How entrepreneurial of you."

"Wow, look how far you can see," said Quinn, pointing toward the Manhattan skyline.

"You can see all three bridges. It's so peaceful up here."

Quinn grabbed Penny around the waist and pulled her in for a hug. "Let's make this the new headquarters and live up here like Queens of the Tower."

"Living on love again?"

"Of course."

"I might take you up on that offer actually," said Penny. "I don't think I want to walk back down into the abyss of evil cherubs."

"Abyss of Evil Cherubs. I'd totally watch that if it was a show and I had Netflix and a screen."

Penny laughed and dumped a pile of paper planes into Quinn's hand. "Here we go."

She shot a single plane into the air, where it fluttered like a dove set free. "It's so pretty," she said, admiring the way it danced and spun in the drifts of wind.

Quinn followed suit and tossed a handful of paper planes into the sky one after the other.

Together, they worked silently and swiftly to set all the planes free, and Penny, elated with the beauty of it, couldn't stop smiling. The planes drifted and swooped around her, just like in her dreams. She let her arms float skyward, held her face up to the breeze, and acknowledged a powerful change in the air as if it were snowing. Each plane, folded from her own hand, was as brittle and ineffectual as a single snowflake, but as a mass, their potential to disrupt and conquer was as exciting as it was overwhelming. Penny whirled in a slow circle, the ecstasy of her achievement beaming into the sky. Each breath filled her with hope and a rush of power as if she owned the world and would forever. She laughed and closed her eyes. This world would be hers once more. She would do everything in her power to make it that way.

Once all of the planes had been released, Penny and Quinn stood hand in hand and watched their delicate creations make a slow and graceful descent. When it was time to leave, Penny found that she wasn't scared at all, and as she made her way through the darkness and down the stairs, she couldn't wipe the smile from her face.

Chapter Twenty-Three

THE WALK BACK to Quinn's loft had been uneventful, and while Quinn crashed into an immediate and deep slumber, Penny spent hours fighting for sleep to come. She tossed and turned and fought against the discomfort in her restlessness until finally her eyes closed and remained that way for more than four hours.

It was the smell of coffee that woke her again.

"Did anyone order room service?" said Quinn, standing beside the bed with a cup in each hand.

"If that's what I think it is, then, yes, I definitely did."

"Coffee for two, madame?"

"Just leave the second one; my lover will be back in a moment."

Quinn laughed and sat on the floor. She sipped her coffee and let her head fall back onto the bed. "So, you didn't run away in the night."

Penny combed her fingers through Quinn's hair and worked out a tangle. "Nope. And I slept like a log."

"Really?"

"Short but sweet. Although that might be the coffee talking."

"I did spike it with an aphrodisiac."

Penny laughed and nearly choked on her coffee. "New rule. No making people laugh when they're drinking black gold. I could have lost a mouthful."

"That would have been a travesty."

"You don't even know." Penny savored the taste of the coffee, which reminded her of simpler times when her morning routine had been definitive, calm, and surprise-free.

"We did well last night," said Quinn. "I wonder what will come of it."

"I don't know, but I want to do it again."

"You're serious about this, aren't you?"

"At least we're doing something, you know?"

"We're definitely doing *something*."

Penny finished her coffee and swung her legs over the side of the bed. "I better get home and make sure the clowns haven't burnt the apartment down."

Quinn grabbed Penny around her waist in an attempt to stop her from leaving. "Anchor attack," she said. "You can't leave unless you can release from my octopus-like grip."

Penny laughed and grabbed Quinn's forefinger, then pulled it slowly upward until it turned white.

"Ow, ow, ow, okay, have mercy, woman," said Quinn.

Penny slipped into her jeans. That smile of hers just wouldn't quit. "So, we're doing it again tonight, right?"

"Penn's Carousel, straight after curfew."

"And you're going to brainwash some minions and bring them along?"

"It's on the top of my to-do list."

"I'll see you later," Penny said. "Don't forget to do your chores."

Penny exited out of the service entrance and was surprised to see the streets full of junior peacemakers holding garbage bags and spears. A few senior guards stood, dotted about the place, whispering to one another in serious communion. Penny tried to stop her creeping smile as she strolled past the hundreds of paper planes, littering the district and filling her with pride and hope.

The sight of the new checkpoint that had sprouted up at the border of the Main Street Park made Penny's buoyant mood dissipate almost as fast as it had arrived. An extra checkpoint would make things difficult with the frequency of her bridge crossing.

As she neared the checkpoint, her panic subsided. Rookie peacemakers, with their quivering hands and shaky knees, instilled a confidence in her that would intimidate every last one of them in their freshly pressed uniforms, starchy and unforgiving. Yet there was one newbie guard who seemed to swagger in the uniform he wore. He had an athletic body with a puffed-out chest and strong shoulders. Penny was ten yards away when the boy turned and revealed his face. At first, Penny didn't believe what she saw. This boy was as familiar as her own blood yet completely different. Was it possible that there could be another person out in the world who looked so much like Sam?

Penny stopped in her tracks and stared at the peacemaker, studying at each feature. The thick brows and the mole on the left cheekbone, the one Sam hated so much. It was only when he caught Penny's eye and held her gaze that Penny knew with clarity that the boy in front of her, the one on the side of the bad guys, was her best and oldest friend.

Sam's face hardened before he whispered to a colleague. He rushed toward her, grabbed her by the elbow, and ushered her swiftly into the shadows of the Manhattan underpass, away from the prying eyes of his colleagues.

"What are you doing here?" he said.

"What am *I* doing here? What are you doing here? And why are you wearing this fucking monstrosity?" Penny plucked at the sleeves of Sam's uniform.

"Keep your voice down," he said, looking over his shoulder nervously. "I'm trying to help you."

"Help me? I don't need help, but you obviously do."

"If you chill out for a second, I can explain it all."

"How can you explain this? Have you forgotten that they reconditioned Simon? How can you justify this? We need you on our side, not theirs."

"There is no other side. This is all there is."

Sam straightened his shirt cuffs, which looked terribly uncomfortable. "We can't beat them, so we have no choice but to join them. That's what Rita says, and I believe her. The sooner you figure that out, the better it will be for you."

Penny shook her head in disbelief. "Rita? Since when are you listening to her?"

"Since she was there for me."

"I was there for you. Trust me; Rita does not have your best interests at heart. She's 100 percent crazy."

"Rather crazy than a traitor. Eventually, you'll have to join, Penn. They'll start to question why you won't, and it's better you do it now than by force."

"By force? Wow, Rita really worked a number on you. I can assure you no one is going to force me to do anything, especially not you."

"You'll end up in a reconditioning unit. Do you want that?"

"Maybe it is what I want. That's obviously where all the good people are ending up. I'd rather be dead than sign up with those rapists and murderers."

"You're so damn stubborn. Don't come asking me for help when you're a walking zombie."

"Well, if I'm a zombie, why the fuck will I care anyway? Kind of reminds me of the time when you came crying to me, and I gave you five hundred dollars to save yourself."

Sam looked guilty.

"What did you do with the money? Did you buy this uniform with it?"

"The uniforms are free," said Sam as he brushed his hands down the front of his pant legs.

"You're disgusting; you actually like it," said Penny.

"Shut up. I don't like it. It's just the smart thing to do."

"But you need a sense of decency, don't you? You need to be able to look at yourself in the mirror and know you're good?"

"I'm good!"

"Keep telling yourself that."

"I'm just trying to survive here. I'm doing whatever it takes to survive."

"You're not surviving. Don't you dare tell me you are surviving. You have it easy. You're just a traitor. How can you align yourself with savage idiots?"

Sam's eyes filled with tears, and Penny felt satisfied.

"Wow," said Sam. "Who are you?"

"I'll tell you who I'm not. I'm not a traitor, and I'm not your friend. You're just a ghost! You're a fucking ghost."

As Sam strode away, regret overpowered Penny. She leaned on the bridge pillar for support and slid all the way down, sobbing into her hands. She'd lost her oldest friend for good; he had become her enemy. She'd lost him to the peacemakers. Along with a big chunk of her heart.

Chapter Twenty-Four

BENNY AND LARRY were relatively sober when Penny walked in the door. They sat at the dining table eating bread with butter and ham. She dumped her satchel on the chair next to her father and took a seat alongside her uncle, emotionally exhausted but relieved to be off the streets and away from the chaos outside. She'd walked the long way via Manhattan Bridge, which had taken her an extra hour but given her time to clear her head and come to terms with Sam's betrayal. As she sat there and watched Benny slowly consume his breakfast with shaking hands, she realized these people were all she had left and felt a great sense of responsibility to look after them.

"You're a civilized lot today," said Penny. She picked up a slice of ham and sniffed it. "Fresh too." She smiled, relieved they'd obviously been selling the bootleg to support themselves. It was perfect timing; with the origami war unfolding, she needed them to start taking responsibility for themselves. If she was honest, she was a bit proud they had been able to feed themselves. It was a big step forward. Almost unbelievable. "Where did you get it?"

"You don't want to know, my darling," said Larry.

He tossed her a slice of bread and pushed the butter toward her.

"Tuck in, my dear. You're all skin and bones. Still as beautiful as the day you were born though."

"Larry, I feel like you're greasing me up for something," said Penny.

"So suspicious," said her father with mock dismay.

Penny loved it when her father wasn't drunk, well, when he wasn't *blind* drunk.

"How's that friend of yours?" asked Benny. "Keeping you out of trouble, I hope."

"Trouble? Me? I couldn't find trouble if I went looking for it."

"Ha," said Larry. "She's like her father, this one. As innocent as a baby duckling and twice as cute."

Benny and Larry peeled into laughter.

"You silly old goon," said Benny, "that's an outright lie. I don't believe it for a second. She's trouble like her mom, this one."

Benny stopped and bit his lip. Larry stared into his bread, falling suddenly silent.

"I mean that in a good way," said Benny as his eyes teared up. "I loved her as much as I love you."

"I know. I know what you mean," said Penny, draping an arm around her uncle and shaking him jovially. She wanted to get the mood back. Without a second thought, she opened her satchel and tugged at the tip of a paper plane protruding from it. "You want to see trouble? Look at this."

She dumped a fist full of crumpled paper planes in the middle of the table but instantly realized her mistake at the worry that crossed Benny's face. "I found them on the bridge; they're all over the place," she lied. "Everyone's talking about an uprising. Well, just a tiny one. A tiny little origami war." She laughed and grabbed a paper plane, unraveled its folds, and ironed it flat with her hand.

Her father reached for a paper plane and slowly unfolded it. She wondered if he would suspect her involvement and feel a rush of pride. She waited for the flash of hope to light his face.

Penny unfolded some more planes and lined them up across the table so her father and Benny could read their messages. "What do you think?" she asked with an eagerness that bordered on desperation.

Benny picked up a plane and read it with a frown.

"The world is burning, and we are the flames," said Larry, reading the propaganda that Penny had laid out for him. "What is this?" He unfolded another flyer. "If we burn, you burn with us?"

"It's just a joke, Larry," said Penny. "Quotes from books and stuff. Obviously, someone is trying to ruffle the feathers of those in charge."

"You better not be mixed up in this bullshit," he said. "You know what they'll do to the idiots on the other end of this?"

Penny smirked. He knew her better than she gave him credit for. She stood and started collecting her planes, swept her arms across the table in broad strokes, and pushed back the simmering indignation.

"I do, actually," said Penny. "Do you know, Larry? Do you know what those assholes are doing to girls like me? No, you don't. You don't have a clue because you're a lousy drunk."

Larry slammed a fist into the table, startling her. "Better a lousy drunk than a suicidal lunatic. You should have stayed on those pills. At least they made you interesting."

Benny started crying.

"Wow," said Penny, bitterness spiraling up from the black hole inside her. "It's no wonder Mom killed herself. Especially if you were as lousy at being a husband as you are at being a father."

The shock in Larry's face mirrored her own dismay at having said such a deeply wounding succession of words. She hadn't known she was capable of such a callous attack. She turned around and walked to her room. Instant regret formed in her stomach like a rock as she went to close the door. There was only enough time to duck behind it when a kitchen chair came hurtling toward her bouncing off the wall, leaving a hole in its flight path.

She closed the door quietly. Took a breath. Then opened it. Slammed it. Opened it again. Slammed it even harder. She dragged a side table over and placed it squarely in front of the door, then collapsed onto her bed, where she sobbed until she felt so empty she feared the smallest wind might blow her away.

Chapter Twenty-Five

THE FOOTSTEPS POUNDING behind Penny as she ran along the bridge walk were so close she could feel them like a whisper in her ear. A menacing wind that chased her every step. The faster she ran, the slower she seemed to go. Every footstep was stuck in treacle until, heavier and heavier, she couldn't lift her feet at all. Yet as she slowed, the chasing shadow hovered. A hot breath on her shoulder. The only safe place, the water below. Her fingers gripped the flimsy wire that scaled each pylon like unruly ivy, and her bare feet teetered on the verge of the bridge, toes twitching with the anticipation of a jump. The shadow monster brought upon her soul a darkness so gloomy that the only option was to jump. She sprang from terror, the moment of freedom only momentarily exhilarating. As her body turned, she looked back at the bridge, at her mother standing there, breathless and full of fear, flanked on either side by Rita, Benny, Sam, and Quinn. The slap of the water was only seconds away when Penny jolted back to reality in a tangle of bedsheets.

The nightmares had become intense since she'd quit the pills, and every dream felt as real as day. The sensation of dropping from that bridge was like a memory. The rush of the wind, the speed of the fall, the regret of the jump. The realization of a fatal mistake. Had her mother suffered these same moments before her life had been taken? Penny shook her head, pushing the thought back to its home in the depths of her subconscious. A small stone, locked safely away and never to be inspected.

Penny pondered the water-stained ceiling. It was a rare thing to wake to the sight of her bedroom ceiling, but even though she was safe at home, a deep anxiety overcame her. She rolled onto her side for a less depressing view, and it took a few moments to register the strange sight of the upturned money box lying carelessly on the floor beside her bed. The lid, recklessly tossed in the opposite direction, lay a few feet away. Had she taken it out? Had she sleepwalked again? She sat up. The room spun for a second but came to a standstill soon enough, and she flicked through her thoughts so quickly her brain buzzed.

She scooped the box off the floor and onto her lap, letting her hand drift from corner to corner. Indeed empty. She pondered the possibilities. Had she spent the money without knowing? Had she taken it out and hidden it without remembering? She traced her memory of the last few days but was quickly confident that she'd done nothing of the sort. With a sigh, the truth of the lost money came to her—a picture of name-brand liquor and a fresh leg of ham. Her father had stolen her money and, even worse, had frittered it away. She dropped the box and stared at the floor, curiously empty of emotion. She had expected nothing less of her father. The bottomless hole inside her expanded until an all-consuming anxiety sparked manic fury.

Penny stormed into the living room but stopped after only a few steps. A fever in the air caught her off guard. Where normally Larry's stupid music would still be blasting, today it was silent. Where normally Benny would be asleep, face-first on the table top or on the couch or on the floor, today he was absent.

Penny strode first to her father's bedroom and was happy to see him sprawled across the floor, snoring. As Penny approached him, she saw the foreshots bottle in his hand. Where was Benny? She scanned the living room and behind the kitchen bench, and with racing heart she barged in through the bathroom door. Benny lay facedown on the tile, a slick of stomach bile, pulpy and pink, traced a path from his chin and across the floor.

Penny fell to her knees and rolled him onto his back. She could tell by the color of his face that he was alive. She'd seen firsthand the color of death. While he was certainly a shade of gray, he didn't have the blue tinge of a corpse. Her relief was palpable, and she eased Benny's head into her lap. He stirred, murmured something unintelligible, and managed to lift his hand a few inches before it crashed back onto the tile. Tears of relief and fear washed down Penny's face. Benny had been more like an older brother than an uncle, and she felt a deep guilt at her inability to protect and care for him in the way he needed.

"Benny," she whispered as she smoothed the sweaty hair off his face. "You're all right. I've got you."

Benny opened his eyes and blinked slowly as if it were a painful task. He lifted his hand again, but this time, Penny caught it.

"I got ya, Benny. You're fine. I got ya."

She held his hand tight and rested her forehead on his, her tears dripping onto his face, dusting his cheeks with her anguish. Benny gripped her hand, and they stayed like that until he opened his eyes and sat up. Penny's legs were stiff and cold by the time she pulled him from the floor and ushered him to the couch to sleep. She laid a blanket over his shoulders and walked away.

Chapter Twenty-Six

PENNY SAT ON her bed for a long time, looking at the wall and allowing her thoughts play before her like a movie. The room felt suddenly small and devoid of air, giving the sensation of being slowly suffocated. She couldn't continue to live in this place with her thieving father and her damaged-beyond-repair uncle. It was all well beyond anything she could manage. The world had become stark after ditching the pills, and she was filled with feelings so real and raw she could almost touch them.

The setting sun cast a slick of orange light, through her broken window, across the floor, and up the wall. Penny opened the closet door and eyeballed the mess. Eventually, she fished out an old rucksack, which she turned upside down and shook. Nothing came out but a few moldy crumbs. She grabbed two pairs of sweatpants, a sweatshirt, a handful of underwear, socks, and any other item of clothing she could stuff into the bag. She checked the bedside table drawer, took out her flashlight, a pack of Nyquil, and the last photo in the world of her mother. She glanced around her bedroom, grabbed her pillow, and realized there was nothing else she needed to take with her, except the empty money box, which she scooped off the floor on her way out of the room.

Her father bristled as she approached the table where he sat, a tic in his neck giving away his guilt as she tossed the empty box down in front him. It rolled across the table, mimicking the sound of hollow footsteps, and came to stop in the middle. Benny, sitting opposite with a blanket around his shoulders, lowered his gaze, and in doing so, registered his own involvement in the theft. His betrayal might be a disappointment she would never recover from.

Larry squirmed in his seat and took a sip of his drink, refusing to meet Penny's gaze.

"I'm leaving," she said.

Larry sipped his drink as Penny observed him, a ghost in his world. Frozen in grief, Penny could do nothing but stare at her father, confused. Her father no longer resided within this shell of a human. All illusions slipped away in an instant. This man had already lost so much, and now that included the only person on the planet who still cared whether he lived or died. Although, she wasn't sure anymore if she really did.

"You have nothing to say," said Penny. "Not a thing?"

Her father continued to ignore her and merely pushed the box into the center of the table.

"Call it a tax," said Larry, finally, with a slur that gave away his drunken state.

"How very mature of you, Larry, to steal from your own kid."

"You're not a kid; you're a fool."

Penny looked at her father and willed herself not to cry. His passivity was raw and sharp, but she deflected it with her own animosity.

"You're a fucking disgrace, an embarrassment. You're nothing." Game, set, match.

Penny grabbed the bag of oranges off the table and tucked it under her arm, followed by the bread and few remaining slices of ham. She turned, marched out the door, and didn't look back. Not even when she heard Benny sobbing.

Chapter Twenty-Seven

IT WAS DARK by the time Penny made it to the carousel. The streets had been relatively empty of people and void of checkpoints, which had suited her mood. She crawled through the hatch, and once safely inside the confines of the carousel, she switched on her flashlight and scoured the perimeter for unwanted intruders. Roving shadows gave the creatures of the carousel a ghostly glow as if they might spring to life at any moment. She wondered at her good sense and questioned her ability to make this place her home without panicking every time she entered, but then, what choice did she have?

She scanned the wall beyond the carousel, and the flashlight illuminated the figure of a person just standing there. Completely still. She gasped. Froze. Fear constricted her voice box. And as she wound up to scream, she recognized the gray hoodie and the curls peeking out from beneath the hood. "Quinn?"

"Penny?"

"Is that you?" asked Penny as the figure approached.

"Of course, it's me. Who else would it be?"

"You scared the shit out of me. Why are you just standing there like a murderer?"

"I wasn't standing there like a murderer. I was standing there like a scaredy-cat waiting to be murdered."

"Well, if that was you hiding, you did a terrible job," said Penny.

"I know. I was like a deer in headlights. I'm so glad it was you. Come on; I was just about to get these lights on. I'll give you a lesson. This way, madame." Quinn took Penny's hand and led her to the generator.

The tangle of electrical cords lying in a pile in front of the generator cupboard seemingly had no beginning or end. Quinn trod over them, and Penny followed suit without question.

Inside the shallow cupboard, they found a mop and a portable generator. It was a large square box with wheels, a handle, and a few lights and switches.

"Here she is," said Quinn, patting the machine as if it was a pet dog.

"It's tiny. I thought it would be, like, I don't know, like the size of a car or something,"

"A car? You're crazy."

"I'll take that as a compliment, thanks."

"Okay, so give me some light over here."

Penny obeyed, illuminating the area.

"You gotta check the gas on the meter here," said Quinn, pointing to a glass window with a red fuel gage. "It's pretty full already, but if you try to start it with nothing in it, you'll blow the whole thing up. I think. Just don't do it." Quinn tapped the window with her fingernail, and the red arrow inside bobbed around with the vibration. "Then you just find all the yellow bits and turn them on." She made light work of all the various knobs and levers until the machine jumped to life.

Penny put her hands on her ears. "It's loud."

Quinn nodded and ushered her backward, out of the cupboard. She closed the doors, and the generator's grumbling faded to a low hum.

Penny dropped her hands, surprised at how quiet it suddenly was.

"They're soundproofed," said Quinn, pointing to the cupboard doors with her thumb.

Penny turned to the lit-up carousel, which draped the room in a comforting orange glow. "I forgot how pretty it is," she said, walking over to one of the angel-covered chariots. She dumped her bag and threw her pillow in. "Home sweet home. You don't mind, do you?"

"What? You're moving in?"

"Pretty much. I can't go home. Those two idiot-clowns are on their own."

Quinn put her arm around Penny's waist and drew her close. "What happened?"

Penny swallowed and looked at the ceiling, willing herself not to cry. She wouldn't waste any more tears on that loser of a father. "I just feel a bit broken, you know? I shouldn't have to look after Larry. He's the grown-up. He's supposed to look after me. Not the other way around."

Quinn nodded and wiped a tear from Penny's cheek. "Well, I'm not having you sleep here all by yourself. You can stay with me at the loft. It'll be great."

"I don't know. We hardly know each other."

"We know enough. Come on. Say yes; it'll be fun. We'll be like a married couple. You can make me breakfast in bed like a proper wifey."

Penny laughed. She loved the way Quinn could pull her out of any dull mood. "Sounds like an amazing opportunity for me. Let me guess, scrambled?"

"What?"

"Scrambled. It's how you like your eggs. I have a theory you don't really know someone until you know how they like their eggs."

"Hang on. Why scrambled? I think I should be offended that you deduced that from my personality. Have you not seen the immaculate state of my living quarters?"

Penny laughed, and then a loud knock from the other side of the carousel made them both jump.

"Oh, good," said Quinn. "They're here. At least, I hope it's them."

Quinn skipped past the screaming horses and jumped off the other side of the carousel, making a beeline for the hatch.

"Hope it's who?" said Penny, following cautiously.

"Our guests, remember?" said Quinn as she walked backward. "It was your idea to round up a bunch of minions."

The light in Penny's brain switched on. It seemed so long ago they'd been zipping paper plane propaganda off the rooftops. A flutter of excitement stirred in her belly.

Quinn disappeared through the hatch, and Penny heard whispers, laughter, footsteps. Many footsteps until, one by one, four squinting faces emerged from the hatch and into the light of the carousel. Quinn held her arms wide and spun around in circles.

"Welcome to Penn's Carousel," she said and hopped up onto the podium next to Penny, who held the pole of a screaming horse in her hands. "Everyone, this is Penn. Penn, this is everyone."

"Hi," said Penny, flicking up her wrist in greeting. "Make yourselves at home.

The two girls and two boys nodded and smiled, but their distraction was obvious. Their awe of the carousel seemed to pull them around its perimeter, like moons orbiting a planet.

One of the girls hopped up onto the podium next to Penny. She wore her hair in two braids, falling either side of her chin, skin the color of burnt caramel. Penny suddenly felt inadequate and small. If this was the quality of Quinn's friends and acquaintances, Penny wondered how she could possibly be interested in a stick insect like her.

"I'm Lucy," said the girl. She held out her hand, and Penny shook it. "Does this thing work?" Lucy swung a leg over the horse and laughed. "Giddy up."

A pang of excitement went through Penny at the prospect of friends, or at least, people who hung out in her vicinity and wanted to have some fun.

"I'll turn it on," said Penny as she made her way to the center control console. She looked at the array of buttons and gear sticks and wondered which one was the On switch.

As if reading her mind, Quinn followed her into the booth and closed the door behind her. "So?" she said, slipping an arm around Penny's waist. "Did I do good? I rounded up all the minions I could muster, just like Miss President wanted me to."

"I'm Miss President now? Who are they anyway?"

"Don't ask me. I just met them today. They could be mass murderers for all I know."

"Really?" Penny felt better knowing these gorgeous people weren't old flames or long-time friends she had to compete with. "So you just picked them up off the street, like, 'Hey, join our uprising.'"

"Literally, word for word," said Quinn.

"How do you know they're not going to turn us in?"

"I don't really, but I've got a good instinct for people, and they don't seem like peacemaker types."

"What if they're spies?"

"There are no spies," said Quinn with a smile. "It's not 1984. We've no reason for spies, at least, not yet. And they've got their shit locked down. They know we're all running scared. No one is doing anything stupid. Well, except me. And now you. And now them." Quinn looked delighted and beamed from ear to ear.

Penny couldn't help but smile along with a flush of embarrassment. She was being childish, of course, there were no spies. "I guess so, but don't you have friends of your own?"

"None that I trust."

Penny laughed and draped her arms around Quinn's neck. She admired her confidence. "So you trust complete strangers more than anyone else in your life?"

"I told you, I've got a good sense for people. I picked you out of the bunch, didn't I?"

"Well, apart from the fact that I'm a walking red flag, I can't argue with that."

Penny looked at the group of ragtag teens Quinn had recruited and agreed the peacemakers weren't smart enough or worried enough to deploy spies into the rundown streets of Brooklyn.

"Let's show them a good time so they don't all leave," said Penny. "How do you get this thing going?"

"Move over, Miss President. This is a job for a professional."

"Shall I go get someone else, then?" Penny laughed as the organ music started up and the ride began to slowly wind around. Their new friends hollered with joy, their enthusiasm infectious. Penny hadn't felt this elated in a long time. She left the control room and jumped on a horse of her own, laughing along. In this moment of perfection, she dared to believe that everything was going to be okay.

The six of them spun themselves silly on the carousel, then set to work creating hundreds of paper plane propaganda.

Penny was mesmerized by the beauty of Eddie and Oscar. They could have fallen straight out of the pages of a girlie fashion magazine, the kind that splashed words like G-SPOT, DIET, and ORGASM on its front cover. When Eddie lovingly tucked a lock of hair behind Oscar's ear, Penny blushed to witness it. She looked at Quinn and smiled. Had she seen her red cheeks? Could she read the longing on her face for her own kind of love like that? It made her blush even more.

"So," said Sara, her golden ponytail trailing down her back, "are you really running for president?" She held one of the leaflets that Quinn had been scribbling on for the troops to fold into planes.

Quinn shot Penny a look. Penny didn't know what Quinn had told them, nor whether or not they expected to get on board with a capable group of rebels who intended to overthrow the government.

"I guess," said Penny. "It's something we're working toward."

"So it's a fake-it-till-you-make-it type situation?" asked Lucy.

"Exactly," said Penny. "I'm not quite pulling off the presidential thing right now, but I'm working toward it. I'm also kind of hoping my boobs are still growing too."

The group stopped folding and looked at her, then burst simultaneously into laughter.

Over the course of the next few hours, they all scribbled a variety of anti-government sentiment onto folded-up planes, and Penny shared her oranges and bread. Penny hadn't laughed so much in a long time. Had any of them?

It was midnight when Quinn decided enough was enough, and they stuffed five bags full of perfectly folded origami jet planes.

"If this drop works," said Penny, "I'm sending a thousand planes off the Empire State."

"That would really get the message across," said Lucy. "It might even reach the Upper East Side and get the attention of the rich and famous."

"Waste of time," said Oscar. "Their eyes aren't on the sky. They've still got Wi-Fi. They don't even know how the other half lives. They're buffered from this shit."

"They know what's happening downtown," said Penny. "They just don't *want* to know."

"Well, a thousand paper planes will be hard to ignore," said Quinn.

She winked at Penny and threw a map of Brooklyn on the floor, which the six of them huddled around.

"So, we're here," said Quinn, drawing a red circle around the spot on the map where the carousel stood. "And we want to get here and here." She scribbled two crosses on the map. "The Williamsburg is good to go. We hit it last night. It's quiet up that way, so I think we'll be fine for another visit. Penn can take the girls."

Penny bit her lip, remembering how creepy the pitch-black walk to the top had been. "Won't it be crawling with peacemakers? Surely, they've traced our planes back to that point."

"I've been up there all day," said Quinn. "They don't have a clue. They've upped their presence around the landing sites, but they haven't thought to trace the flight paths. I don't think they've realized how we're doing it just yet."

While slightly relieved, Penny couldn't shake her unease, like a tiny rock stuck in her shoe.

"I'll take the boys and hit the Hub," said Quinn. "It's not as tall, but it's smooth sailing toward the Hudson. We'll get these things far and wide."

Penny studied the map, tracing her finger along the trail Quinn had drawn. "So, we can head up together along Flatbush." She was happy in the knowledge they'd all be together for most of the journey. "And split off at Lafayette. It's basically spitting distance between the two buildings."

Oscar placed his fingers in a *V* formation on the map between the two buildings.

"Well," said Oscar, "if three blocks is your idea of spitting distance, then you're dead right."

Penny laughed. This was going to be fun.

Chapter Twenty-Eight

THE WALK TO the drop zone was mostly silent and especially tense, without a moon to light the way. When they finally came to a stop at the Lafayette turnoff, the sense of relief among the group was undeniable.

"Don't use the flashlight unless you have to," said Quinn. "And run if you see anyone. Anyone, okay? Civilian or not. People out past curfew are up to no good."

"Like us," said Penny.

"Worse than us," said Quinn.

Penny liked the way Quinn attempted to protect her, but she was nothing like a porcelain doll in need of care, despite her petite appearance.

"Meet you back at the loft, right?" said Quinn.

Penny nodded and kissed her, but as she moved to walk away, it took all of her courage to let her fingers slide from Quinn's. She wasn't exactly scared—it was something else, like the world was on a tilt. Something about the night didn't feel right, as if there were eyes in the shadows, watching her every move. But before Penny had a chance to verbalize her fear, Lucy and Sara had intertwined their arms on either side of her and dragged her off toward the Williamsburg Tower with a hop in their steps and smiles on their faces. It wasn't long, though, till the tense silence rolled back in as Quinn and the boys disappeared quietly into the shadows, and the girls were on their own.

Penny stopped when they came to the scaffolding that shrouded the lower half of the tower and pointed skyward. "Follow me up, but watch the jump at the top. The windowsill is slippery as fuck."

Penny adjusted her messenger bag, full to bursting with paper planes, and hopped onto the scaffold with minimal effort. The girls trailed in her shadow with surprising deftness, and a roll of nerves tumbled through Penny's belly. When she reached the top and stood before the step-across, she was just as alarmed as she had been the first time.

Without looking down, she stretched out her arm, and sprang across the daunting gap. Her foot skidded a mere inch, but the anticipation of probable death almost killed her.

Adrenaline coursed through her veins, and the buzz of being alive made her laugh. She pulled her flashlight from the top of her satchel and illuminated the huge room, running the light around its walls, up and down, side to side, looking for rough sleepers or serial killers.

"Penn," said Sara from the scaffold. "Are you in there?"

"Yep, come across," said Penny, stretching her arm across the void.

Sara took her hand and crossed first, followed swiftly by Lucy until all three of them huddled together.

"There's a small drop-off." Penny aimed her flash toward the floor. "I'll go first, then shine the light for you to follow."

Penny paused to scan the interior one last time, peering carefully into each shadow. The girls' anxiety was off the chart, as if it were a whole other person in the room.

Lucy clutched Penny's elbow. "What are you looking for?"

"Nothing." Penny tried not to think about all the possible axe murderers, serial killers, and peacemaker guards who might be roaming the shadows.

Penny finally stepped into the room and helped her friends down. They made their way hand in hand across to the stairwell, Penny leading with the flashlight up front and Lucy at the rear with her own light trailing in their wake.

"Is this super creepy, guys?" asked Lucy.

"It's fine." Penny tried to keep her voice from quivering. "I was just here last night."

"Well, it seems creepy to me," said Lucy.

Penny stopped short of the stairs and shone her flashlight up through the middle of the railing. The shadows shrank and grew at odd angles as she swept the light along the bars of the stairwell—near impossible to tell the shadow of the rail from the shadow of someone's leg.

"Well, up we go, I guess," said Penny, her enthusiasm waning by the minute.

"It's a long way," said Sara.

"The adrenaline will get us up there." Penny was so on edge she felt she could probably bend a metal pole if she had to.

She took the first step, setting a swift pace to the top. Lucy and Sara had no choice but to follow or stand alone in the dark. Their footsteps echoed throughout the building despite their attempts to go quietly. Penny swept the flashlight wildly in front of her as she moved forward. With every twist and turn of the light, she expected nothing less than to see a murderous human jump from the blackness and kill them all while Quinn's words ran nonstop through her head: *Run, just run. Run, just run.*

Her relief at making it to the top alive was exhilarating, and though she was desperate for air, Penny felt like she could keep going for at least another ten floors as the adrenaline surged through her blood. She bowled through the exit door, shoulder first, and the three of them fell onto the balcony. Penny held her arms above her head, the flashlight beamed into the sky, and she smiled at the other girls.

Lucy broke into laughter. "I was literally shitting my pants the whole time."

"Ew," said Sara. "You literally do not know what literally means, do you?"

"It means totally," said Lucy.

"Literally, it doesn't," said Penny.

Sara draped her arm around Penny's shoulder, and as they laughed together, a rush of kinship swept across Penny like none she'd ever known before. She had no family left to speak of, but these girls would be a good replacement, and life was looking up.

"Let's do this thing," said Penny, dumping her satchel onto the ground. If she flapped her arms a couple of times, she might just lift off with the sudden lightness of her being both physically and emotionally. Penny grabbed the first paper plane and pulled out its wings. "First flight, cleared for takeoff." She gently released it.

The three of them watched in mesmerized silence as the plane drifted peacefully out across the sky, dropped a couple feet, looped around itself, and continued farther across the skyline.

"It's never going to land," said Lucy.

"Amazing," said Sara.

With a surge of pride, Penny picked up another. "The trick is not to force it too much, just kind of set the little guy free."

"Like a butterfly," said Lucy as she held a paper plane on the palm of her hand.

"You've got to give it a bit of help," said Penny. "It's not actually a butterfly."

Sara laughed at Lucy and then shot her plane off with the full force of a javelin thrower at the Olympics. "This is literally the best thing I've done in years," she said.

"Literally?" asked Penny.

"Literally," said Sara.

"You guys—" Lucy picked up another plane. "—shut up and get going. These butterflies aren't going to free themselves."

For the next fifteen minutes, Penny, Lucy, and Sara quietly shot three hundred paper planes off of the Williamsburg Tower, and when it came time to leave, they weren't scared anymore. The girls laughed and chatted all the way back down the stairwell, elated with the success of their mission. They hoisted themselves onto the window ledge, and Penny guided them back onto the scaffold.

Penny crouched on the wide ledge, and as she did so, her hand dropped onto something soft. She pulled away and shone her flash next to her. She froze. It was a hat. A peacemaker hat. She stared at it as if it were a snake about to bite. Had this been here last night? Was there a peacemaker hiding somewhere in the building, or was it simply a trophy stolen by a rough sleeper and then abandoned?

She swept the flashlight across the ledge, and to her horror, in the corner next to the stairwell stood the Lanky One, the junior peacemaker who had only a week earlier threatened to kill her.

At first, she thought he was a statue with the way he stood so still. But then a smile grew on his face, and he grinned at her so menacingly that she dropped her flashlight and leaped across the scaffold. She descended so rapidly she didn't even feel the scrapes and bangs as she slipped down the rails to the bottom.

"Are you okay?" asked Sara as she dropped off the scaffold and landed near Penny's feet. "You flew down that thing so fast I thought you were being—"

"Run," said Penny as she grabbed Lucy by the elbow and pushed Sara forward. "Just run."

The girls obeyed without question, and they all whipped through the darkness without pausing for breath.

They finally came to an uneasy halt when they reached the Hub and huddled in the shadows, gasping and peering into the night on high alert for danger.

"What was it?" whispered Lucy. "Were we followed?"

Penny shook her head. "I think I saw something in the building. I think I saw someone."

"Was it a peacemaker?" asked Lucy.

"Yeah. I mean, I don't know. I think so."

Sara shook her head. "Are you sure? Why would a peacemaker be inside a derelict building on their own? They always work in pairs. It's policy."

"Policy? How would you know?" said Penny, suddenly alarmed.

"Doesn't everyone know?"

"Well, I didn't know," said Penny, a little more defensively than she'd intended. Had she been wrong to trust Quinn? How did she know these girls weren't spies? The bubble she'd been floating in had just popped. Was she being reckless? A frisson of doubt crept up her spine, and her breath was short. Panic percolated below the surface.

Lucy and Sara swapped a look that Penny couldn't decipher.

"You probably just saw a weird shadow or something," said Lucy as Sara nodded in agreement. "There's no one around."

Penny was sure of what she had seen. She considered relaying the entire story to the girls but could tell by the way they turned their bodies away from her that they'd moved on. She realized, with a stab of disappointment, that these two girls were besties, a tight twosome. There was no room for her in this relationship.

"They could still be in there," said Sara, resting her hand on the wall of the Hub.

The alley was deserted, but Penny struggled to focus. How long had the Lanky One been following her? He'd preempted their trip up the Williamsburg, but how could he have known unless he'd heard them planning in the carousel? She racked her brain and tried to remember those moments. They'd been full of excitement and laughter, and it was entirely possible he could have crept into the carousel and heard every word. The light of the carousel only extended so far before it dropped into shadows. A shiver ran up her spine. What else did he know? She needed to talk to Quinn. Where was she?

"How do you think they got in?" asked Penny as she ran her hand along the rough brick, searching for a miraculous anomaly. A secret hatch perhaps, like the one at the carousel.

Lucy shook her head. "I'm not keen on going back into a creepy building again tonight, and next time, I vote we all stick together."

Penny bit her lip, taking Lucy's comments as a vote of no confidence.

"Me too," said Sara. "We can use the boys as shields if anyone attacks us."

Lucy laughed.

"So," said Penny, "do we stay and wait? Or do you think they've already gone?"

"Let's just go," said Lucy. "They're probably long gone."

"Yeah." Sara rested her head on Lucy's shoulder. "I need to sleep."

"We're headed toward Prospect Park," said Lucy. "Which way do you go, Penn?"

Penny thumbed her hand in the opposite direction. "Dumbo—the complete opposite direction." She tried to hide her rising panic. It was a long way to walk in the shadows all by herself, and she didn't know any shortcuts.

"Are you going to be okay? Walking by yourself?" asked Lucy.

"Of course. I do it all the time."

"Cool." Sara reached over and hugged Penny. "That was fun."

"I can't wait to see the aftermath," said Lucy.

"No one will probably even notice," said Penny, but the girls had already started walking away.

"Take care," Lucy said before disappearing into the night.

Penny stood in silence and listened to the street sounds. She willed her legs to move, but they were glued to the spot. She couldn't stay there all night. At some point, she'd have to get home. She looked left and right. Swallowed the wall of panic that rose up. Counted down from three and ran.

Chapter Twenty-Nine

PENNY WAS BREATHLESS by the time she reached the service entrance to Quinn's loft. She stood with her back to the graffitied roller door and looked for moving shadows. As far as she could tell, she was on her own, and the only thing chasing her had been the ghost in her head. She took a deep breath, confident to have escaped the Williamsburg Tower faster than the Lanky One had been able to follow.

With the alley quiet and shadows unmoving, she crouched and rolled the door up a few inches. It was dark beyond it, which meant Quinn was still out. As Penny pulled the door up to shoulder height, a flap of fabric caught her eye—navy cotton, a heavy drill fabric hooked onto the wire that protruded from the rim of the door. The same wire that had gashed her the first night she entered Quinn's loft. It seemed long ago now. She pulled off the fabric and caressed it between her fingers. She didn't re-member seeing Quinn in anything navy, but she slipped the strip into her back pocket. Whatever it was she'd ripped, Penny would be happy to fix it up. She wasn't the best seamstress in the world, but she had a good darning stitch under her belt. She smiled and ducked under the door, careful not to let the wire stick her.

She guided the roller door downward and let it go about an inch from the floor. It slammed shut like a crashing cymbal despite her attempt to control the noise.

A shiver ran down her spine as soon as the door came too. Something felt off. She could hear a breath that wasn't her own. Quinn? Then the single fluorescent bulb that swung from the ceiling flitted into life.

She squinted with the sudden brightness, and a flash of panic froze her in place. Standing next to the roller door was the Lanky One. He had a fresh rip in the shoulder of his uniform and a small white bandage over the bridge of his nose, framed between dark eyes. His hat sat firmly atop his head, and he tipped it theatrically at her, like a doorman at the Ritz. His smile, sleazy and entitled, gave away his thinly veiled animosity.

Penny reached for the door and managed to slide it upward a few inches before he slammed it down with his boot.

"That's what I like about you," he said. "You're feisty." He looked at the paper plane in his hand, straightened its folds, and sailed it gently toward her. It swooped, dropped, and hit her in the chest. The Lanky One took off his hat and set it down on the workbench next to him. "Who the fuck do you think you are?"

Penny inched backward, her mouth dry, and her head empty of coherent thought. The Lanky One took a step toward her.

"I'll tell you who you are," he said. "You're a Number. Like the rest of them. A dirty little faggot Number lover. A traitor, a double traitor."

The Lanky One was taller than Penny remembered, and while he towered over her, he was also triple her size in bulk. Penny took another step back, and the Lanky One shot his hands out in front of him like he was trying to give a child a fright.

"Boo!" he said, and Penny flinched in response, sending him into a fit of laughter. "Jumpy, huh? Little Red Riding Hood is scared of the Big Bad Wolf?"

Penny shook her head and took a step back.

"Well, you goddamned fucking should be, darling." He took another step forward. "Your drunk-ass daddy ain't here to protect you. Neither is your Number girlfriend. The second thing I'm gonna do after I cut your tits off is get that little shit's ass deported the fuck out of 'Merica."

"Where are you going to deport her?" said Penny. "To the dirty little hick town you're from?"

Penny's fear subsided, and a bitter fury replaced it. But quicker than she could form a thought, the Lanky One had his hand around her throat, and she was staggering backward. He thrust her against the shelves, which clattered hysterically as a heap of cutlery and dishes fell to the floor. Penny gripped the Lanky One's hand with both of hers and dug her nails in, gasping for breath.

He put his face right up to hers, noses touching. "I've told you once, I've told you twice. Shut the fuck up."

He let her go, then, and laughed as Penny fell to her knees. She was surprised to find the guttural groaning filling the room came from her own voice as she gulped at the air.

"Darling," said the Lanky One, holding out his hand, "let me help you up."

Penny rocked back on her heels and grabbed for the shelf behind her as he laughed at her. She pulled herself to her feet and looked around the room. It was only four strides to the door that led to Quinn's room, and she made a dash for it. She was on her third stride when the Lanky One grabbed her by the hair and pulled her backward.

"Not so fast, darling. We've got a score to settle," he said.

He twisted her around to face him, and before she had a chance for her vision to adjust, he punched her on the cheekbone. The force of it spun her around and threw her to her hands and knees. The taste of salt and marrow dripped into her mouth. She wiped her nose and a lick of red stained her sleeve. She scanned the floor for a weapon. Nothing but a broken bag of flour trickling its contents onto the floor.

The Lanky One grabbed her around the waist and hoisted her off the floor. She swung her knees up in front of her and kicked off the wall with all the strength she could muster. The Lanky One flew backward, and they both crashed into the shelves on the other side of the room.

When Penny felt his arms loosen, she crawled as fast she could toward the safety of Quinn's loft.

The Lanky One grabbed her foot and yanked her toward him. She desperately searched the floor for a weapon and came upon a shard from a broken plate next to a handful of flour. The Lanky One dragged her close and flipped her over as if she weighed nothing. She threw the flour in his face, and a plume of dust floated in the air, making them both choke.

"Fuck!" He gripped her foot and pulled her even harder, but when she got close enough, she slashed the porcelain shard across his cheek. He screamed and released his grip.

Penny scuttled away, in awe of the skin peeling off his face. Her fingers were bloodied, cut from the shard that lay on the floor at the Lanky One's feet. She searched frantically for another weapon, anything she could find, and picked up a pen. Gripping it tightly, she shuffled backward like a crab with it held in front of her.

The Lanky One laughed suddenly and sat on his haunches. "What are you going to do with that? Draw all over me?" He dropped his chin and looked at Penny as if he were a wolf about to pounce. "Now get over here, you little bitch," he said, and he came at her in one hefty blow that laid her flat to the floor.

A spark of stars and a dull thud came as her head smashed on the floor. She was unable to get a full breath, her chest tight, as the Lanky One dug his knee into her torso and grabbed a handful of her hair. Pinned beneath his mass, she pushed to no effect, could only stare at the veins that ran down the side of his neck bulging with life and fury.

Penny still gripped the pen in her free hand and plunged it directly into the side of his neck—into the vein, once, twice, three times, four times—again and again and again. She was surprised how deep it went each time, and she kept going until the Lanky One loosened his grip on her hair. Penny waited for the next blow to come and end her life, but the Lanky One just stared at her with a frozen look of shock, while a shower of blood spurted from the wound in his neck. He tipped sideways, all the way, until he landed on the floor.

Penny cupped her hands over her mouth and held her breath, astounded at the amount of blood pouring from his body. She crawled to the far side of the room, until the wall wouldn't let her go any farther, and stared in horror and fear. She scooped a butter knife off the floor and held it in front of her. Just in case he came back to life for that one last blow sent her way.

Chapter Thirty

PENNY HAD BEEN sitting in the corner long enough that her attacker's blood had congealed in a puddle. It covered half the floor and pooled around the shelves, utensils and equipment lying upturned and scattered across the tiles. The door rolled up and crashed down again, and although she sensed Quinn's presence, she didn't take her eyes from her bloodied attacker.

Quinn whispered words Penny didn't comprehend, then took the knife from her hand and scooped her into her lap on the floor, cradling her in her arms. Penny buried her face in the nook of Quinn's neck and sobbed into her jacket, not only for the life she'd taken but for everything. For all her losses, for her lost mother, her broken father, for the betrayal of her friendships, for her divided country, for all the hate and turmoil in the world. She cried for it all until she felt like she was floating away. The pain came next, starting from the top of her head and spreading down her body, first as a dull ache and then as a sharp stabbing pain that wrapped around the side of her face and into her brain and shot out the bottom of her toes.

Quinn pushed Penny's bloodstained hair back from her face and kissed her on the forehead. A circle of warmth emanated from this kiss and then faded away. Quinn lifted Penny gently onto the dough-bench and stroked her face. Penny witnessed the horror on Quinn's face, and she knew what had happened to her was real.

"I'm so sorry," said Quinn. "I shouldn't have left you alone."

Penny shook her head, unable to speak. She stared at her hands, clasped in her lap and covered in blood. Quinn lifted Penny's chin, her eyes full of tears but also something else, something sharp that gave Penny a seed of strength.

"Is he dead?" asked Penny, but she already knew the answer. The guy hadn't moved in a long time.

Quinn nodded, keeping her eyes fixed on Penny's.

"There's so much blood," said Penny.

Quinn nodded.

"I didn't mean to kill him."

"I know."

"He just wouldn't stop."

"I know."

"I just needed him to stop."

"Shhh," said Quinn. "I'll fix it."

"How?"

"Just focus on you. I'm going to put you in the shower, okay? And you're going to stay in there until I'm done."

Penny glanced at the Lanky One's dead body, and her eyes filled with tears again.

"Don't look." Quinn scooped Penny into her arms like a child being cradled.

Then Penny was moving, drifting in deep dark space, safe.

Quinn carried Penny through the bakery kitchen and into the small pantry that Roy had converted into a bathroom for her. The toilet was on one side of the room and the showerhead on the other, with a little curtain partitioning the space into two tiny halves.

Quinn turned the shower on and helped Penny remove her blood-soaked clothes, which she dumped into a pile beyond the bathroom pantry. Penny had never been less self-conscious in her life. She didn't care that Quinn saw how skinny she was, that her boobs had shrunk another size, that her toes were weird, that her hip bones protruded at masculine angles. The only thing she cared about was washing the blood off. If only she could wash off the dirt that couldn't be seen but stuck to her like an invisible cloak of muck. And it was caked on thick tonight.

Quinn took her hand and popped her under the shower, not appearing to care that her own clothes got wet in the process. "You're safe now," she said. "I'm going to clean up, and then I'll be back. Do you want me to leave the door open?"

Penny shook her head.

"You're going to be all right," said Quinn. "Okay?"

Penny nodded, and the door shut softly behind Quinn as she left the small room.

Penny dropped to her knees and rolled onto her side as the warm droplets rained down on her. The water pooled in pink puddles around her, and Penny felt her old self wash away down the drain. She wondered who would emerge from the shell of her body when Quinn came back to get her. All she knew was that something had died alongside the man she had killed, and she suspected it might have been her soul.

PENNY WAS SITTING on the closed lid of the toilet seat when Quinn opened the door. She'd turned the shower off and now stared at the tiled wall, taking long slow breaths. The steam-filled room made her feel like she was sitting in a cloud. Roy had put a lot of effort into this secret bathroom for Quinn. Penny ran her finger over the walls and thought how lucky Quinn was to have someone who cared about her so much.

"How are you doing?" asked Quinn.

"I'm okay." At least, she had no more tears to cry.

Quinn wrapped a towel over her shoulder with one hand. The other held a set of neatly folded clothes.

Penny dried herself without standing and then put the clothes on as Quinn handed them to her one by one, watching her with worry in her eyes.

Penny slipped on one of Quinn's shirts, a pair of underpants that were too big, and jeans that she tightened around her waist with a shoe-lace. Finally, she zipped up a black hoodie. The clothes smelled like Quinn, as if Penny was in her constant embrace.

Quinn placed Penn's shoes on the floor next to her feet. "I wiped them clean, but I don't have a pair that will fit you."

"It's fine," said Penny. "Honestly, I'm fine now; I really am." It was a lie. A big one. She would be forever scarred, hollowed as if someone had scraped out her insides with a spoon. But what choice did she have but to stand up and keep going?

Quinn crouched before Penny and gently placed white socks on her feet one by one, followed by the bloodstained shoes.

"What are we going to do about him?" asked Penny. "His body, I mean?"

"Don't worry about it. I've got it all sorted. Why don't you go to bed, and I'll meet you in a few hours? Once I get rid of him."

Penny shook her head. "It's my mess. I'm going to clean it up." She could see by the look on Quinn's face that she wasn't going to accept it. "Besides, I don't want to be alone. Not here. Not now."

Quinn's face softened. "Okay. You sure you're going to be okay though?"

"I'm fine," said Penny as a hard shell started enveloping her. "So what's the plan?"

Quinn led Penny back into the service bay, where she'd killed the Lanky One. Penny stood at the door and looked around the room, astonished. The blood was gone. The body was gone. The shelves had been righted, everything in its place, apart from a large wheelie bin in the middle of the room with *Roy's Place* stamped on each and every side.

"He's in there," said Quinn, pointing to the bin as nonchalantly as if she were a tour guide.

"So, what now? Just dump him in the Hudson?"

"Pretty much," said Quinn.

Penny felt sick. "So, we just wheel him down in the bin and toss him in?"

"That's the plan. At least, the best I could think of. I guess I've seen them do it in the movies."

Penny wasn't filled with confidence, but what else could they do? "Okay, let's do it."

"Let's do it," said Quinn. "But if we meet anyone on the way, let me do the talking."

Penny was happy to let Quinn take the lead. She placed her hand on top of the bin and suppressed the urge to raise the lid and look inside.

Quinn hoisted the roller door halfway, poked her head underneath, checked the alley left and right, and then pushed the door all the way up. "Let's go," she said.

She heaved the wheelie bin onto its edge, and Penny pushed from behind as the noise of the wheels scraping along the pavement echoed off the buildings like rolling thunder. Its wheels kept catching in the pavement cracks, so they dragged it onto the road where it glided down the smooth asphalt with ease. The streets were empty of life, and except for a lifted curtain in a derelict apartment block on Pearl Street, they had a clear run.

Penny couldn't imagine what the punishment would be for causing the death of a peacemaker, even under self-defense, but she knew there would be no mercy. Quinn, seeming to sense her urgency, sped them to a slow jog.

They shimmied the bin onto the paved trail at the dog park and followed it all the way to the water. Penny panted from exhaustion, but adrenaline pushed her until they stood at the water's edge.

Penny placed her hands over her face.

Quinn slipped an arm around her shoulder. "It was you or him, Penn. You or him."

"Yep. Isn't he just going to float?"

"I filled some flour sacks with Spam and tied them around his waist."

"Spam?" Penny looked at Quinn and burst out laughing. "I'm so sorry; that's not even funny. I don't know why I'm laughing. This is just awful," she said, manic with emotion.

"What the fuck, huh?" said Quinn.

Penny put her hand on the bin. "Let's do it before someone comes."

"Okay."

"Do I need to say something?" asked Penny. "I've never done this before."

"And you think I have?"

"No. Of course not—"

Quinn took her hand. "I know this is really intense, but that fucker was going to hurt you. This is on him. You don't owe him any last words."

Penny nodded. She opened her mouth to speak, but tears welled, and she didn't want to cry anymore.

Quinn and Penny cajoled the bin to the edge of the Hudson. It was only a two-foot drop to the water, but they'd have to toss him with heft to get him to roll fully to the bottom of the sloping cement wall.

Penny lifted the lid and let it fall back. The bin was full of empty flour sacks, the Lanky One buried somewhere beneath. She took a breath and saw Quinn watching her intently. "I'm okay," she said, "really."

"Ready, then?" said Quinn.

"Yep."

"One, two, three. Go."

Penny and Quinn tipped the bin over the ledge with all their might and held it fast until the body rolled out and tumbled into the water. His eyes were still open, and they watched Penny as he plunged into his watery grave. He looked like a little fat man with the Spam-filled flour sacks duct-taped around his torso. Penny crouched beside the bin, hand over mouth, and followed those dead eyes until they disappeared into the murky waters of their new home.

Chapter Thirty-One

QUINN DRAGGED PENNY to her feet, and without another word, they made their way back through the dog park and up to the Pearl Street Triangle. The bin was much lighter but harder to maneuver with nothing in it. It twisted and spun, as if of its own accord, like a prisoner trying to break free from its captors. This bin knew some things.

As they turned into the service alley, relief rushed through Penny, and she hoped she could now forget what had just happened. Quinn parked the bin at the corner of the alley, tucking it discreetly among a collection of other bins. Looking at Penny, she exhaled with a shake of her head, grabbed her hand, and guided her down the alley toward Roy's service entrance, less than fifty feet away. But as they neared the door, a pack of kids rolled into the alley, singing, shouting, and presumably drunk.

"Oh, great," whispered Quinn. "What the fuck is this?"

"They just look like kids," said Penny.

"Kids in uniform."

Penny's concern grew when she saw the uniform of her attacker adorning the bodies of these kids, who looked to be no more than thirteen.

"I don't like this," said Quinn. "Let's turn around." She gripped Penny's elbow and swung her swiftly back the way they had come, but as they walked toward the bin bay, another group of uniformed kids entered from that direction. They whooped and hollered at their friends coming from the other side, who whooped and hollered back.

"Shit," whispered Penny.

"They're just kids. We can manage them."

"It's like fucking *Westside Story* out here," said Penny. "How many of them are there?"

"Twenty at a guess." Quinn's face was as rigid as stone; she hadn't even looked this worried when they'd been rolling a dead body halfway across the city. This situation was more serious than Penny had initially thought, and then she spotted the knives that hung from their belted waists, sheathed in elegant brown leather and emblazoned with the word *Triumph.*

"Shit," said Penny. "They're giving kids knives now?"

"Part of the uniform," whispered Quinn.

"But they're so young. Do they even know what they're signing up for?"

"Doesn't matter. It's got to be good if they give you a pretty knife. It's every twelve-year-old's dream."

"And the booze?" whispered Penny, staring at the name-brand Johnnie Walker Black that was being passed down the line.

"Just don't look at them," said Quinn. "They haven't spotted us yet; stick to the shadows."

Quinn dragged Penny close to her, and they stood silently with their backs against the wall. But the kids had seen them and gathered around them in a menacing semicircle.

"Look at these faggots," said a small boy who swayed on his feet and looked to be about eleven years old.

"They're not fags," said another kid. "That one's a boy."

"Ugly as fuck too," said another kid.

Penny gripped Quinn's arm. The kids weren't terribly menacing, but they were aggressive, buoyed as a pack.

"Hey, guys," said Quinn, trying to defuse the situation. "Partying tonight?"

"Fucking right we're partying," said one of the boys, and they all erupted into drunken howls.

"Hang on, hang on," said another boy. "They *are* faggots! Chick faggots."

"Dykes! Look at her. Do you fuck bitches, dyke?"

One of the boys stepped forward, right in front of Penny. He was tall for a kid and met her eye to eye. The other boys hushed, watching. The leader of the pack.

Penny smiled at him, at this pathetic kid, a revolting spoiled brat. "Who I choose to fuck is none of your goddamned business."

"It is my business when you walk around like a faggot all in my face," said the Leader.

"And what would you know about fucking? You're barely out of diapers."

"I know plenty about fucking. I'd fuck you if you weren't an ugly dog-ass dyke."

"You wish," said Penny as she looked at Quinn, whose face was stone-cold serious.

Confidence rushed through Penny, but she'd severely underestimated the swiftness of the boy's wrath. Before she knew it, the kid had grabbed her in a headlock and was pulling her along the alley and out of Quinn's reach. She grabbed the kid's arm, which gripped her tightly around the neck, and squirmed to free herself, but her arms were quickly fastened behind her back and tied tightly with a drawstring wire that dug into her wrists.

"Penny!" called Quinn as they descended on her next and promptly tied her wrists behind her back. "Let us go, you little motherfuckers."

"I think we got ourselves a couple of traitors," said the Leader.

"What are we going to do with them?" asked one of the kids with a nervous shake in his voice that gave away his angst.

"We're going to let them off with a warning," said the Leader. "But first, we'll shave their heads. Remind them who's boss when they look in the mirror each morning."

"Just let us go," said Quinn, "and we won't report you."

"Report us to who?" said the Leader. "Hang on. Check it out." He stepped close to Quinn, almost matching her in height. "Are you a Number? You look like a Number—a faggot Number. A two-for-one!"

"This is fucked up," said Quinn.

The Leader started howling then, and his pack of minions followed suit.

"Let's go," said the Leader; then he stormed up the street and left his gang in charge of dragging Penny and Quinn by the hair up the alley.

"Let me go!" said Penny, but her voice was lost among the hollering. She tried to resist, but she was helpless without the use of her hands.

"Penn!" said Quinn from somewhere behind her.

They were dragged a couple of blocks eastward, up three flights of stairs, and into a luxurious apartment with marble floors and high ceilings. Music suddenly erupted, and the kids jumped around like a pack of wild animals while Penny and Quinn were plonked onto beautifully carved antique chairs with dark polished wood. The kids made fast work of tying them to the chairs, pulling out wire coils from clips on their belt. Penny had no idea that pockets of luxury like this existed in the Leftover Boroughs. Who were these people?

"Don't wreck the chairs," said the Leader. "My mom will kill me."

Penny laughed. Was this a ridiculous dream? She was suddenly exhausted beyond anything. Then, as her smile grew wider with the absurdity of the situation, her laughter rolled out in an unstoppable ball of emotion until some kid came over and slapped her across the face, which, of course, made her laugh even more.

These kids couldn't hurt her; she was sure of that. No thirteen-year-old kid could hurt her any more than she'd been hurt in the past, and now she was going to have her head shaved in atonement for all her sins. She deserved this. In fact, it was perfect.

"Are you okay?" asked Quinn, who'd been tied to a chair at the opposite end of the sprawling dining room.

Penny nodded as her laughter wound down, and a few tears leaked from the corner of her eye. She looked around the beautiful room made from marble and chrome, black and gold. Vintage and modern. Penny had never seen anything like this place. In fact, she couldn't believe people really lived like this.

Penny heard the sound of the clippers before they touched her head, and she closed her eyes, letting them take her hair. As it fell to the floor around her, so did the weight of the world. When she opened her eyes and saw Quinn watching her, she was overcome with a sense of peace. The kid who'd been tasked with shaving her head looked nervous, not only to be cutting her hair but to be near her. Penny stared at him until she caught his eye, and then she smiled. He licked his lips in a nervous twitch, took one last stroke over her head, and disappeared behind her.

The other kids thrashed and jumped around the room to the music, pointing and laughing occasionally, but then it all stopped as suddenly as it had begun.

"Your mom's home!" yelled one of the kids over the din as he peered through the elegant drapes, his forehead pressed at the window. "She's out of the car; she's coming up!"

"Fuck!" said the Leader. "Everyone get the fuck out!"

The music came to a halt, and the kids raced about the place grabbing jackets and shoes and bottles until no one was left except the Leader, Quinn, and Penny.

He pulled his knife and pointed it at both of them simultaneously, the fear on his face certain. "Get the fuck out." His voice cracked.

"You gotta untie us, if you want us to leave," said Penny.

"Don't try anything funny," he said as he sidestepped toward Penny.

"Either way. I'm happy to have a chat to your mom," said Penny. "In fact, that's a good idea. Let's do that."

The Leader's eyes welled up, and he quickly cut Penn's hands free. She rubbed at the red marks strewn across her wrists.

"You're fucking traitors," said the Leader as he freed Quinn's hands. He prodded the knife at the air in front of Penny. "Just get out."

Quinn grabbed Penny by the elbow and led her toward the door. "Let's go. We don't need trouble, after everything."

Penny knew what she meant. The Leader's mother was likely not any better than he, himself.

They passed a grand mirror in the foyer, and Penny stopped, slipping her hand free of Quinn's. She studied this new version of herself, running her hand across her soft yet bristly scalp. Her neck, now bare, was elegant in its nakedness. A ballerina neck that she'd never noticed before. Her face, with its sharp angles, had fresh dark bruises from her fight with the Lanky One. They offset the color of her eyes, blue and glistening from either fatigue or tears, she couldn't tell. She looked battered but strong, and she thought she'd never looked more beautiful. The girl that had woken up that morning was gone. In her place was a woman with a power that she'd never known she possessed until this very moment.

"Hurry up," said the Leader, with tears in his eyes. "Just get out, just go!"

Penny looked at the boy in the reflection of the mirror as he rocked from foot to foot, and felt a rush of resentment, followed swiftly by pity. She would remind him who was boss every time he looked in this mirror. She balled her fist and punched the glass as hard as she could, directly over the place that reflected the Leader's face.

"Penn!" said Quinn from the doorway, where she stood half in, half out.

Penny looked at her cut knuckles and let the blood drip through her fingers and onto the floor.

The Leader was crying now, and she watched him with hardened eyes as she walked slowly out the door, a trail of blood dripping in her wake.

"What the fuck, Penn?" Quinn gripped her hand and pulled her toward the stairwell.

Penny smiled as they passed by an elegant-looking woman in an extravagantly furry coat—the assumed mother of the Leader.

"She's like a caricature," said Penny.

"What?"

"Of rich people."

"What are you talking about?"

Penny turned and walked backward for one last glimpse of this rare species. The mother turned at exactly the same time, no doubt, with a similar thought in mind. Power flowed through Penny as she registered the fear on the woman's face, and as Penny descended the stairs, euphoria overcame her. This was the beginning of something big; this was the beginning of everything.

Chapter Thirty-Two

NEITHER PENNY NOR Quinn spoke another word until they were back in the service bay of Roy's bakery. It smelled of bleach and was cleaner than Penny had ever seen it.

Quinn slammed the roller door shut and padlocked it from the inside. "Are you okay?"

Penny nodded, but she wasn't entirely sure how she felt. "It's like it never happened."

"It happened," said Quinn. "Don't forget it, okay? Never forget. This is our turning point. This will fuel our fire."

Penny nodded but was surprised Quinn felt that way. She'd been sure Quinn was going to chide her and tell her enough was enough. She was relieved, in a small way, as she felt the nagging thoughts of shame, regret, and fear creep into the periphery of her subconscious, chipping away at her resolve.

"I'm sorry they cut your hair," said Quinn. "I should have done something. There were just so many of those little fuckers."

"It's okay," said Penny. "At least it's low maintenance."

Quinn didn't smile at her attempt to make light of the situation, and Penny wondered if she'd heard it at all.

"Come on," said Quinn, "Let's get out of here before anything else happens tonight."

She opened the door to the loft and guided Penny through first. Penny climbed into bed, and every single ache and pain made itself known as she pulled the blanket up. Her head thumped, her cheek stung, her ankles were weak. Her knuckles hurt, and her arms were numb, but she was finally safe. She let out a sigh and tried to relax, but her brain buzzed with all that had happened. She didn't even notice Quinn roll onto the bed next to her until she wrapped an arm around her waist and nuzzled into her neck.

"I think we should quit with the paper planes," said Quinn. "It's getting too dangerous."

"What? I thought we were never forgetting? I thought we were fueling a fire?"

"We are," said Quinn. "Well, I am anyway. The old-school way, ink on cement. It's too dangerous for you. I'll do it alone."

Penny sat up, despite her exhaustion. "Hold up. No way. I'm just getting started. We're just getting started."

"You'll get yourself killed. They're serious out there. It's not a game."

"I know it's not a game. I know that more than anyone and definitely more than you."

"Well, you weren't acting like you knew that with the peacemakers tonight. It's almost as if you liked provoking them."

"Oh, come on. You think I enjoyed being tied up and having my head shaved?"

"That's not what I'm saying. It's just that you didn't seem that scared. You didn't seem worried."

"I wasn't worried," said Penny. "They were just kids, just idiot kids."

"We're lucky they were just kids. We were totally at their mercy."

"You think I don't know that? I was right there alongside you."

Quinn sighed and ran a hand over her face. "I don't want to fight about it. I just don't want anything to happen to you; that's all I'm trying to say."

"You can't protect me every second of the day. I've lived my life to this point without needing you."

"Don't be like that, Penn."

"I'm not quitting, and quite frankly, I'm disgusted that you could ask me to. The whole thing was my idea. Mine."

Penny was aware of the whiny tone her voice had taken and blushed at the tantrum she was having.

"Let's talk about it when we've had some sleep," said Quinn. "Neither of us is thinking clearly."

"Oh, I'm thinking clearly. In fact, I've never been clearer about anything in my life." Penny rolled away from Quinn, tucking her feet up under her knees, making sure not a single patch of her skin was touching Quinn's. Quinn really knew how to push her buttons.

Penny was never going to quit, and there was no way Quinn could make her.

Chapter Thirty-Three

WHILE PENNY HAD fallen asleep easily, her dreams had been full of blood and violence. When she startled awake, drenched in sweat, the Lanky One watched her from the comfort of Quinn's chair. They stared at each other for a second, ghost and human taking the other in, but in the blink of an eye, he was gone, and the events of the night before came flooding back to her. She pulled her knees up to her chest, wrapped herself in a hug, and buried her face in the folds of her elbows. With her mind racing, she was unable to focus on a single coherent thought.

Quinn lay motionless beside her, and Penny absentmindedly let her hand drift over to come to rest on her stomach. Instantly comforted, Penny watched as her hand rose and fell with Quinn's every breath. A rare moment of total peace.

"Morning," said Quinn.

Penny jumped out of her skin. "Shit, you scared me. I thought you were asleep."

Shaking her head sleepily, Quinn pushed her fingers through Penny's, then yanked her close, making her unfurl from her ball and onto Quinn, laughing.

Quinn kissed Penny's hand. "What were you thinking about?" Her voice quivered as if she was still half asleep.

Penny nuzzled into Quinn's embrace, their faces only inches apart. "I have a new slogan for the paper planes—'Eye for an eye.'"

Quinn's smiled faded into a disapproving frown. "I thought we were going to take a break from all that. I thought we agreed."

Penny shook her head. "We didn't agree on anything. Nothing at all. Why are we even having this conversation? Who do you think you are to tell me what I can and can't do?"

"Whoa. Take it easy." Quinn untangled her fingers from Penny's and threw the blanket off. "Why are we still fighting about this? You're being so unreasonable."

"Me, unreasonable? Well, you're being totally selfish."

"Wow. Selfish." Quinn stood and slipped on a pair of jeans, followed by a T-shirt picked up off the floor.

"Oh my god, you're being such an ass," said Penny as she crawled to the end of the bed and stared at the empty chair the Lanky One's ghost had been sitting in. She took a deep breath and rubbed her head, alarmed at the absence of all her hair.

Quinn sat next to her and threw a Pop-Tart on her lap. Penny picked up the packet, enjoying the way the foil crackled in her hand. She opened it and took a bite. It was sweetly satisfying and helped her aches and pains.

"Sorry," she said, the Pop-Tart having a positive effect on her mood. "I have authority issues."

"I'm not trying to tell you what to do. I'm not the boss of you."

"And don't forget it," said Penny, trying to forge a smile.

"I'm just worried, and I don't want to lose you. I don't have anyone else."

Penny's eyes filled with tears, and she blinked them back. She didn't want to cry; she didn't want to soften. She wanted to hold on to her simmering resentment a little while longer. She wanted to bathe in the injustice of it all. She wanted her bitterness to boil up into a fury that she could unleash on the world. "Me too," she said finally. "You're all I've got, but this is important. Don't you think?"

"To a point, but I don't think it's worth risking our lives over."

"Well, I do."

Quinn stared at her feet, defeated. An invisible wall sprang up between them. "We're not even making a difference," she said. "The paper planes are all for nothing."

"It's only because we've just started. We will make an impact. We'll start our uprising."

"And what if we do start an uprising? Then what?"

Penny took a bite of her Pop-Tart and chewed it carefully, savoring its flavor. Swallowed. "I don't know; then we rise up. It's not going to blow over. You saw those little shits last night. They're going to grow up into big shits, and when they do—look out."

She finished off the last of her Pop-Tart and pulled on the jeans Quinn had given her.

"I'm not going to stop, and tonight, I'm hitting the Empire State, with or without you."

"Without."

"Pardon?"

"I said, without. You're going to have to do it without me." Penny wasn't expecting that Quinn would let her go alone. She'd thought Quinn wanted to protect her. "Fine." She slipped her feet into her shoes, overwhelmed with dread. Abandoned again. "It's not a job for the softhearted anyway."

Penny walked to the door but paused before letting herself out. She bit her lip, reeling in the wake of her overly harsh words. She turned to observe the wreckage of her attack, expecting to see a wounded soul staring forlornly after her with puppy dog eyes. But Quinn sat quite comfortably on the ghost chair, her nose buried nonchalantly in a book—George Orwell, *1984.*

Penny almost laughed with the absurdity and shook her head. "Are you researching that for new catchphrases?" Her voice dripped with sarcasm. "War is peace? Freedom is slavery? Ignorance is strength? Kind of suits your attitude right now." She watched the effect of her verbal attack on her enemy, satisfied.

Quinn's eyes pierced through the pages like a hot sword, as if willing them to burst into flame. "You're so fucking mean sometimes," she said.

Penny stared at her, desperately fighting against falling at Quinn's feet and apologizing, begging for forgiveness, begging for her love. She willed Quinn to look at her. To smile, to wish her luck, to say she loved her, to say she would come with her. But Quinn simply licked her finger and flicked the page with all the drama and intensity of someone who really meant it.

"I guess I'll see you around then." Quinn finally looked up from her book, expressionless save for hint of disdain.

"Whatever," said Penny, mirroring her disgust. She didn't move, her feet rooted to the spot, and she desperately waited for Quinn to beg her to stay.

They stared at each other, reflecting back their pain and pride.

"Feel free to leave." Quinn suddenly swept her open hand through the air like a magician performing a trick.

"Fuck you too." Penny slammed the door behind her. Quinn was deadweight anyway and unable to go where Penny was headed—back into the real world where cowards were punished and only the brave survived. Penny was on her own again, just how she liked it, just how she needed it, just how she deserved it.

Chapter Thirty-Four

THE PEACEMAKERS MILLED about in the streets, asserting their presence, bored yet proud and reveling in the power their uniforms gave them. The younger ones held long garbage spears, which they used to pick up the hundreds of paper airplanes that had made their way down from the sky, spreading across the city. Civilians loitered in pockets of ten or twelve, quietly inspecting the paper planes and talking in hushed whispers, peppered with an occasional outburst.

"Open your fucking eyes!" screamed a voice from a small crowd up a back street. This was followed by a rush of footsteps as the peacemakers scrambled to find the source of the outburst, to no avail.

The civilians hushed and busied their eyes on the sky or in one another's hopeful faces as more phrases broke the silence of the day.

"I am not a number!"

"Rebel, rebel, rebel!"

"My voice is my weapon!"

Penny's face hurt with the beating she'd suffered. Her smile was small and much like a scowl, yet hope sprouted from the pit of her stomach and rose into her throat.

A cool breeze dusted her scalp, and she pushed her fingers across the dewy fur of her new hairstyle. She would need to invest in a warm hat. Her pants hung off her, and Quinn's sweatshirt was so long it came well below her thigh. She was a ghost in this outfit, and her ability to walk like a man elated her. Such freedom she'd never felt before. The fear of sudden attack, all but gone. The hungry stares from men who presumed she was an object of their gratification. She took a breath, straightened her shoulders, and walked with newfound confidence.

The carousel, far from the main streets of Brooklyn, was a quiet wasteland, but Penny loitered for a few minutes in the fall sunshine to make sure she hadn't been followed. She was surprised when she crawled through the hatch to find her headquarters lit up with studious groups busy at work, writing, drawing, and folding.

Oscar was side-straddling a plastic horse when they locked eyes. He stared at Penny, blank-faced, before recognition set in. He jumped off the carousel and strode toward her, his hand halting his gasp.

"Are you okay?" he asked as his eyes swept over her shaved head and bruised face. "What happened?"

Penny leaned into his shoulder, and he wrapped an arm around her. She'd known this guy for less than twenty-four hours, and already he felt like the brother she'd never had. His gentle concern touched her deeply. A tear rolled down her cheek, not from pain but for all the love she'd ever been deprived of and had ever tried to give, only to have it thrown back in her face.

Another pair of hands came to rest lightly on her shoulder, followed by another. She swallowed her tears, took a breath, and looked up, leaving a damp patch on Oscar's sweatshirt.

Lucy, Eddie, and Sara all huddled around her, gasping at the cuts and marks on her face.

"What happened?" asked Lucy.

"Fight with a lawnmower," said Penny, but her attempt at a joke fell short, not even garnering a smile from one of them.

"Are you okay?" asked Sara.

"Where's Quinn?" asked Eddie.

"Guys, give her some space." Oscar swept his arm in a wide arc, and the three of them stepped back, worry on their faces.

"I'm fine," said Penny. "Really, I am. I just—" She trailed off as her head really began to thump.

"She just doesn't want to talk about it," said Lucy. "Right?"

Penny nodded.

"But Quinn's okay?" asked Oscar.

"She's fine," said Penny, "but she quit this morning. We're on our own."

The four of them exchanged glances, and while she knew they were desperate to know everything, she was too exhausted to rehash the events of the previous night.

"She would never quit," said Oscar. "I don't believe it."

"She did, so believe it," said Penny with irritation she hadn't meant to portray. "Anyway. We don't need her. We just keep moving forward, and tonight, I want to hit the Empire State."

"Tonight?" said Lucy. "Are you up for that?"

"I know I look like shit," said Penny, "but I'm ready for a fight, and the fight starts now."

"You're the boss," said Oscar. "Do you want to meet all your new crew?"

Penny nodded and was swiftly ushered over to the group of worker bees as if she were the queen drone. It was obvious from the look of excitement on their faces that the rumor mill had already begun to build her reputation as a force to be reckoned with. The group of students Oscar and Lucy had rounded up looked to Penny as if she were a great goddess to be admired as they nodded in awe at her battle wounds and close-cropped hair. They smiled and shook her hand and told her how amazing she was. But it all meant nothing to her. They might as well have been reciting a shopping list for all she cared. Oscar set them back to work with renewed energy, and as they scribbled and folded, their eyes darted in Penny's direction, desperate for her approval.

Penny didn't even bother to excuse herself and simply turned her back and retreated to the carousel control center. Despite their kindnesses, she knew nothing but hollow sadness, and she shut the door without another word.

Chapter Thirty-Five

PENNY SAT AT the console, gazing out the control window and into the carousel bay. A grim fever of self-hatred gripped her soul as she pondered the meaninglessness of it all, but then a shadow approached. Quinn? Penny held her breath as the figure walked into the light, and hope faded to disappointment. Sam. No surprises there. He'd never been able to stay mad at her for too long. His weakness had always been his veiled love for her.

Penny considered hiding under the console bench. She wasn't sure she was ready to forgive him, despite their lifelong history. Penny sighed. Sam knew her better than anyone. Who else did she have left if she didn't have him? She hopped to her feet and walked out to meet him, trying hard to keep her tears at bay.

The volunteers stopped what they were doing and stared at the handsome guy in the peacemaker uniform. Oscar stood behind Penny, a bodyguard, ready to attack if need be.

Penny's resolve for a frosty greeting failed instantly, and she fell into Sam's outstretched arms. They held on to each other as if they were the only two people left on earth, and without a single exchange of words, all was forgiven.

Sam kissed Penny's forehead and lifted her chin to run his thumb gently across her bruised and battered face. "Who did this?"

"Friends of yours."

"Does it hurt?"

"Not much. I'm a tough bitch; you know that."

"You're a pain in the ass, is what you are."

"As long as I'm your favorite pain in the ass, I'm happy."

"Always. Jesus, though, it's a flaming roller coaster having you as a best friend."

Penny smiled. She'd forgotten how much Sam hated the sound of swear words. She loved how his sweet soul flinched and shrank away whenever she swore in front of him. How she'd missed teasing him. "I'm just glad you're here. How did you find me?"

"I followed you."

"You what?" Penny shook her head. "Why would you need to do that when you could just walk with me? I don't get it."

"I know, I know. I'm sorry, but you know I can't be seen with you. It would compromise us both."

"Us both?"

"I'm just trying to keep us safe."

"So you're not here to join us?"

"Join you? Penn, I'm here to tell you to stop."

Penny stepped back, preparing for yet another disappointment. She braced herself for the bullet of pain. "Stop? Why would you think I'd ever stop?"

"Just hear me out. Please, please just listen for a second."

"Listen to what? It doesn't matter what you say. Your words are wasted."

"They know all about your paper planes, and they're really not happy."

"Do I look worried?"

"No, you don't. That's the problem. You should be worried. You should be shaking in your flaming boots."

"Flaming boots. Jesus, when are you going to grow up? You can't even handle a fucking swear word. Wake the fuck up, Sam. If this is what they did to me, imagine what they did to Simon. Or have you forgotten about him?"

"Of course I haven't forgotten about him, but he's fine. He's home. Rita found him and brought him home for us. He's even working on the door again. He's the only doorman left in Two Bridges. He's doing better than ever."

"Rita?" said Penny. "How did she do that?"

"Don't underestimate her. She's got some powerful connections."

Penny already knew this, but things were beginning to make more sense.

"No shit, Sam. If you didn't know that by now, you're a total fool. You know she owns you now, don't you? She collects people. Pretends to save them, and then they owe her."

"I don't owe her anything. I chose to become a peacemaker. It's a good fit for me."

"Rita manipulated you."

"That's rich, coming from the pill popper who almost got me killed."

"Wow. I don't even know what to say. Why did you even come if you truly feel this way?"

How many times in a day could her heart break?

Sam sighed and pushed his hand through his thick mop of hair. Regret was clear on his face, but it didn't change anything. Rita had done a good job recruiting this one. "I still care. I just want to help."

"If you really care, you'll just leave me alone." Penny turned then and walked away. She didn't want Sam to witness how much she both hurt and loved him. Why was it so hard to let him go?

"So, this is how it ends, after everything we've been through together?" said Sam.

"Don't let the door hit you on the way out." Penny didn't even turn to face him. A final sword delivered to his back. She knew that would really hurt him, and that knowledge empowered her.

"When did you get this mean?"

Penny paused to consider the words that would deal a nice final blow. "I got this mean when I was disappointed by everyone I know. That's when I got mean."

Sam stared at her for a second as if trying to formulate words to match her spite but just shook his head and turned toward the exit. "Don't come crying to me when they come for you, Penn. Do you really think you're changing anything? They don't give a damn about your stupid paper planes. Don't think for a second that this crap is working. They're gonna come for you and swat you away as easy as a swarm of kitchen flies. And when they catch you, it won't be because I told on you; it'll be because you are sloppy and careless and a fraud. You're an embarrassment."

Sam smiled a big sarcastic smile that turned his beautiful face ugly with spite, yet Penny felt as small and painfully inadequate as he'd intended. A ringing in her ears accentuated each footfall as Sam walked away from her.

Penny watched the hatch slam shut, and she burned with a loathing so intense that she flew across the room. She would not let him get the last word. As she bowled through the hatch, the brightness of the sun momentarily stunned her. She blinked aching eyes as she sought out Sam's retreating figure, but words wouldn't come, only nausea. She stopped and closed her eyes, crouched until she felt the ground beneath her hands. She dug her fingers into a crack in the cement and took a few slow breaths, waiting for the spinning world to come to a stop.

"Fuck you, Sam! Fuck you!"

Sam was already a blurry figure in the distance, getting smaller with every second that passed. Penny rolled onto the ground, stretched out flat on her back, and stared at the sky as blue and crisp as a summer day. She would never be able to fully let Sam go. They were connected in a way she couldn't explain, like they were tied at the heart. But they had to let each other go, at least for now. She hoped against all odds they would find a way back together. Somehow. Some day.

The cold crept in fast, slithering into her bones and freezing her from the inside out, sucking out any last fight she had left. Maybe if she lay on the ground and stared into the great abyss of the universe for long enough, maybe she would wake from this hideous dream and find herself on the grass at Jane's Carousel as a five-year-old, her mother gently stroking her hair in the sunshine. Maybe everything, absolutely everything that had come after, was just one awful nightmare.

Chapter Thirty-Six

WORRY WAS EVIDENT on Oscar's face when he poked his head through the control room door. His eyebrows sat high on his forehead, his bottom lip tucked under his front teeth. "Can I come in?"

Penny nodded without looking up from the control panel, where she'd been lazily tracing a path along the metal surface between the buttons and knobs.

"You've been in here for three hours," said Oscar. "You should come out and get some fresh air. Well, maybe not fresh air—"

"I like it in here. It's my new bedroom, I guess."

"Are you going to tell me what happened?"

"One day, but not right now. It hurts to even open my mouth."

Oscar touched her shoulder, his concern trickling down Penny's arm, right into her heart.

"How are things going out there anyway?" asked Penny.

"They're fine. Our crew are an enthusiastic bunch. I stopped counting paper planes at seven hundred and twenty-four."

"Really?" Penny looked at him, and the act of doing so seemed to ground her. Here she was, in her carousel with someone who seemed to truly care. *Stop wallowing.*

"We're well on our way to a thousand. Do you still want to hit the Empire State?"

"Yeah. I really do."

"We'll do it, then, if you're up for it." Oscar's enthusiasm was catching.

"I've been thinking about that," said Penny. "The peacemakers are swarming the Brooklyn streets because that's where they think the uprising is coming from."

"And they'd be right."

"Dead right. So, let's split up into pairs and hit a bunch of low-rises across Brooklyn. Spread far and wide, and while you and your group hit Brooklyn, keeping the peacemakers distracted, I'll head over to the Empire State and get the business done. Spread this fucker like a virus."

Oscar nodded slowly, clearly not enthused by Penny's plan. "Okay, but shouldn't we stick together?"

"And risk all of us getting caught? No way. I'm in this thing for the long haul. We have to be smarter about how we do things."

"I guess so, but it's not as fun going off in pairs."

"It's not supposed to be fun. It's not a game."

Oscar bit his lip.

"I'm not telling you off, Oscar," Penny said. "I'm serious now. Focused. This is war. This is an origami fucking war, and I'm going to do it until it kills me."

"Okay," said Oscar. "I'm in. I..."

Penny didn't hear anything else he said because standing suddenly in the shadow of the carousel was Quinn. She seemed to have appeared, like a ghost.

Quinn scanned the room, a frown set on her face, but Lucy was by her side like a swift wind and pointed in the control booth. A whisper, a nod, and Quinn was on her way.

Penny felt woozy, like she might pass out.

Oscar touched her shoulder. "Do you want me to stay?"

She shook her head and looked at Oscar with a smile. "I'm fine," she said as Quinn opened the control room door.

"I'm right out there if you need me," said Oscar.

"You're better than a guard dog, but not as barky."

Quinn and Oscar passed each other at the door with a handshake and a shoulder pat, a glance and a nod, a moment of comfort passing between them. An invisible hug.

Quinn pulled the door shut behind her. "I'm an idiot," she said.

"Yes, you are, and I'm still mad at you." Penny decided in an instant she wasn't going to keep up the mad-girl ruse for much longer. If she was honest with herself, she wasn't angry with Quinn. In fact, Quinn was the only person she *wasn't* angry with. "You're just lucky I happen to like idiots. A lot."

"Like, how much?" asked Quinn. She took a seat on the stool next to Penny and nuzzled her face into Penny's neck.

"Don't push your luck. I could change my mind at any given minute," said Penny.

Quinn kissed the top of her head, and they held each other without speaking, hope and optimism surging in Penny.

"So, we're all on for tonight?" asked Quinn. "The Empire State?"

"Are you coming?"

"Wouldn't miss it."

Penny wanted to jump for joy, and if her body hadn't ached so much, she just might have done. With Quinn by her side, they could do anything, topple any kingdom.

"By the way," said Quinn, "I have something for you."

"A present?"

"Yep, but it's outside."

"So, what are we waiting for?"

Quinn took Penny's hand, and together, they left the bubble of the control room.

Penny was aware of all eyes on her as they walked across the room. A hush fell over the crew as they carefully packaged up paper planes into satchels and bags. When she and Quinn met in the shadows, the tension fell away, and Quinn squeezed her hand as she led her through the hatch.

The sun was setting across the Manhattan skyline, a perfect fall evening as the sky tapered from indigo to pink. Quinn draped her hand around Penny's waist and pulled her in gently.

"Perfect night for a paper plane drop," said Quinn.

"A penny for your thoughts."

"Exactly, and I'm never letting her go."

"Ouch," said Penny, cupping her left cheek. "Don't make me smile; it hurts."

"In that case, think unhappy thoughts because this thing is going to make you grin from ear to ear." Quinn grabbed Penny by the shoulders and nudged her around in a half circle to the black moped that stood a few yards from the hatch entrance.

Penny's mouth dropped open. "No way," she said, running her hand along the handlebars.

"Yes way." Quinn tipped the bike toward her so she had to take it up with her own hands.

"It's amazing. Where did you get it from?"

"It's Roy's old delivery bike. From before the division, when he had a proper baking business."

"Does he know you have it?"

"More than that. He knows I'm giving it to you, and he fully supports our little project."

Penny was speechless.

"He's on our side," said Quinn with a smile, her eyes sparkling in that way they did when she was up to something.

"Is it really for me?"

"You earned it."

"I did?"

"You did."

"I love it. So, so, so much." Penny flung her leg over and nestled into the seat. Quinn copied her, gripping Penny around the waist while resting her face on the bridge of Penny's shoulders.

"Oh," said Penny. "I see it all so clearly now. You want a chauffeur. Someone to shuttle you around town."

"You caught me. Seriously though. This will be good to keep you out of trouble."

"Or get me in deeper."

"Well, we're already in it pretty deep. We're in so deep. Like, really, really deep."

"Things have certainly escalated somewhat."

"Somewhat, indeed," said Quinn. "So, we can test-drive her to the Empire State tonight."

Penny hopped off the bike and leaned it carefully against the wall, then threw her arms around Quinn. "I'm happy. It's been a long time since I've been happy."

Quinn held her close as they watched the sunset. It was eerily quiet as the day fell away to night. Amidst the towering buildings, the Empire State rose, the beacon of the city, and Penny could hear it calling her name.

PENNY ARGUED WITH Oscar for half an hour before he finally conceded to her plan. She'd insisted that the Empire State wasn't safe for all of them, and it was better to disperse the troops to distract the peacemakers and keep them in Brooklyn. It was, admittedly, a good tactic, but more than that, the Empire State was her dream. If she was honest, she didn't want to share it with the others, and she argued stubbornly until Oscar gave up.

The safest spot to cross into Manhattan would be across the Williamsburg Bridge, which meant they'd have to ride the Queens Expressway halfway across town. At curfew, this would be mostly empty of both cars and peacemakers. Penny threw her leg over her bike as Quinn draped herself with three satchels, crisscrossed over her chest and hanging at either hip. She hopped on the back half of the bike seat, which dropped an inch under her weight.

Penny looked back at Quinn and got the giggles. "You look so ridiculous. Ouch, my face!" She cupped her still tender cheek. "I don't even know if you can ride with a Heffalump on the back."

"Well, you don't want me driving."

"I don't?"

"I'm not the most coordinated when it comes to two-wheeled vehicles. It's lucky I made it here in one piece, to be honest."

"Aren't you lucky to have a little chauffer to ferry you around?"

"I'm pretty sure I'm onto a good thing here. Let's get this show on the road. Giddyup, horsey."

"Giddyup," said Penny, and after a wobbly start, they were away, cruising down the empty expressway. It seemed all the complications of Penny's life blew away with the wind that rushed by. There were only two things that mattered. Her origami war and Quinn.

Chapter Thirty-Seven

THE ENTRANCE TO the Empire State Building sat between a boarded-up pharmacy and a derelict deli. The deli's window boards were long since gone, and the interior was mostly bare apart from a few broken chairs. The bench seats had been ripped free of their stuffing, and puffs of white cotton lay scattered across the floor like clouds. Penny parked her bike in the shadows of the deli, and looked up at the silver plaque that ran the length of the boarded-up doors to the Empire State Building: 350, Observatory Entrance.

"This is it," said Quinn.

Penny ran her hand across the wooden boards, then gave them a push. "How are we going to get in? This is some strong wood."

"Don't worry; I've got a key."

"Really?"

"Of sorts." Quinn flashed a smile and pulled a small metal bar from her bag.

"That's the cutest crowbar I've ever seen," said Penny. "I'm not sure it's cut out for this job though."

"One way to find out." Quinn dug the wrench under the wood and jammed it in with her fist. She pushed and pulled and dug all the way along the side of the wooden wall until it creaked in defiance.

"Do you need some help?" asked Penny.

"Stand back, darling. This here is serious work."

"So you want me to go back and get Oscar, then?" Penny smiled and shone her flashlight at Quinn, who grinned in return and handed her the wrench. Penny dug her fingers under the top edge of the board and heaved with a strength fueled by adrenaline and fear. With a crack that echoed through the streets, the board fell from its perch and thundered to the ground.

Penny staggered backward. The board had missed her toes by an inch. "Yes!" she said, jumping up and down. "We're in." She looped her arms around Quinn and kissed her on the lips, then threw her head back and laughed. How could life get any better than this moment?

"So far, so good," said Quinn.

Broken glass crunched under Penny's feet as she walked into the entrance. "It's so beautiful in here. I haven't been here since I was a kid."

"Me neither. Look at this place."

Penny moved her flashlight across the floor and up onto walls, highlighting the beauty of the art deco interior. The marble flooring was pristine, and chandeliers still hung in place, untouched by looters.

"It looks like they locked this place down before anyone could vandalize it," said Quinn.

"Probably the only thing anyone's done right."

"This way." Quinn pointed to a sign that read Stairwell.

"How long do you think it's going to take for us to climb eighty-six flights?"

"Long."

Penny stood at the bottom of the stairs and peered upward. She felt no fear in this building and was elated to begin their ascent. They climbed at a reasonable pace, chatting, hand in hand.

Penny told Quinn about the woman who'd tried to jump off the top and was blown back inside by a gust of the wind that ultimately saved her life, and Quinn told Penny that the lightning rod at the top had originally been a docking station for zeppelins. So then, Penny told Quinn about a secret door on the 102nd floor that lead to a private balcony with no safety bars.

"And that's where we're headed," said Penny. "I know you're afraid of heights."

"Everyone's afraid of heights this high up."

When they got to the 102nd floor, they discovered the secret door was not so secret after all.

"It's right here," said Penny, shining the flashlight on the metal door, which had a large sign that read To Level 103.

"They're making it too easy for us," said Quinn.

Penny grabbed the door by its handle and pulled. "Hurry up; this ain't no summer camp."

"Yes, ma'am." Quinn saluted her as she followed her up the last set of stairs.

Penny's nerves kicked in when they got to the final door. "Here goes." She opened the door.

They stepped onto the balcony, and Penny was surprised at how little wind there was so high up. The landing was less than three feet wide, and the rail seemed awfully inadequate, considering the drop.

"You're right," said Penny. "Everyone is afraid of heights this high up."

"Especially when there's hardly any barrier. I feel like the right gust of wind could just sweep me over."

"Don't say that; you're freaking me out."

"You're freaking *me* out."

The drop from level 103 would have toppled them onto the viewing deck at eighty-six, but it was still a decent enough drop to kill a person.

"Look how dark it is," said Penny. "It's so weird to see all the skyscrapers without any lights. No one working late. Or working at all, for that matter."

"It's creepy, that's for sure."

"Do you think anyone can see our light?" asked Penny.

"Maybe, but it probably just looks like a tiny star."

Quinn always knew exactly the right thing to say.

"A tiny star," said Penny. "I like that."

Quinn handed Penny one of her satchels. "Now for the fun part."

Penny and Quinn began shooting the paper planes off the side of the building as they walked slowly around the perimeter of the deck.

Penny was careful not to get too close to the sides as she didn't entirely trust herself not to fall off.

"Penn," said Quinn, "what do you think that is?"

A convoy of flashing trucks rolled through the streets, heading toward the Empire State. Their sirens wafted up like wolves howling in the wind.

Penny didn't like the urgency in her voice; she also didn't like the fact that she was draped over the low rail, pointing toward the street below.

"I can't see the street below," said Penny. "That stupid viewing platform is in the way."

"Let's get down there and check it out," said Quinn. "I don't like it."

Penny and Quinn dropped their satchels and tore down to level eighty-six. It took them less than a minute to get there, but they didn't need to go onto the viewing platform to know they were in trouble. Voices shouted from below, followed by footsteps echoing up the stairs. The peacemakers were coming for them.

"Shit," said Penny, "how long do we have?"

"The runners can do it in twenty."

"What runners?"

"The marathon runners. They used to do it every year. It doesn't matter."

Penny turned in circles, looking for an escape.

"Calm down," said Quinn, grabbing her by the shoulder. "We've got time to think. Just think."

Penny nodded and tried to order her racing, jumping thoughts, tried to catch a single coherent one.

"How do they know we're here?" said Quinn.

Penny swallowed and shook her head despite the looming dread.

"I thought you said we could trust him," said Quinn.

"Trust who?" asked Penny, knowing exactly who she meant.

"You know who I mean."

Penny shook her head. "We can—we can trust him. Sam would never put me in danger. Never."

"I knew this would happen," said Quinn. "I knew it."

"So why come, then, if you're so right about everything all the time?" Penny crouched and put her head between her hands. She was stupid to have trusted Sam, but she never thought he'd be capable of such spite.

"Penn," said Quinn, laying her hand gently on her shoulder. "We're in some serious trouble, but we can get out of this."

Penny nodded. When she got to her feet and saw Quinn surveying the streets below in a calculated manner, Penny knew she'd only come to protect her. Quinn had figured this would be the likely outcome, and she'd come anyway. To protect her.

"Okay, so they know we're in here," said Quinn. "The paper planes will still be coming down."

"And the only way out is the stairs and elevators."

"Surely, there's got to be another way."

"We need to start going down," said Penny. "Go as far down as we can and then hide. They can't check every single floor."

"But there's nowhere to hide. These are empty floors. They won't stop searching till they find us."

"There are eighty floors," said Penny. "They can't search all of them. Maybe we can blend in."

"Blend in? How exactly are we going to blend in?"

"Like I said. We—we blend in. We run right into the middle of them and pretend we're part of them."

"No offense, but that's a shit idea," said Quinn. "That's way too crazy, even for you."

"We can do it."

"We're not even wearing uniforms."

"It's dark; no one will notice, at least at first. We have to try," said Penny. "I'm not going to sit here and wait to be captured, no fucking way."

Quinn nodded. "Shit, this is so fucking crazy."

"Trust me," said Penny. "They're not catching us. I promise."

Penny grabbed Quinn's hand and pulled her toward the stairs. Quinn resisted at first, but she dragged her anyway. They ran down as far as they could until the encroaching footsteps became so loud Penny was sure they were less than two floors away.

"This way," said Penny, ducking into an exit door on level forty-six. "We're going to race out of these doors when we see them, okay? Turn your flashlight on."

"Fuck." Quinn shook her head.

"I know—We're going to find hiding places and wait them out. Really good ones and not move until they're gone."

"That's never going to work. Please, no. No, no, no."

"Trust me, okay? Do you trust me?"

Quinn took Penny's face in her hands and kissed her once, twice, three times on the lips in a manner so heartfelt it made Penny want to cry. "You know I do. You know it. I love you."

"Don't tell me you love me now. Tell me after. Tell me when we're free."

"I'm telling you now," said Quinn. She then grabbed Penny's hand and dragged her toward the boarded-up elevators on one side of the wall. "There's always a service shaft at the end of the row." Quinn released

Penny's hand and crouched in front of a small metal grate. She stuck her fingers in the slots and pulled hard enough to remove the panel from the wall, revealing a cavity just big enough to house a scrunched-up adult.

"I'm too big," said Penny. "I won't fit."

"You will. You have to. Quick."

"Where will you hide?"

"I'll find somewhere. Get in, and I'll shut you in tight. Don't make a sound again."

Penny reluctantly wedged herself into the gap in the wall with Quinn's gentle guidance, and they shut the panel.

"See you on the flip side," said Quinn. "We got this."

"We got this."

Penny touched the grate, but Quinn had already slipped away. The sound of peacemakers storming the stairs got louder and louder, and Penny watched in anguish as Quinn put her hands behind her head and dropped slowly to her knees.

"No!" said Penny and banged her fist against the grate. But she went immediately silent when peacemakers engulfed the area in a floodlight, lighting up the room as if it were day. Penny's breath came in short gulps. She shimmied as far as possible against the wall as she could, watching as they roughly forced Quinn onto her stomach and cuffed her hands behind her back. The peacemakers hollered in triumph and dragged Quinn out the exit door.

Penny went still as a single peacemaker halted at the door and stood silently alone. Something about the way they stood there, cocking their head to the left as if able to hear her breathing. A demon on the hunt for blood.

Then without hesitation, the figure scanned the room with their flashlight and made a beeline for her service vent. They shone their flash directly into the vent, directly into Penny's eyes, temporarily blinding her.

Penny didn't squint; she didn't want the peacemaker to have the satisfaction of seeing her pain. Penny channeled all her animosity into the beam of light. She was surprised when the peacemaker switched off the flash and moved closer to the vent. So close, their heads could have been touching if not for the metal grate separating them. Then quietly, as if in a dream, the peacemaker spoke.

"I'm sorry," he said. "It was a mistake to join them; you were right. But I'm in too deep now."

Penny recognized the voice as Sam's straightaway. As her eyes readjusted, the shadows on his face became more visible. Fresh bruises. A swollen eye. She understood his pain.

"Did they hurt you?" Penny lifted her hand to the grate.

"I miss you," said Sam.

"Those fuckers."

Sam stood up and sniffed. "Stay here till it's light. Then go see Rita. She'll get your girlfriend back. Just—just be careful of her though. Everything is so fucked up. And know that help from Rita will cost you, and you won't know what that cost is until she comes looking for it. You can't say no to her. You wouldn't dare."

"What? Sam, wait," said Penny as his shadow scurried off into the darkness.

She had so many questions, but now she had a purpose. And that purpose was to wipe out all the peacemaker cowards.

Chapter Thirty-Eight

THE DULL MORNING light leached in through the windows, illuminating the vast open space in which she was hiding. It took a few moments for Penny to figure out where she was. Had she been sleepwalking? Her body ached, and her arm had a bad case of pins and needles—she was stuck in the vent system. The reality of her life came flooding back. The murdered peacemaker, the traitor that was Sam, her new bike, the Empire State, and Quinn, who had sacrificed herself to save her.

Penny kicked out the grate and crawled across the floor, then sprawled onto her back, stretching out her limbs. The ceiling, covered in millions of tiny dots, momentarily mesmerized her. She rolled onto her feet and felt like she'd traded her body in for that of a sixty-year-old. The street below was draped in gray tones, and she rested her forehead on the window, considering her options. There were no visible guards, but she didn't care if she was captured now. At least, if she were, she would be with Quinn.

She crept down forty-six flight of stairs and stopped at the very bottom. It was eerie yet beautiful, as if she'd stepped into a photograph. Fearlessness flowed through her veins as she strode along the marble floor, her feet tapping as she went. The wooden plank that Quinn had torn down was secured against the doorframe but not fastened, and it only took one big kick to knock it down.

The street was as dead as a ghost town, and her bike was still where she'd left it, toppled on its side but no damage done. She rode the FDR Expressway all the way back to her father's apartment in Two Bridges, but instead of going home, she turned down Market Slip and headed directly toward the Church of Rita. It was too early for any queues to have formed, but Penny knew Rita was in there. The pink Land Rover parked out front gave her away. Penny dumped her bike on the sidewalk and banged on the door until one of the flush-faced twins finally opened it.

"Hey Rob," said Penny, pushing past him with ease. "Is your mom in?"

"Um, I'm Drew."

"Hi, Drew, is your mom in?" Penny smiled and looked him up in down in his new peacemaker uniform.

"Look what the cat dragged in," said Rita as she wandered out of the kitchen, throwing a tea towel over her shoulder. "I love what you've done with your hair, darling. Come to see if my eyes are open?"

Penny attempted a smile and wondered how much groveling she'd have to do to get Rita back on her side.

"The thing about lab rats," said Rita, "is that they're stupid as fuck, and no matter what you do to them, as long as you've got that hit of pleasure-seeking goodness, they just keep coming back for more. Now are you a lab rat, or are you the scientist?"

"What?"

Rita laughed. "I think we both know what you are. Don't we, darling?"

"Sorry, Rita," said Penny, trying to channel as much remorse into her voice as possible. "I wasn't in a great place. I should never have disrespected you that way."

Rita raised an eyebrow and smiled. "I don't believe a word you've said, but you're here for a reason, so let's get to it. Boys! You're in charge." She turned to Penny. "Follow me, honey."

Robert and Drew high-fived each other, seemingly delighted to have been given the task of looking after an empty, derelict building.

Rita rolled her eyes, then led Penny into the kitchen, leaving the two boys to play-fight together in the main room.

Rita pulled out a chair from the kitchen table and directed Penny into it. "Now, to what do I owe the pleasure of your visit?"

Penny bit her lip. Rita was being very nice to her, considering their last conversation. "Um, I heard you rescued Simon."

"Did you now?"

"And I wondered if you could do the same for me? For my friend?"

"Friend, huh. Now why would someone who walks around with their goddamned fucking eyes closed help you?"

There it was. Rita had invited her in only to play games. Penny didn't have time for this. If Rita couldn't help, she'd need to find another way. She stood up. Pushed her chair in.

"Okay," said Penny, "thanks for your time."

"Hold it, darling; take it easy," said Rita. "We've both said things we regret, right? Now sit down and tell me about this friend of yours."

Penny sat. "Her name is Quinn—Quinn Austin—and she was taken by peacemakers last night from the Empire State."

Rita raised her eyebrows. "I see. And what was she doing in the Empire State? Not spreading messages of hate, I hope."

"On the contrary," said Penny. "She was spreading messages of *hope.*"

"Well, it's all subjective I guess, isn't it," said Rita. "You say tomato; I say tomahto."

Rita sat forward, drummed her fingers on the table, and stared at Penny—really looked at her as if she was reading a life story in her face. She then sat back and beat both hands on the table at once, making Penny jump.

Rita smiled and nodded knowingly. "I'm going to help you. Yes, ma'am, help is on the way," she said as brightly as if she'd just declared it to be Christmas.

Rita reached into her handbag and pulled out a black brick that looked like a walkie-talkie but was actually a large radio phone. She punched in some numbers, held it to her ear, and stuck her finger in the air. She stared at Penny as if she was trying to pause the world.

"Howard, darling," said Rita. "It's your lovely wife." She laughed, then, as she and the man on the other end exchanged pleasantries.

A ball of nerves rolled around Penny's stomach; this seemed too easy. Far too easy.

"Now, a girl named Quinn Austin was captured by a troop in the Empire State last night," said Rita. "Hang on; you don't even know what I'm going to say."

Rita's finger hung in the air, along with Penny's breath. "Correct. I want her found, and I want her delivered to me."

Pause.

"Because I say so, that's why." Rita nodded and smiled at Penny as if she had everything under control. "Oh, rubbish. She's not high profile at all; she's just a girl. The person in charge isn't going to be sending their own propaganda off the top of a building. The person at the top is someone like you or me, sitting behind a desk, handing out directives. Not some random kid. And if they don't know that, then they shouldn't be running the regime."

Rita winked at Penny, and she began to understand that Rita wasn't just the wife of a businessman; she was deeply involved in the Division regime and deeply dangerous because of it.

Penny swallowed. But was she good or bad? Could she help or hinder? Penny had no idea. She also had no choice. It felt like the whole planet had come to a stop.

"Right. Good," said Rita. "We're on our way."

Chapter Thirty-Nine

RITA SAILED THROUGH all the checkpoints in her oversized pink Land Rover with CUPCAKE plates. The peacemakers all knew her by name, and Rita flirted shamelessly with every one of them. Occasionally, their eyes would dart across to Penny, who sat nervously in the passenger seat, but none of them ever asked for her particulars. It wasn't until they crossed the Harlem River, into the Bronx, that Penny asked where they were going.

"We're going to the jail barge at Hunts Point."

"The Boat?" said Penny. "But that's a reconditioning camp." Panic swept across her.

She'd heard of the infamous juvenile correction facility for what they called "troubled" kids. It was the kind of place angry parents threatened to send their children if they didn't clean their room or do their homework.

"She's not troubled!" said Penny. "Call them and tell them to stop, please."

"Oh, she's troubled all right, and clearly, you are too, with a haircut like that. Don't take it personally, hon. They've started preventive reconditioning now. Just in case."

"Jesus, Rita. What the fuck is that?"

"Now, I'm not saying I agree with it," said Rita. "It's a fail-safe method to rewire the brains of all the youth Numbers who end up in state care. It's all about minimizing gender confusion. We have a real opportunity here to create a society of heaven on earth. Man, woman, and child all doing the proper and godly thing we were put here to do."

"What the fuck are you talking about? What the fuck is happening?"

"My darling, what I'm talking about is seeing the positive in the negative. This virus has created the perfect set of circumstances for us to finally create the world of our dreams. A pure world. A world in God's vision. Finally, we have the means to be able to set people on the right track without their silly misguided minds steering them on the wrong one. We are giving the lost a new life to live. A proper, respectable life."

Penny remained silent, fighting the urge to argue. Things were much worse than she'd ever imagined, and her main focus was to get Quinn and get out.

When they arrived at the facility, they were waved through the barriers without so much as a sideways look, then ushered toward an important-looking man in full military dress, backed by a posse of guards. Rita's face hardened, and she sucked in her lips as if she'd eaten a bitter lemon.

"Lieutenant Dickhead is on duty," she said. "What does he want with this business?"

Penny was surprised that Rita had taken on the nickname she herself had come up with. As Lieutenant Dickhead strode toward the car, she shrank as far back into her seat as possible in the hope he wouldn't notice her. The lieutenant held his arm in the air, motioning for Rita to stop.

"For fuck's sake," said Rita with a smile on her face. "What does this asshole want now?"

Rita waved at the lieutenant and slowed to stop. Lieutenant Dickhead gestured for her to wind down the window, and she obeyed with a sigh, then threw her elbow out the window, leaning toward him. "Morning, Lieutenant Dixon," she said.

"Rita," said the lieutenant with a nod of his head.

"How lovely to see you this fine day. How are Lorna and the kids?"

"Fine, thank you, Rita," said Lieutenant Dickhead through pursed lips.

"Good, good, darling. You must pass on my warmest regards."

The lieutenant bristled with Rita's niceties, and Penny could tell there was no love lost between the two of them and that the small talk pained him greatly.

The lieutenant spotted Penny and ducked his head to inspect her. He opened his mouth to say something, but Rita spoke first.

"Now, about this girl," she said. "I expect she's ready for collection?"

"The girl—" he started.

"Orders from the top, Lieutenant," said Rita. "We're all just doing what we're told." She shrugged and feigned a look of cluelessness.

The lieutenant stared at Penny, and Rita took a deep breath, her impatience obvious.

"Yes," said the lieutenant, "the guards have her ready on the dry, but—"

"Good," said Rita. "Let's make this quick. I have hungry mouths to cook for."

Rita wound up her window and drove toward the barge that towered beside the dock, an oversized block covered with mesh and wire. It had a few tiny square windows dotted around its perimeter but mostly looked like a grim floating prison.

"Insolent piece of shit," said Rita. "If Lieutenant Dickhead thinks he's the king of the world, he's got that all wrong. Very wrong."

There was a lot of foul language bandied about for someone so invested in the church, thought Penny. How clever she was. How fooled Penny had been.

Rita unbuckled her belt and pointed a diamond-clad finger in Penny's face. "Now don't move." She hopped out of the car and stormed off to meet the gang of troops that had gathered at the entrance to the Boat.

Penny squinted into the crowd and spotted Quinn standing behind the guards with her hands tied in front of her. Rita threw her arms about, pointing every which way until a peacemaker untethered Quinn's wrist. Penny clenched her fists and cheered Rita on silently even as Lieutenant Dickhead strode up to Rita and engaged in what looked like a lively argument. Rita slipped her arm through the crook of Quinn's elbow and led her on a quick march to the car as the lieutenant fumed behind her, his face turning visibly red.

Rita opened the car door and stuffed Quinn into the back seat, where she promptly fell face-first onto the seat.

"Quickly, my darling," said Rita. "Things seem to be turning to custard rather fast."

Penny jumped into the back seat and grabbed Quinn's hand.

Rita hopped into her seat and managed to turn on the engine before Lieutenant Dickhead was upon her and knocking on the window. Rita wound it down.

"Who's the girl?" said Lieutenant Dickhead.

Penny untangled her fingers from Quinn's and slid her hand discreetly back into her lap.

"Well, not that it's any of your business, Jim," said Rita. "This is Penny-Ann, my best cupcake assistant, aren't you, darling?"

Penny smiled, happy he hadn't recognized her from the checkpoint all those months ago.

Rita pinched her cheek, a little too hard. "She looks a mess," she said, "but boy can she pipe those cakes."

"I'll need to see her ID," said Lieutenant Dickhead.

"You'll need nothing of the sort, Jim, and I most certainly hope you're not thinking of biting the hand that feeds you, my darling?" Rita smiled then, her best shiniest smile. "Now get this barrier open like a good little lieutenant."

Rita waved her hand out the window to the guards manning the barrier. "Whip it up, boys; we're good to go."

The guards started to lift the barrier, but the lieutenant raised a hand to stop them. "The girl stays," he said.

"The girl does no such thing."

"We have reason to believe the girl has information to help the cause."

"Oh rubbish, Jim," said Rita. "Now open this goddamned barrier and open your fucking eyes. Right the fuck now, Jim. Right the fuck now." Rita slammed her hands on the steering wheel and stared at the lieutenant with deeply unsettling disgust.

Penny realized then that Lieutenant Dixon was one of Rita's lackeys. What did he owe her that she wielded so much power over him?

Rita raised an eyebrow at the lieutenant, and he spun on his heel and ordered the barrier open.

Chapter Forty

NONE OF THEM spoke a word until they were well clear of the facility and had crossed back into Harlem.

"Well," said Rita, "that was quite the palaver."

"Can you fix her?" Penny asked. "Will she be okay?"

"Look what a mess you've caused. But you can't possibly imagine what you've gotten yourself into, sending those silly little paper planes off the top of buildings."

"You know about that?"

"Darling, please."

"It's just a bit of fun. It was just a few paper planes."

"It was more than a few paper planes, and you know it," said Rita. "All kinds of riffraff have come out from the woodwork and are swarming the streets as we speak. So, darling, it's more than a few paper planes. It's a revolution. The Leftovers are swarming with little revolutionaries, my dear. The peacemakers are having a hell of a time keeping the riffraff under control. I'd be remiss if I didn't say I'm a little proud, my darling. You've created quite a little drama out there in the world."

Penny bit her lip and let Rita's words soak in. Had they really started a revolution?

They rode in silence for the rest of the trip back into Manhattan. Penny held Quinn's hand tightly and waited for her to return the grip, but she remained unresponsive. Her eyes rolled back, and her neck, too weak to support her head, lolled from side to side. She wasn't there. She was a zombie, and it broke Penny's heart.

"We did it, babe; we started a revolution," she said.

Quinn stared back at Penny, and a single tear rolled down her face.

Penny kissed her once, twice, three times on her mouth.

"I love you, I love you, I love you," she whispered. "Do you hear me? Do you see me?"

Rita peered into the rearview mirror, catching Penny's eye without a trace of empathy in her own. "You got your revolution. How does it feel? It came at quite the price, don't you think?"

"Is she going to be okay?" asked Penny "Please, tell me; is she going to be okay?"

"She'll be better than ever, honey. I'll make sure of it."

Rita's words didn't comfort her at all. "Why did you help me? Why would you go through all that for me?"

Rita smiled. "Because I collect people, and when I collect them, I own them, and when I own them, my life is rich with opportunity and choice. I have all kinds of people ready to do just about anything for me." Rita winked at Penny. "And when I say jump, they say, 'How high?' Don't they, darling?"

After Rita drove through the last checkpoint before the Manhattan Bridge, she stopped the car and turned to Penny, and finally showed some kindness. "I'll take the girl to the church. Fix her up. Nurse her to health. Okay?"

Penny nodded and gazed out over the bay as a low rumbling sound grew ever louder.

People were marching across the bridge into Brooklyn, carrying huge rainbow-colored paper planes and banners and singing, "I am not a number."

Penny took Quinn's face in her hands and looked in her eyes.

Rita leaned back through the middle of the seats at an awkward angle and pushed open the back passenger door.

"She owes me, you know," said Rita. "And so do you. Now get the fuck out of my car."

Chapter Forty-One

THE STREETS WERE full of people milling about in large groups. Penny stood at the edge of the bridge and let the crowds jostle around her as she watched Rita drive away. She felt empty in the midst of all these people's freedom. Hollow. Like a ghost. The rain fell lightly on her shoulders, and no one seemed to notice the impending storm but her.

What had she done? Quinn had been right. The sacrifice was too much. The pain was too unbearable, and her revolution had come at a price far too big for her to bear.

Penny opened her arms wide to let the rain, cold and sharp, fall on her face. Her breath came in gasps. She dropped to her knees, suddenly weak with fear.

And she screamed as loudly as she could until she thought she would explode into flames. And then she screamed again and again and again, her guttural howls lost in the rumble of the masses chanting, "I am not a number," over and over again.

Penny cried into her hands until she was empty of everything, until she was a ghost, a skin, to be picked up on the wind and blown away like dust. She had lost everything.

"I am not a number," she whispered as the chants rushed in to fill the void of her pain. "I am not a number."

And she said it again and again, louder and louder, until she was screaming at the top of her lungs. Then she stopped and listened and looked at the faces, each and every one.

"I am not a number," they yelled.

"I am not a number."

Epilogue

IT TOOK A moment before the sensation of skin versus pavement kicked in. Arms wrenched behind her back, shoulder sockets on the verge of popping, shirt ripped, back scratched raw. The alcohol clouding Penny's reality was a godsend—cheap cooking wine, stolen from Ron's bakery a little bit at a time and stored for her own personal use.

She'd started stealing the wine once Quinn's scent had worn off the pillow and Penny had understood they might never see each other again. At first, it was small swigs of wine while working in the bakery, mixing up the sourdough for the cinnamon rolls. Over time, the pours of wine, stashed in recycled jam jars, became larger and larger until she had a whole corner of Quinn's old bedroom stacked with booze. While Penny had loved the way Ron had taken her under his wing after Quinn had been ripped from their lives, it had been an overwhelming experience. The stark reality of Penny's everyday life working in the bakery as Quinn's replacement had saved her yet left her broken. Every day was a struggle, and her future was nowhere to be seen.

Quinn had been missing for 256 days. The soft edge that the stolen wine provided gave Penny a crutch to cope with the infinite hopelessness of her existence.

Rita and her soup kitchen had disappeared from Two Bridges promptly after she'd made her promise to fix Quinn. Without Rita, Penny had no hope of reuniting with Quinn. Sam's family had moved to Queens, and her father and Benny were dead to her. Life was just an experience in survival, and the stolen wine gave her fleeting moments of hope that maybe, if she was lucky, Quinn would come back, and a future would exist for her after all.

The midnight bridge walks had become an obsession, the place where she and Quinn had first met.

"Find me. Find me. Find me," Penny would whisper as she lay on the edge of Brooklyn Bridge, drunk and desperate with the hope that Quinn would stroll by with a bag full of dead spray cans, exhausted from rebellion, and fall into her arms.

"You're here," Quinn would say. "I've been looking for you. I love you. I miss you."

The fantasy was deep and romantic, but despite the fleeting imagined reunion, it always ended in the same heartbreaking realization that Penny was crazy and alone.

This new sensation, then, of being dragged along the bridge walk was a punishment she knew she deserved, and she welcomed the pain—an external misery to match the agony she felt deep inside her bones.

The peacemaker slapped her till she opened her eyes. He looked at her with such disdain that Penny spat in his face. Her saliva barely left her own mouth and dribbled down her chin.

"Disgusting little bitch," he said as Penny broke into laughter.

The sky above her, filled with so many stars since the blackouts had begun, laughed along with her, and she rejoiced with her own starry cheerleading team and realized how drunk she was. She laughed again, but a rush of melancholy overcame her, disappointment as the punishment came to an end. But no sooner had she wished for more pain than her arms were pulled behind her back, hands cuffed, body arching, and head hanging forward. Resigned. Bad girl.

The tears that came next surprised her. How had she ended up here? The physical pain couldn't even compete with the pain inside her. The unbearable aching, the infinite darkness that constantly threatened to overwhelm her mind. The nightmares of demons in her dreams. And, as if she'd summoned an angel out of thin air, a shadow approached.

A voice, soft yet commanding whispered in her ear. The words made no sense, but the tenor of the voice gave her such comfort that her tears stop rolling. She was uncuffed, scooped up, cradled, and moving. Her arms fell around the neck of this savior, and she allowed her face to rest on his chest. A peacemaker badge jutted into her cheek, but all her instincts knew to trust.

"I've been looking for you everywhere," said her savior.

Penny didn't even need to try to focus her drunken eyes. She knew this man's voice and that she was safe with him. Who would ever have guessed Lieutenant Dickhead-Dixon would be her saving grace? He buckled her into the passenger seat of his car, into comfort and safety.

"It's a long drive," said Lieutenant Dixon. "Get some rest."

Penny's words, thick in her throat, were impossible to push out in a coherent way; a few swallows and they were all but gone. Eyes closed shut, and she was still alive. Breathe in. Breathe out. Surrender like a leaf floating down a river.

It was the smell of coffee that dragged her from her nightmares. Her bones ached from every joint as if fighting to escape the prison of skin holding them in place. The brightness of the morning sun hurt her eyes. She was in a car, her head pounding, her mouth dry, and the lieutenant staring at her, holding a cup of coffee under her nose. His face was soft, and while nothing had notably changed about his appearance, his eyes were hollow and his suffering plain to see.

Penny reached for the coffee with a shaking hand. "Thank you," she said, and she truly meant it. Small kindnesses were few and far between.

Lieutenant Dixon didn't reply. He sipped his coffee in the driver side of his SUV, while staring at a fence that protected a dense forest beyond.

Penny wondered momentarily if he had plans to kill her. She smiled at her own stupidity to blindly trust anyone who might scoop her off the pavement and put her in their car. Her lack of fear surprised her as did her lack of caring about what happened to her. She was a ghost anyway.

"Are you ready to make a difference?" said the lieutenant.

He didn't look at her, and he stared so intently into the wooded forest beyond the fence that she couldn't help but be astounded by his drama. A rumble of joy erupted from deep inside her. Laughter. Real laughter.

"To make a difference?" she said, unable to contain the laughter. "Hi, by the way. I haven't seen you since I reconditioned your girlfriend and ruined your life, and now I've kidnapped you and I'm about to kill you and chop you into a million pieces, but here's a last coffee before you die. Please and thank you. Amen."

Lieutenant Dixon couldn't help but smile. His shoulders dropped, and he leaned back in the seat, brushing his hands through his hair, and then he laughed. "I really have always admired your moxie."

"Moxie! That's so old-fashioned. I love it. Reminds me of Rita."

"Rita? Well, we have a lot to talk about."

"Do we?"

"Don't we?"

"Not as far as I'm aware."

Penny took a sip of coffee. Its heat filled her soul, but its punch made her sick to her stomach after a night of wine and fight.

"I can take you to Quinn," said Lieutenant Dixon.

Penny's body reacted before her mind had a chance. She opened the car door and tumbled onto the road. Her legs gave way as she hurled onto the gravel. Yellow bile dripped down her chin and spilled onto her shirt.

Lieutenant Dixon didn't rush to help her, taking his time to get out of the car. He came to a stop in front of her as she balanced on her hands and knees, staring at the ground in anticipation of another gush of stomach acid. "She's okay," he said, "in case you're wondering."

Penny wiped her mouth with her sleeve and stared up at the guy. "In case I'm wondering? Are you serious?"

The lieutenant shook his head and sat next to Penny. He buried his head in his hands and sobbed, "I don't know how it all got so fucked up."

"How? How it got fucked up? It's been fucked up since the beginning. Don't you realize that? Since they divided us all, since they started randomly reconditioning any human who had a pulse for the joy of life."

"The joy of life? What's that?"

"Wow. You're so depressing."

The lieutenant went silent, staring at his hands, and slowly shook his head. Penny could almost see the pain seeping out of his skin. She crawled over to him, plonked herself by his side, and rested her head on his shoulder. His pain was something she was familiar with, to an extent that it felt like comfort. She wanted to crawl inside him and soak in his anguish.

"You're not the only one who lost someone," said the lieutenant.

"What do you mean, lost?"

"I mean lost, taken, reconditioned, broken."

"Why did you bring me here? What is this place?"

The lieutenant wiped his nose with his sleeve. "Well. It's best I just show you."

He stood up and stretched out his hand. Penny paused before she placed her palm in his. His eyes, full of pain, said everything she needed to hear. He wore his heartbreak like a flashing neon sign, and she felt a deep affinity with the pain he carried. His grip was warm and strong as his fingers curled around hers, and he pulled her to her feet.

"Follow me and stay close. Don't breathe a word," he said before spinning on his heel and making an abrupt beeline for the barbed wire fence.

Penny did exactly as told. In silence, she watched as he used a pair of wire cutters to make a hole in the diamond-crossed metal gate. He kicked at the wire with his military grade boots and fashioned a raw gate from the cutting. Without a word, he held it open with one hand and ushered Penny through.

The other side of the fence was a different world. The grass was not as green, the sky gray, the colors muted. Imagined or real, Penny's heart broke a little more, and she wasn't sure why.

"This way," said the lieutenant as he traipsed on ahead as if she didn't even exist.

Keeping up was a challenge, with his long legs and a gait as huge as a giant's, yet as soon as she caught up to him, he stopped.

Penny had been so focused on sticking with him that she was unprepared for his sudden halt.

The dense forest they'd been navigating cleared, and Penny was surprised to find herself teetering on the edge of a grassy bank, with wild forest giving way to a lookout.

The lieutenant crouched and motioned for her to do the same. She fell to her knees, still woozy from the night before and crawled beside him. Safety. The drop-off was relatively small, only ten feet or so, but it offered a view of a large camp, crowded with ugly fabricated buildings.

"There," said the lieutenant.

But Penny had already seen her. The girl in the red uniform. It wasn't a uniform she'd seen before. Simple, long pants, and a white T-shirt tucked into a smart leather belt. Almost stylish if it weren't for the other fifteen people wearing the same thing.

Penny covered her mouth with her hand, both for comfort and to stop from yelling out.

Quinn looked the same but different. Her unruly mop of hair was pulled back in a bun. Penny had never seen Quinn wear her hair that way, and it was unsettling.

"They call them zombies," said the lieutenant.

Penny had momentarily forgotten where she was and who she was with. She stared at the lieutenant, confused.

"The ones in the pajamas," he said. "The ones they're walking around the yard."

Penny hadn't noticed the others. They ambled in pairs, one red uniform with one pajama-clad zombie. Quinn simply crouched on the cliff-edge, observing attentively.

"It's from the reconditioning. This is where they take them to be reprogrammed. It's Rita's project, and it's got legs. This is where they took my boy." The lieutenant stared down at the courtyard, but before he could say any more, out strolled the lady in pink.

Penny's breath caught, and darkness curled in at the edges of her vision. She stood, hands on hips, hunched over, and began pacing. She didn't know what her body needed, only that she had to move.

"I'm not feeling well," she said. "I don't feel well at all."

The lieutenant wrapped an arm around Penny. "I understand, but I need you to be strong. It's important."

Penny stared at her bare feet. Her toenails had a tiny bit of color left on the ends from the bottle of red polish she'd found in Quinn's goodie box. The nail polish had served as a way to emotionally deal with Quinn's absence.

Penny nodded.

"I want our people back," said the lieutenant. "I need you."

"Why? I'm no one."

The lieutenant smiled. "You, my dear, are a force to be reckoned with, and together, we are going to start a war."

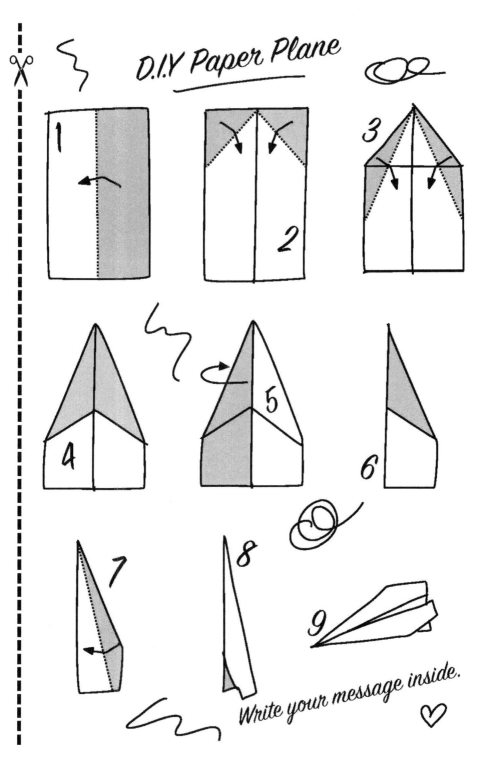

D.I.Y Paper Plane

Write your message inside.

Acknowledgements

It took a whole village to write this book—scratch that—a whole country—a whole *world*, in fact. Apparently, I'm quite good at procrastinating, and while I love writing, I find the process of cleaning up my own messy words quite a task.

So, thank you, to my friends and family who, in varying degrees, picked me up off the floor, endured my rants, watched me find a million fun things to do that wasn't sitting at my laptop and working. Those who had to tell me off or coax me to sit with my laptop by means of chocolate or red wine or bribery and corruption. The ones who listened to and applauded my wins and fails. Who laughed and danced and cried and dreamed alongside me. Who looked after my kids, and kept me going when my confidence had all but dried up.

Big thanks to Harris Keenan for his fabulous illustrations which are just the bee's knees.

Finally, the true ring master, Elizabetta McKay and her incredible team at NineStar Press, who not only taught me a great deal about myself as a storyteller, but endured the trials and tribulations of my technical incompetency behind the wheel of ridiculously complicated editing software.

But, the gold medal of thanks goes to my kids, Harry and Emmy, for embracing our unconventional life and never making me do their laundry.

About Toni J. Spencer

Toni J Spencer is an avid daydreamer and eternal optimist. When she's not encouraging her two children to jump on the couch, eat with their fingers, or understand the power of using swear words in context, she writes. Toni has several award-winning short stories under her belt, and once the procrastinating is done and dusted, plans to turn most of them into novels.

Despite calling New Zealand home, Toni considers herself a citizen of the world and dreams about the day when she can once again stuff her backpack full of short-shorts and furry jackets and head out in search of adventure and friends unmet.

Origami War is Toni's first published novel and was mostly written in the witching hour during a serious bout of insomnia. She figures she'll have plenty of time to sleep when she is dead.

Email
tjspencerwrites@gmail.com

Instagram
www.instagram.com/tjspencerwrites

Facebook
www.facebook.com/tjspencerwrites

Tiktok
www.tiktok.com/@tjspencerwrites

Connect with NineStar Press

www.ninestarpress.com

www.facebook.com/ninestarpress

www.facebook.com/groups/NineStarNiche

www.twitter.com/ninestarpress

www.instagram.com/ninestarpress

Printed in Great Britain
by Amazon

83843033R00132